T0130166

**For the price of honor, he must walk away from the woman he loves . . .**

Orphaned young, Sir Ronan O'Connor left behind a childhood of loneliness and brutality to join the Knights Templar, vowing never to return to Ireland. But now a mission to transport a cache of Templar armaments for King Robert the Bruce forces the knight back to his homeland. Under his protection on the journey is an Irish nobleman and his daughter, Lathir McConaghy. Trained in combat, Lathir will bend to no man . . .

After the death of her betrothed in battle, Lathir guards her heart fiercely. Until an attack at sea forces her and Ronan to rely on each other for their survival. In the storm-filled days adrift at sea, a passionate bond forms between Lathir and the fierce warrior. In a realm torn by treachery and turmoil, they fight for their future even as secrets threaten to destroy their mission, and any chance at love.

# Also by Diana Cosby

# Forbidden Realm

*The Forbidden Series*

# Diana Cosby

**LYRICAL PRESS**
Kensington Publishing Corp.
www.kensingtonbooks.com

LYRICAL PRESS BOOKS are published by
Kensington Publishing Corp.
119 West 40th Street
New York, NY 10018

All Kensington titles, imprints, and distributed lines are available at special quantity discounts for bulk purchases for sales promotion, premiums, fund-raising, educational, or institutional use.

Special book excerpts or customized printings can also be created to fit specific needs. For details, write or phone the office of the Kensington Sales Manager: Kensington Publishing Corp., 119 West 40th Street, New York, NY 10018. Attn. Sales Department. Phone: 1-800-221-2647.

Lyrical Press and Lyrical Press logo Reg. U.S. Pat. & TM Off.

First Electronic Edition: April 2020
ISBN-13: 978-1-5161-0888-6   (ebook)
ISBN-10: 1-5161-0888-4   (ebook)

First Print Edition:  April 2020
ISBN-13: 978-1-5161-0890-9
ISBN-10: 1-5161-0890-6

Printed in the United States of America

*It's my deepest honor to dedicate Forbidden Realm to my daughter, Stephanie Cosby, who is the most incredible, talented, and loving woman. She's truly a blessing in my life.*

*I love you so much, Stephanie. Dare to dream, but more, dare to go after your dreams! I believe in you!*

# Acknowledgments

My sincere thanks to Cameron John Morrison, Kathryn Warner, and Jody Allen for answering numerous questions about medieval Scotland and England, and to Fra Lavery for his insight into Ireland. I would also like to thank The National Trust for Scotland, which acts as guardian of Scotland's magnificent heritage of architectural, scenic, and historic treasures. In addition, I am thankful for the immense support from my husband, parents, family, and friends. My wish is that everyone is as blessed when they pursue their dreams.

My sincere thanks to my editor, Esi Sogah; my agent, Holly Root; production editor Rebecca Cremonese; copy editor Randy Ladenheim-Gil; and my critique partners, Kathy Altman, Michelle Hancock, Cindy Nord, and Ella Quinn for helping Rónán/Dáire and Lathir's story come to life. A huge thanks to the Roving Lunatics (Mary Beth Shortt and Sandra Hughes), Nancy Bessler, and The Wild Writers for their friendship and support over the years!

A very special thanks to Sulay Hernandez for believing in me from the start.

# Chapter One

*Scotland, March 1309*

The late afternoon sun provided little warmth as a frigid blast of wind hurled past Sir Rónán O'Connor. He glanced toward Stephan MacQuistan, Earl of Dunsmore, a friend and a fellow Knight Templar, then nodded to the guard holding open the intricately carved arched door of St Andrew's Cathedral as they strode past.

The rich scents of frankincense and myrrh filled the air as he halted inside, then dusted off the thin layer of falling snow from his cape. However thankful to be out of the cold, unease rumbled through him at King Robert's request for his presence, more so that it involved the Earl of Sionn, a powerful Irish nobleman.

A soft groan sounded as the guard pulled the entry door shut, then the man glanced to the earl. "My lord." Then he turned to Rónán. "Sir Rónán, King Robert is meeting with the Bishop of Dunblane. He bids you to wait in the solar until I bring word that he will receive you."

Rónán nodded.

The guard stepped back. "If you would follow me."

"'Tis unnecessary," Stephan said. "My wife is there. I will show him the way."

"I thank you, my lord." The steady pad of steps faded as the guard departed the massive entry and headed toward a nearby corridor.

Waning rays of golden sunlight streaming through an ornate arched window entwined with torchlight illuminated the grand interior. In awe, Rónán studied the massive columns lining each side of the cathedral. He glanced toward the nave, framed within the rows of highly polished pews leading to the chancel adorned with carvings of Christ and other well-crafted tributes honoring the Lord surrounding the grand altar.

"'Tis beautiful," he breathed, "and incredible craftsmanship. Nay doubt Templars were involved in the construction."

"Aye, 'twas my thought the first time I came here." Stephan headed in the opposite direction the guard had taken. "This way."

They passed a fresco mural of Christ. "With the significant number of clergy and nobles arriving for King Robert's first parliament," Rónán said, "I should have expected to find you here."

"I arrived two days ago with the Bishop of Dunblane. We are to listen to the Bruce's strategy for quelling the English and Lord Comyn's resistance, and to offer insight."

"With Lord Comyn believing he is the rightful claimant to the Scottish throne, 'tis a fight he will never abandon. Unlike King Edward II, who hasna the taste for power like his father."

"Indeed," Stephan agreed. "'Tis the blasted lords who have the young sovereign's ear and press him to continue the battle to conquer Scotland."

Rónán shot him a wry smile. "Nay doubt they are furious that King Philip of France has recognized the Bruce as the King of Scots."

A satisfied look settled on Stephan's face. "'Tis certain that news put a burr in their arse." He nodded respectfully to a monk garbed in a brown robe as he passed, then glanced at Rónán. "I didna expect to see you here. Did you travel with one of the representatives in support of King Robert?"

"Nay. 'Tis an unexpected trip. I was at Tiran Castle, attending Sir Cailin's wedding—"

"Wedding?"

"Aye." In brief, Rónán explained having been sent to aid Cailin in reclaiming his birthright, Tiran Castle, and discovering Cailin's father hadn't been murdered in Cailin's youth as he'd been told by his treacherous uncle, but was alive and locked within the dungeon. Then, Rónán told Stephan the unusual circumstances of their friend meeting and falling in love with Elspet McReynolds.

Stephan shook his head in disbelief. "'Tis remarkable."

"Indeed. I was there, and I am still stunned by the extraordinary chain of events." Thoughts of their friend—also a Knight Templar—made Rónán smile, more so due to the happiness Cailin had found in his lovely and spirited bride. "'Twas after the wedding when the king's runner delivered a missive that the Bruce requested my presence in matters concerning the Earl of Sionn."

The faint murmur of voices echoed from down a corridor, and the scent of venison, onions, and herbs sifted through the air.

Rónán's stomach rumbled, a reminder he hadn't eaten since dawn. But that would have to wait until after he'd met with his sovereign.

His friend guided him down another hallway, this one smaller but as grand. From the ornately framed paintings, the discreet carvings straddling the walls, 'twas clearly the king's private area.

"Have you ever met the Earl of Sionn?" his friend asked.

"Nay, only heard that he is a man well respected by his warriors." Learned during a time in his brutal youth he'd rather forget, a place filled with naught but pain and fear. Nor did he ever intend to return to Ireland, a promise he'd kept after his adventures had brought him to join the galloglass, where a year later he'd met and given his vow to the Brotherhood in France. He'd sailed away with a Templar crew and never looked back.

Cold fury lanced his gut as he thought of the Knights Templar, who'd been betrayed by King Philip, of the false charges leveled upon an elite Christian force who'd displayed naught but the highest ideals and principles for nearly two centuries.

Yet, for all the French king's conniving to replenish his coffers with Templar wealth, in the end he'd claimed naught but a pittance of their gold.

Warned in advance of King Philip's nefarious intent, Rónán, along with a sizable portion of the Brotherhood, had loaded most of the Templar treasures aboard their ships and sailed from La Rochelle before the arrests began. Five galleys and their crews had headed to Scotland, led by the fierce warrior at his side. The remainder of the fleet had traveled to Portugal.

Though a year and a half had passed since the arrests had begun, heartache still filled Rónán at the loss of men who were like brothers. Nor could he forget the brutality endured by those still imprisoned in France.

"During my last meeting with King Robert," Stephan said, drawing Rónán from his somber musings, "he mentioned that he is seeking support from Ireland."

"'Twould explain why Lord Sionn is here, but not the reason the Bruce would request my presence."

"Perhaps the king seeks a trusted Irish adviser."

Rónán shot his friend a skeptical look. "As I havena been in Ireland since my childhood, that I doubt."

"But with your Irish roots, along with our king's Templar ties, a motive that makes sense."

Learning King Robert was of the Brotherhood over a year before had left Rónán stunned. Stephan's reasoning could indeed explain why the monarch had asked him here, a rationale Rónán prayed was wrong. The very thought of returning to the land of his youth chilled him.

"If Lord Sionn has joined the Bruce's cause," Rónán said, shoving aside the dreaded possibility, "Lord Comyn and the English will be irate." His friend grunted. "There is that."

Paces ahead, torchlight illuminated a statue of Jesus, and another of the Virgin Mary.

"I regret to have missed Sir Cailin's wedding," Stephan said.

Rónán smiled at memories of his friend's marital vows. "You would like Elspet. In addition to being beautiful, she is an intelligent and strong woman. A fine match for Cailin."

Humor twinkled in his friend's eyes. "Mayhap a union in which our king had a hand?"

"A thought I considered. Though Cailin protests that fact, he canna deny that King Robert sent him to meet with her father." In brief, Rónán explained.

Sadness edged Stephan's face as he passed below an arched, stained-glass window softly illuminated by the last rays of sunset. "I regret the lass had to endure such treachery from her liege lord and stepbrother. That justice has been served, and she and Cailin have found love, is what is important."

"Indeed."

Eyes softening with humor, his friend arched a brow. "Mayhap 'tis why the king has called you here, not to have you meet the Earl of Sionn, but to announce the lass you are to wed."

At his friend's teasing, Rónán shook off the claw of dread sliding through him and forced himself to shrug. "With the Bruce preparing for his first parliament and nobles and clergy arriving in force, I far from think he has time to ponder the future of an unwed knight."

"Mayhap." Stephan waggled his brows. "But the earl has a beautiful daughter, one who accompanied him to St Andrews."

Far from worried, a smile touched Rónán's mouth. "A woman who I will never meet, nor will she play a part in my life."

"Given the dangerous situation created by those seeking to dethrone King Robert, that her father allowed her to travel with him is surprising." Stephan shot him a wry look. "Unless her presence here, like yours, was requested by the Bruce."

"I am without a title, a rank her station demands when she weds. Nor does this conversation hold any relevance. 'Twas only the Earl of Sionn who was mentioned in the Bruce's writ." He held up his hand as Stephan started to speak, missing their verbal spars over the years, appreciating that regardless whether his friend had reclaimed his father's title, their strong bond of friendship hadn't changed. "As for a reason she accompanied her father, I remember another stubborn lass who confronted our king in her efforts to accompany our force as we sailed to seize her home."

Stephan turned a corner, the waning sheen of colored light sifting through the crafted glass window lending a demure cast over the corridor. "'Twas a different circumstance."

"Indeed, but unlike you, I willna marry the lass, much less meet her," Rónán said, amused at his friend's attempt to make him worry about Lord Sionn's daughter. "Speaking of beautiful women, when I first saw you in the stable, you mentioned that Lady Katherine is here. Nor have I congratulated you on the birth of your son."

Pure joy swept Stephan's face. "I thank you. Three years ago, I never could have imagined myself married with a child; now I canna imagine myself without them. And King Robert has agreed to be Colbán's godfather."

"Wonderful," Rónán said, surprised by the tug of envy. Why? He'd never pondered thoughts of marrying, much less of having a family. That his friend had found both was a blessing, but not a life for him.

With Scotland far from united, the years ahead would be dedicated to fighting beneath King Robert's standard. Though Rónán had somehow managed to retain a sense of humor and an appreciation for friendship, 'twas a foil against the bitterness in his heart, one forged by his brutal youth, many battles fought, and of witnessing too many of his friends dying beneath a blade.

A familiar trickle of laughter sounded from an open door ahead, an elaborate crucifix centered above the entry.

"'Twould seem," Stephan said, "that my wife has found something to amuse her."

Recalling Katherine's humor during the time they'd spent aboard ship with Stephan and the other Templar knights over a year before, an idea sprung to mind. "Does your wife know I was summoned by the king?"

"Nay, neither of us were informed you were to arrive. The only reason I saw you was because I was outside when you rode in."

"Is your son with her?"

He shook his head. "Colbán is asleep in our chamber, his nursemaid nearby."

"Then," he said with a smile, "wait here and let me surprise her."

His friend chuckled. "If you think you can. I doubt you will get the best of her."

"We will see. 'Tis time for me to pay her back for the last prank she played on me." With stealth, Rónán crept to the entry, but his view was blocked by a large carved statue. He peered between the figure and the wall.

A slender woman stood with her back to him. She had long blond hair, and wore a stunning blue wool gown that hung to her ankles. Celtic designs braided in gold decorated the hem, a *sgian dubh* secured at her waist, and an intricate silver torque encircling her neck.

Though over a year had passed, he'd recognize Katherine anywhere. Pride filled him as he thought of their time onboard the Templar cog. And when attacking her castle to reclaim it, she'd proven over and again that she was a woman who, when determined, could accomplish all she set out to achieve. To find a lass of such integrity, oh, were he to be so fortunate...

Stunned, he smothered the thought. Nay, he sought naught but the life of a warrior. That his friends had found women to love was a fate he didn't seek.

The soft murmur of another woman's voice had him glancing over, but with his limited view, he couldn't see farther into the room. Nor did it matter. Rónán glanced back at Stephan.

Down the corridor, a smile curved his friend's mouth as he leaned against the hewn stone wall and folded his arms across his chest.

Turning, Rónán focused on Katherine's back. With a plan in mind, he crept around the statue and started to lay his hands over her eyes. "Guess wh—"

In a blur of movement, blond hair slapped his face as a woman he'd never seen before whirled to confront him. He caught a brief glimpse of smooth features and glittering eyes a second before her leg swept out and hooked his knees.

Off balance, Rónán caught her shoulders to steady himself.

She jerked back.

Air rushed down his throat as they started to fall. Blast it! He shifted his body, taking the brunt of the impact as they landed.

Sprawled atop him, gray eyes narrowed with fury, she unsheathed her dagger.

God's truth! Rónán caught her wrist. "Lass—"

"Release me!" she warned.

Her rich, lyrical brogue had him hesitating. With the Bruce's first parliament soon to be held within these walls, he'd expected to find travelers from Ireland. So why did her body pressed to his, combined with the wild flash in her eyes, make him hesitate? "With pleasure." He caught her blade with his free hand, jerked it away, then let her go.

Her breath coming fast, she scrambled up.

Considering the speed and accuracy with which the woman had withdrawn her *sgian dubh* and aimed it at his throat, she must be trained in combat. Nor was he surprised by this discovery. 'Twas naught uncommon for women in Ireland to hold rank, be educated, and trained for war.

"My mistake for surprising you," Rónán said, pushing himself to his feet. He extended her weapon to her handle first.

Eyes wary, she snatched her dagger.

"Sir Rónán?"

He glanced right to find Lady Katherine stepping toward him, her eyes warm with surprised welcome, the reaction he'd anticipated a moment before.

"Whoever this stranger is," the lass snapped, "he has the manners of a lout."

"Lady Lathir," Lady Katherine said with a chuckle, her voice growing fond. She walked over and rested her hand upon his arm. "May I introduce you to Sir Rónán, a friend and a man I would trust with my life."

The lady took an almost insulting length of time securing her blade, then gave him a cool nod. "Sir Rónán."

"Sir Rónán," Katherine continued, "I am pleased to introduce to you Lady Lathir. Though you two have just met, I believe that you will get along well."

With the daggers shooting from the other woman's eyes, that Rónán doubted. Intrigued now that their scuffle was over, he studied her. Wary gray eyes, ones he noted had a hint of lavender, held his without apology. She was fair, even-featured, with lush lips. A beauty by all standards. And she'd felt very soft and womanly in those brief moments she'd lay upon him on the floor.

Most women would have jumped or screamed at his unexpected presence, but like a trained knight, she'd gone on the attack. A mystery. Nor did this incident hold importance in the scheme of things. Once he'd spoken with the king and was given his mission, he would depart and, thankfully, he and the lass would never see the other again.

But he did owe her an explanation. "My lady, I regret startling you. Lady Katherine and I have a history of playing pranks upon each other. As you have a similar appearance and height, and I heard her voice, I believed you were she." He offered her a warm smile that had charmed many a lass. "I had meant to surprise her."

"I see," she said, her words clipped.

From her cool manner, he suspected otherwise. He shifted his gaze to Katherine. "'Tis wonderful to see you, my lady."

"And I you." Katherine smiled. "I wasna informed you would be here."

"Which is what I explained to Rónán when I saw him," Stephan said as he entered the solar. He crossed to his wife, then nodded to Lady Lathir.

"My lady, 'tis good to see you again. I regret the confusion. These two can be like scrapping siblings trying to outdo the other."

"Lord Dunsmore," she said, her tone warming to a sincere welcome. "The knight's action is inconsequential, and as he explained, 'twas a mistake." She took a step toward the door, a tight smile on her lips. "Nay doubt you wish to reminisce with your friend."

Worry filtered into Katherine's gaze. "Please stay. Once Sir Rónán learns that—"

"An explanation that is unnecessary. Enjoy your reunion. We will talk later." She nodded. "If you will excuse me."

With exquisite grace, she exited the solar, her blue robe swirling around her slender curves with a royal flare. Without a glance toward him, Rónán noted, though he found himself watching her departure. As the last tantalizing wisp of the lass disappeared from view, he grimaced.

"She is a bit skittish."

"Nay, anxious," Stephan said. "En route, her party was attacked a league outside St Andrews. During the fray, two men rushed Lady Lathir."

"God's truth," Rónán hissed, "they tried to kill her?"

"We believe the warriors meant to abduct her for ransom," Stephan said, "or to use her to force her father to withdraw support for King Robert."

"But," Katherine said with pride, "she killed them both."

Given her skill with her blade, that he believed. "Serves the scoundrels right, and explains her reaction when I snuck up on her."

"It does," Stephan said.

Katherine poured a cup of wine, held it out to him. "She is just now beginning to relax."

"I wish I had known."

"You couldna," Stephan said, "but during your stay at St Andrews, you can speak with her again."

"I will make a point to make amends before I depart." A point he hadna counted on including in his schedule, but 'twas proper. "Were Comyn's men behind the attack?"

"King Robert believes 'twas some of John of MacDougall of Argyll's men, still hidden about and seeking retribution after their stinging defeat at the Pass of Brander," Stephan said. "That they somehow discovered Lord Sionn was traveling from Ireland to meet with the Bruce and were determined to stop him."

"Lord Sionn?" Rónán repeated, a sinking feeling in his gut as he recalled her brogue. "What has Lady Lathir to do with the earl?"

Katherine laced her fingers together. "She is Lady Lathir McConaghy, his daughter."

Bloody hell. If the powerful Irish noble learned of the incident, Rónán hoped he found it amusing. As for King Robert, he surely would find hilarity in the misstep.

Katherine walked to a table by a grand stone hearth. A banner displaying a red lion rampant sporting blue claws and tongue, woven on a yellow background, hung centered above. Beeswax candles seated in skillfully crafted holders flickered a soft golden glow on either side. She poured three goblets of wine, then returned.

Rónán thought of when they'd first met, her fiery demeanor one he'd admired, more so when, in the end, she'd fallen in love and married his close friend. So much had changed since, except that their love had prevailed, and now they had a son.

He accepted a cup, waited until she'd handed her husband his, then lifted his forged vessel. "A toast to your son. I wish Colbán God's blessings."

Pride filled their eyes as Stephan and Katherine raised their goblets and drank.

She lowered her cup, her countenance glowing with a mother's love. "Colbán is a handsome lad, with his father's good looks and—" Laughter shimmered in her eyes. "—also his stubbornness."

Stephan grunted. "The willfulness, my lady wife, comes from you."

At their teasing, the last of Rónán's tension eased. He'd missed his friends, and would enjoy the time with them until he departed.

A soft knock sounded at the entry.

"Enter," Stephan said.

The king's runner stepped inside. "My lord, my lady." His gaze shifted to Rónán. "King Robert requests your presence."

\* \* \* \*

Rónán entered the throne room. Through an arched window, inky swaths of the oncoming night marred the fading shimmers of orange-gold painting the sky. The warm spill of golden light, along with the torches placed inside sconces positioned upon the wall, illuminated the chamber. In a massive stone hearth sparks popped from the fire and swirled within a plume of smoke before disappearing up the chimney.

Stepping onto the plum carpet, he strode toward King Robert, seated upon his throne. Behind him stood intricately carved columns, and stone lions stood positioned discreetly on either side of the platform. A powerful setting for a formidable monarch, a man who'd gained his loyalty and respect, and, as a fellow Knight Templar, one he would die to protect.

Over a year had passed since Rónán had been part of Stephan's crew that had sailed to the monarch's stronghold, Urquhart Castle, and learned the Bruce was part of the Brotherhood. A tie that had proven critical. King Edward I had gone to great lengths to ensure Scotland was excommunicated. But the religious exclusion secured by the English monarch, and the Scottish clergy's refusal to acknowledge it, had allowed King Robert to offer all Knights Templar entry into his realm with impunity. A move that had strengthened King Robert's efforts in reclaiming Scotland's freedom.

Before the dais, Rónán halted. That the Bruce had made time to see him during the harried preparations for his first parliament revealed the grave nature of the mission.

He bowed, then met his king's gaze. "I am here as you commanded, Your Grace."

Shrewd eyes held his. "How fared the contingent you led to aid Sir Cailin?"

"We arrived in time and aided him in overthrowing his uncle and seizing Tiran Castle." Pride filled him. "And to discover his father, the rightful Earl of Dalkirk, was locked within the dungeon."

The formidable ruler's eyes widened. "God in heaven, 'tis a miracle."

"'Tis." He handed the king the writ from Cailin. "'Twill explain the events."

"I thank you."

"I have more news you may find of interest," Rónán added, "Sir Cailin has wed Elspet, the stepdaughter of one of your loyal confidants, Sir Angus McReynolds."

The king's eyes widened with satisfied delight. "A fine match, one I would have encouraged had I the time."

Aware of the king's penchant for matchmaking, and confident the ruler had indeed played a hand in his friend's marriage, Rónán only nodded. "Though," he continued, damning the news he was next to impart, "I regret to inform you that both Sir Angus and Elspet's mother were murdered during these events."

Anger whipped across the monarch's face. "Is the bastard who killed them dead?"

"Aye, Your Grace." He gave a brief explanation of what had occurred.

King Robert blew out a rough exhale and took a moment of silence for their sacrifice. "I will be happy when Lord Comyn accepts me as Scotland's king and English ambitions to seize our country end. The latter," he said, his voice dry, "given the young king is far from concerned with issues of war, but a matter of time."

The Bruce stood, strode to a table, and lifted an elegant glass carafe. Dark amber liquid sloshed inside. Mouth grim, he filled a pair of goblets inlaid with a Celtic weave, a ruby centered between the breaks in the complex design.

The king handed him a cup. "The Earl of Sionn has arrived at St Andrews. Unknown to most, he is a trusted Templar supporter and has a large cache of Templar weapons hidden in his realm. Arms I need to force the English from Scotland and quell Lord Comyn's attempts to seize the throne."

Which explained the powerful Irish lord's presence. Rónán took a sip and recognized the potent slide of *uisge beatha*, the spirit distilled by the monks of the Border Abbeys.

"With your expertise in strategy, battlefield experience, and Templar background, you will accompany the earl to his home in Ireland and oversee the transport of the Templar cache to my castle in Aberdeen."

"Aye, Your Grace." Blast it, the last thing he'd ever intended was to return to Ireland. There was naught in his homeland he wished to ever see again. Even the nightmares that had haunted him as a child were long since gone. He would find comfort in that his time in Ireland would be short. Nor did he miss the pride in the king's voice at the mention of the recently captured northern stronghold, boasting an easily accessible seaport to the north. "When do we leave?"

"At first light." The monarch took a sip from his goblet, then shot him a hard look. "The earl's party was attacked about a league from St Andrews by a band of John MacDougall of Argyll's men."

"The Earl of Dunsmore explained the details of the assault, Sire. With John MacDougall of Argyll's forces severely cut, and his begging the young English king for supplies, 'twas a brazen move."

"'Twas. I have ordered a contingent to accompany your party to ensure you reach their ship. My guard will remain in port until you have sailed. Once at sea, keep watch for English ships intent on severing my attempt to gain Irish support. If they see Lord Sionn's cog departing Scotland, they will attack."

Rónán nodded. "Aye, Your Grace."

His face relaxed, and he sat back. Mischief sparkled in the king's eyes as he swirled the amber liquid in his cup. "Did Lord Dunsmore also mention that Lord Sionn has a beautiful daughter?"

At the king's measuring look, Rónán stilled. Was he the subject of the king's next matchmaking ploy? No, he was being oversensitive. His thoughts shifted to Stephan's amusement at Rónán's thwarted attempt to surprise Katherine.

"Aye, we have met," Rónán said with reluctance.

The Bruce set down his goblet. "How so?"

In brief, he shared the chaos of his and Lathir's encounter.

With a smile, the king laughed. "An intriguing way to meet a lass. She is a strong and intelligent woman." He took a deep drink. "One who needs a man of caliber at her side."

Rónán cleared his throat. "With the dreadful impression I made, Sire, I assure you, I have far from earned her favor." Her *sgian dubh* pointed at him was, he recalled grimly, proof.

"Mayhap a feisty lass is exactly what you need."

In midsip, Rónán almost choked on the powerful spirit. "I am here to serve you, Your Grace, not seek a wife." God's truth, he needed to change the subject before his sovereign became enamored with the idea of pairing him with Lady Lathir.

With the monarch's power of persuasion, ability to bestow upon him a title, and Lord Sionn's Templar ties, 'twould take little to convince the Irish noble to agree to such a union. The disappointment of having to leave in the morning and not spend more time with Stephan and Katherine faded against thoughts of escaping before the king decided he and the earl's daughter should wed.

* * * *

A thin mist clung to the air as Lathir dismounted. The strong scent of fish, decaying seaweed, and salt filled the air as the first rays of sunlight struggled through the dense overcast.

She glanced around, thankful to arrive safely at their ship, anxious to be out to sea. After their party's attack days before, only when the shore faded from sight would she relax.

"I will take your mount, my lady," her personal guard said.

"I thank you, Gearalt." The soft thud of hooves on dirt and the guards' voices rumbled around them as she joined the tall, stocky man who'd raised her.

Blond hair secured behind his neck in a leather strip framed his intimidating features, and his face settled into a harsh frown as he strode toward the ship. Eyes sharp with intelligence shifted toward her. "You were quiet during the trip."

"I am anxious to be home." The truth.

"The attack still troubles you."

She grimaced and said with equal candor, "I doubt that I will ever forget taking a life, regardless whether 'tis an enemy and deserved."

He grunted, leaving her to her silence. Nor would she reveal that what disturbed her as well were her dreams the previous night of Sir Rónán. Something about him had left her unsettled. Several times she'd woken with images of him filling her mind.

To be fair, their first meeting had been something, well, unusual. In those few heated moments, how could she not notice his well-muscled form, confident air, or grayish green eyes that pierced her with such intensity 'twas as if he could see to her soul. His every move proclaimed him a warrior, a man who did naught without purpose, and one who, with his smooth words and manner, no doubt drew many a woman's eye.

Since her betrothed, Domhnall Ruadh mac Cormaic, had died in battle against the English more than two years before, never had another man earned more than her passing interest. That this Irish knight had the audacity to invade her dreams was unacceptable.

Though they hadn't spoken since they'd departed St Andrews, she was aware that he rode with their soldiers.

Unwittingly, she glanced around and found him. The knight was talking with the leader of the contingent King Robert had provided as protection for their journey to their cog.

Her father followed her gaze. "The Bruce speaks highly of him."

Lathir sighed, understanding his intent. A year after Domhnall's death, he'd advised her 'twas time to seek another man to wed. Her heart still hurting, she'd refused, doubting she'd ever recover from the heartbreak. Nor had he given up pressing her on the issue, a frequent discussion that left her weary. The knight's lack of title mattered little to her father. He judged men by their caliber, not the title they bore. For a king's favorite, nobility could be granted with but a wave of the hand.

Lathir met her father's gaze, blinked. "Of whom?"

His lips thinned. "Sir Rónán O'Connor."

"Which," she said as she started up the gangway, "I would expect of the knight as King Robert chose the warrior to oversee the transfer of arms."

"Lathir—"

"Father, my marital status, or lack thereof, isna one I wish to discuss, more so," she said, keeping her voice low, "as we prepare to sail."

A deep frown settled upon his mouth. "'Tis time for you to marry."

"I dinna need a man to accept responsibility for the realm of Tír Sèitheach when the time comes."

"You are as stubborn as your mother," he blustered.

She arched an amused brow. "Mother said I acquired my obstinacy from you."

"Aye, she did," he said, his face softening. "I miss her and want you happy."

An ache built in her chest, and she lay her hand upon his arm. "I know, Da."

He covered her hand with his, winked. "What do you say we set sail and return home?"

She smiled. "I would like that very much."

\* \* \* \*

"The fog is thicker than mud," Rónán said as he stood at the bow of the *Aodh*, scanning the thick, dense gray that had moved in several hours after they departed. The soft slap of waves against the thin layer of ice upon the hull played in eerie harmony to the ghostly cries of distant gulls.

"Aye," Lord Sionn agreed at his side, sounding equally displeased. "Nor with the wind having decreased to a light breeze in the last few hours have we traveled far."

"'Tis clearing overhead," Lathir said from her father's other side. "Mayhap the fog will break soon."

Rónán rolled his shoulders and wished that unease didn't trail up his spine as it was wont to do in times of danger.

He allowed his gaze to skim over her plaited gold hair, adorned with a weave of silver, accenting the silver torque around her neck clasping an emerald at the base of her throat, before meeting her gaze. "Fog formed over the sea is not something that tends to fade beneath the sun's rays. I expect we may be in the thick of it for a while."

She gazed at him and opened her mouth as if to answer, then looked away, leaving him to wonder what he'd done anew to offend her.

A distant creak, the faint rattle of a chain, and the muted tangle of voices echoed in the gloomy setting.

On alert, Rónán scanned the dense swath toward the sound. "Someone is out there." He glanced toward the earl and said under his breath, "Did you leave ships farther from port for protection?"

"Nay," the earl replied, his jaw tight. "We saw several English ships en route, but they were at a distance, and we were still in Irish waters."

"King Robert warned me that the English are determined to sever any attempt for the Irish to support his cause."

"Aye, but they will fail," the noble replied.

A soft splash sounded, this time closer. The outline of a ship sailed into view, men running to the rail, their swords drawn.

Lathir gasped. "Their standard is English."

"God's truth," Rónán hissed, "prepare for an attack!"

# Chapter Two

Engulfed within the dense fog, wood groaned and splintered as the English cog slammed into the side of the *Aodh*.

Feet braced against the shudders rumbling through the ship, Rónán damned the lack of wind, which would have allowed them to evade the attack. He faced the crew as they lined up against the rail, weapons drawn.

"Dinna allow the bastards to lash their ship to ours."

Even as he said it, the enemy swung onto the deck of the *Aodh*, thick lines of rope in hand.

Lord Sionn lunged forward and drove his sword into an attacker's chest.

The man stumbled back; the noble shoved him over the side, then whirled to face the next aggressor.

Paces away, Lathir slew a warrior trying to tie a line onto their cog.

Rónán slashed an attacker, turned toward the next.

Amidst the clash of blades, several warriors managed to secure the English ship alongside the *Aodh*.

The vessels scraped as a swell rolled beneath. Rónán kept his balance while he defended against another invader.

"Attack!" the English ship's captain boomed.

Enemy forces poured onto their deck. Shouts, the roar of men, and screams of pain filled the air.

Rónán cursed the sheer number of fighters boarding their vessel, more so the number continuing to surge from the English ship's hold. God's truth, 'twas far from a simple cog designed to keep watch of the coast, but as his sovereign had warned, a warship assigned to halt Lord Sionn from aiding the Bruce.

He glanced at Lathir.

Determination narrowing her eyes, she wielded her blade against an opponent. Their weapons scraped free. As her foe raised his sword, she drove her *sgian dubh* into his heart. On a gasp, he crumbled. Appreciation filled Rónán as she secured her dagger, spun to meet the next aggressor.

"Fire at the bow!" one of their crew yelled.

"Another fire at the stern," Lord Sionn roared as he slashed his sword across his enemy's neck, then swung at the next invader.

After disposing of the next attacker, Rónán caught a blur of flames climbing up the wooden mast and engulfing the sail. A cool gust hurled across the deck, fanning the flames of the fires spreading across the deck. God's truth, the bastards were casting torches onto the *Aodh*!

The tang of the sea melded with blood as another swell rolled beneath the *Aodh*. Rónán glanced around. Though the English had suffered significant losses, the Irish noble's men lay scattered across the deck, but a handful alive.

"Father!" Lathir shouted.

At the panic in her voice, Rónán turned. Two Englishmen were dragging Lord Sionn toward their ship. Rónán drove his blade into his attacker, then jerked his weapon free. He kicked away the next charging warrior, and hacked through the melee toward the noble.

Lord Sionn's gaze met Rónán's as a third guard pulled his struggling form onto the enemy ship's deck. "Protect Lathir!" he roared.

The crush of enemy men blocked Rónán's view of the noble. Blast it, there were too many Englishmen between him and the earl. He glanced toward Lathir. Her teeth were clenched, and both fear and determination glittered in her eyes as she backed away from the four Englishmen trying to surround her.

Terror surging through Rónán, he lunged toward her, slaying two of the guards by the time he'd reached her. "Place your back against mine."

She coughed in the smoke. "My father!"

"We will rescue him." How they would do that was another matter. That the enemy hadn't killed the noble outright offered a thread of hope that they intended to hold him for ransom. Nor at the moment was that their greatest concern.

"Seize the earl's daughter," an Englishman yelled.

As the man reached for her, another swell rolled beneath the cog. The *Aodh* listed. Stumbling back, the assailant caught the rail.

Smoke billowing around them, Rónán grabbed the side of a partially burned small boat secured near the bow. He caught Lathir's hand, tugged her against him as she started to slide past him. "Hold on to me!"

"'Tis sinking; return to the ship and sever ties!" the captain yelled. "We set sail for Ireland!"

A warrior still gripping the rail called back, "What of the earl's daughter?"

"We have the earl," their leader replied, "she isna important. Hurry!"

The remaining warriors hurried to their ship. Once the last man climbed aboard, one of them severed the lines.

\* \* \* \*

Choking on the stench, Lathir clung to Rónán as thick flakes of the charred sail tumbling within soot-laden smoke engulfed her. She tugged her cape over her mouth, tried to make out her father on the enemy ship through the billowing rolls of foul murk.

With the next swell, the *Aodh* lurched upright.

Rónán hauled her back. "Look out!"

A strip of the flaming sail swirled past, landed a hand's length away, slid in a fiery trail down the angled deck.

Tears clogged her throat as the ship disappeared into the fog. "They are leaving!"

His grip on her tightened as she instinctively fought his hold. "They are, and we canna stop them now. 'Tis imperative you be calm."

"Calm?" Riotous emotion burning in her chest, Lathir took in the horror of the bloody bodies strewn about the deck, men she'd trained with, had grown up with. Not a single one lived. She wanted to cry, but anger won out. Grief had no place now. "My warriors are dead, the *Aodh* is ablaze, and the small boat, our only hope of escape, is destroyed. Once the ship goes down, we will die!"

As if mocking her, the cog groaned, then gave a violent shudder. The deck dropped a foot and buckled, exposing the hull, the fire creeping up large portions of the damaged wood.

A burst of wind hurled past. Yellow-red flames clawed skyward on a growing roar, consuming wood with merciless disregard as fire swept across the deck.

Heat built around them.

Lathir coughed into her cloak.

"Help me shove the small boat overboard," Rónán yelled. "Mayhap we can keep it afloat until we reach land."

Charred planks clung to the small craft, and flames spurted from the side. Regardless of her doubts of the vessel's seaworthiness, she gripped the side, shoved, prayed.

Another gust buffeted her. Then, as if the heavens were granting an unspoken wish, a cold droplet pelted her face, then another.

Relief welled in her throat as beads of rain and ice pinged off the deck. Beneath the torrent, bursts of whitish-gray smoke spewed in the twist of black with an angry hiss. "'Tis raining!"

Covered in soot and blood, with ferocity a stamp on his features, Rónán stood on the deck gazing skyward. At this moment, to her, he seemed invincible.

The next swell rolled beneath them; surrendering wood groaned as the cog was shoved up.

Charred decking broke free, plummeting into the smoke-filled hull in an awkward twist.

"Saint's breath," Lathir gasped, stumbling against him. "The ship is breaking up!"

Rónán caught her as another shudder wracked the cog. "Hold on!"

Timber cracked.

The sodden planks beneath them collapsed.

A scream erupted from deep in her throat as they fell, the smoke billowing around them a macabre backdrop to the blur of flames and the stench of charred wood.

Pain raked her as she slammed against the knight, and then the vessel's hull.

Another loud crack sounded overhead.

Heart racing, she looked up.

An ember-laden chunk of the upper mast broke free, spiraled toward them.

Rónán shoved her aside, then dove to join her.

Embers spewed in a reckless cloud as timber slammed in a fiery heap paces away.

Gulping a deep breath, she stared at the blazing hull where they'd lain moments before.

He pushed to his feet, pulled her with him. "Let us go."

"Where?" She fought another a wave of panic. "We are sinking!"

Face streaked with smoke, sweat, and blood, he cupped her chin, his gaze intense. "The ship isna going down, or at least not any time soon." He released her. "Look around. The storm is quenching the fire."

Pushing soaked locks from her face, Lathir scanned their surroundings and saw he was right. Smoke billowed skyward, but ice pellets and rain were clearly having a smothering effect. She swallowed once. Twice. Inhaled to regain control. By slow degrees, relief shriveled beneath an agonizing reality. "T–they have my father," she choked out, "while we are adrift on a half-burned cog. One—" On an unsteady breath, she took in the charred planks along the hull, then paused on where the fire had burned through the upper deck. "—one that could break apart with the next swell."

Expression grim, Rónán nodded. "Aye, but we are alive."

Her throat clogged with shame at her outburst, by the truth of his statement. "You are right."

"Lathir, 'tis okay to be frightened."

She fisted her hands, nails digging into her palms at the compassion in his voice, the understanding. "I am a warrior, not a weak-kneed fool."

"You have earned naught but respect in my eyes. Come. Let us determine the cog's seaworthiness, make repairs where we can, and then decide how to proceed."

His practical tone soothed her. "You think the English willna return?"

Icy rain slapped the knight's face as he glanced at the dark churning clouds, then his solemn gaze shifted to her. "With your crew dead, the *Aodh* on fire as the English departed, and a storm moving in, nay doubt they believe that by now we have perished."

She nodded at his reasoning as the icy mix slid down her face. "Aye, an assumption we must use to our advantage."

The howl of wind roared overhead. Waves slammed against the cog, and with each crash, the half-charred vessel groaned beneath the assault.

Soaked, Lathir glanced toward the small boat they'd clung to for a short while. Burned and in pieces, any chance to use it to escape was lost.

Still, she refused to give up hope. Against the odds they'd survived.

Rónán made his way to a pile of upturned buckets, grabbed two. "Help me put out the remaining fires."

Pushing past the fatigue from the battle, she went to work.

By the time they'd extinguished the last of the flames, the storm had moved out, leaving behind a somber peace. A fitting mood as they'd said a quick prayer for the bodies of her warriors as they'd given them to the sea.

Exhausted, Lathir wiped the icy rivulets from her face. "A barrel of fresh water remains near the bow, and the cooking pot is still hanging mid hull."

Face marred with soot, fatigue, and blood, Rónán tugged a blackened tarp free from the ties that had managed to survive. He stared at the various crates. "We have ale, salted beef, oatcakes, and bread."

"And a bag of flour here, and—" She pointed to a thin line with a forged hook that'd been stashed with the provisions. "We can catch fish."

He nodded. "And have more than enough to survive until we can reach shore."

"However long that takes. Between the fog and the storm, we dinna know where we are, or where the English have taken my father."

"Once ashore, it willna take long to discover our location. As for your father, I heard the captain shout that they were heading for Ireland."

Hope flared even as she pointed out, "Ireland is vast. They could have taken him anywhere."

He lifted the container of ale, placed it near the crates of food. "The English control several southeastern ports. It makes sense they would take Lord Sionn to one of those locations."

"Yes. Of course." Eager to be on their way, she helped him move the salvageable food stores together, then secured them as best they could beneath the tarp.

Rónán's strategic deductions, the way he'd fought during battle with incredible precision, and against every catastrophe kept calm and maintained his focus, reminded Lathir of the galloglass, Celtic fighters whose mere name set fear into their invaders' hearts.

Mayhap he was of the ferocious ilk? Regardless, 'twas clear why King Robert had selected this brave knight for this critical mission. As much as she hated to be dependent on anyone, especially a man, if anyone could help her find her father, 'twas him.

She pushed to her feet, wiped her brow. "With the challenges we face, once we reach shore, 'tis best if we travel to my home, Wynshire Castle. There I can raise a force to find and free my father."

"As much as 'twould be best to sail to your home, I dinna trust the *Aodh* to survive another storm. When the opportunity arises, we must run the ship aground."

She nodded, pressing a hand to her stomach. It was inevitable, she told herself, that for their safety, her family's cog would have to be sacrificed.

He stood from a crouch, stretched. "Many years have passed since I sailed these waters. Are you familiar with the Irish currents?"

"Very."

His expression held none of the skepticism she equated with men who doubted her abilities. Instead, he seemed to accept them.

"To the best of my calculations," he said, "before the attack, we had rounded the tip of Scotland and were heading west. The question is how far we traveled after."

She grimaced. "Indeed, until we are again underway, between the local current and the tides, we will be pushed north or northeastward."

"Let us mend the sail as best as possible and secure them to the remnants of the mast." Wood snapped as he started toward the partially charred ladder, began to climb. "As we worked on deck earlier, I noticed the rudder is unscathed."

"Thank God." With a sense of renewed hope, she followed him up the ice- and rain-slicked ladder to the top deck and began gathering pieces of rope to make repairs.

Hours later, streaks of orange and red filled the clearing western sky. Wiping her brow, she glanced at the makeshift sail they'd rigged on the remnants of the burned mast. It wasn't pretty, but it should hold, as should the patches they'd made to the side of the ship using sodden rags wrapped around shards of wood, or whatever could be scrounged to stay the influx of water.

Now, thankfully, they were taking advantage of the stiff breeze and headed west toward her home.

Exhausted and with muscles aching, Lathir climbed down the ladder to the hull. She moved around the charred debris with care to the iron pot straddling the fire on three forged iron rods. How long had it been since she'd last eaten? She couldn't remember.

She leaned over the water they'd warmed over the fire and splashed her face clean of soot as best she could. Feeling refreshed, however slightly, she collected one of the woolen blankets they'd recovered from the unmarred supplies and wrapped it around her shoulders.

The pad of steps on the ladder sounded.

She glanced at Rónán as he reached the bottom. "I began to wonder if the rain would ever quit," she said as he settled beside her. "Not that with the storm dousing any remaining embers am I complaining."

Lengths of brown hair clung to the side of his face, the invading shadows of the night and the golden flicker of flames casting his eyes in shadows. The hard cut of his jaw reminded her of a pirate, his muscular form that of one seasoned in battle.

He was a man to admire; how could she not? Nor could she begrudge the way he took charge without hesitation. Traits no doubt that had attracted many a lass's glance. With his confidence and quick decisions, he was clearly a warrior who'd faced many a battle, and a man who would no doubt leave a woman well-pleased.

She frowned inwardly and shook off the intimate musing. Since Domhnall's death, never had a man caught her eye.

Grief built in her chest as she remembered her betrothed lying in her arms, blood draining from his chest as he fought to take his last breath. Though two years had passed, she still struggled against the pain of losing a man who was more than a man to wed, but a friend.

Rónán edged closer and lifted his hands near the flames, drawing her attention. "A boon in that, with the destruction and significant portions of the hull charred, if any ship spots us from a distance, they will believe the cog is adrift and unworthy of interest."

The tang of dried meat and herbs she'd tossed together scented the air as Lathir stirred the bubbling stew, and her stomach growled. "That we are headed toward Ireland is what matters."

"'Tis." Grim-faced, he lowered his hands.

"Given our current pace, I suspect we are well off the northeast coast. Far away from where you believe they have taken my father."

"Aye, nor can it be helped. 'Tis a blessing we are still afloat."

"'Tis, but I worry we should come ashore in the realm of Tír Kythyr, where our travel will be dangerous." Lathir filled two cups with stew, handed one to Rónán. "'Twill take us a few days travel on foot to reach my home."

Without her father, an inner voice whispered. When more fear encroached into her thoughts, she clung to Rónán's reasoning that if the English had wanted her father dead, they wouldn't have dragged him onboard their ship.

Was he hurt?

Suffering?

Or was he sprawled in a rancid cell, dying?

Face pale, she shoved aside her food, and Rónán muttered a silent curse. She was thinking about her father. Which, at this moment, he could do bloody naught about. Nor could he overlook that as dire as their situation, he could have been stranded with someone far less worthy. He admired her resourcefulness and general calm, which now contrasted sharply against the ferocity she'd displayed in battle.

Deliberately, he turned their conversation to her comments of moments before. "Why will traveling be dangerous? Does Tír Kythyr support the English?"

"Aye." As if distracting herself, she collected several pieces of plank fragments, wedged them within the dying flames. "'Tis safest if we travel by the cliffs until we reach my home. If we are forced to move deeper inland, we should travel only at night. God help us if they find me on their land."

Dread seeped through him at the prospect of returning to Ireland. He grimaced, remembering the age-old disputes between the clans. Years had passed since he'd thought of the divisions in Ireland, the politics of the land.

"After over a century, one would think the bitterness between the clans would have faded."

She arched a curious brow. "You have been to Tír Kythyr?"

"Through it," he evaded, cursing the slip. He set down his cup of stew. "A long time ago."

With night stealing the last wisps of day, she studied him, her gray eyes sharp with intelligence.

No doubt his vague reply had piqued her interest. Nor could that be helped. His past was one he wished to remain buried deep. Every man who entered the Knights Templar had a story, his own dark and unfit for hearing.

"Over the next few days," he said, shifting the topic, "we will make sacks to carry the supplies we will need once we reach shore."

She nodded. "I am ready to have land beneath my feet."

"As I. How do you feel?"

Eyes heavy with fatigue, she offered him a weary smile. "As we were securing the makeshift sail to the damaged rigging, I was wondering if I would ever be warm again."

A shiver whipped through him as he remembered how they'd battled the wind-driven rain, each knot made during the storm a victory. "Aye, the wind cuts right through your clothes and down to the bone." He looked at the makeshift bed they'd fashioned. "With our sail naught but glorified rags, the ship doing naught more than lumbering in the swells, it may take several days before we reach land."

"I hope 'twill be less."

"As I."

She added another broken plank to the small fire. "Though the wind is still strong, at least the storm has moved on."

"The choppy seas should calm during the next few hours."

A groan sounded overhead.

He frowned. "I need to check the rudder to ensure we are still heading west. Finish eating while I do."

"I have little appetite. Nor," she continued as he opened his mouth to tell her to stay, "did I see you finish your food." She pulled free the blanket that was wrapped around her. "I shall go with you. As agreed, I will take my turn with the rudder while you rest. Besides, I suspect if I fell asleep, you wouldna awaken me 'til morning."

An issue they'd argued over earlier. On a sigh, Rónán set aside his bowl. Stubborn lass. He sheltered the coals within the deep cavern created in the sand; even if the seas grew rough during the night, no embers would roll free, causing a fire.

He lit one of the tapers he'd found wrapped in a waxy cloth, pushed to his feet, and extended his free hand.

She accepted and stood.

He tossed the blanket over his shoulder and started toward the ladder. Her steps laden with fatigue, she walked at his side.

Tightening his hold on the taper, he climbed. An erratic dance of candlelight fractured the blackness as they made their way up. Near the top, he blew out the flame to conserve wax and prevent any ship, however distant, from seeing the light.

He wedged the taper in a split plank, climbed on deck, scanned the horizon. "We sail beneath a full moon, and it looks as though we are still heading west." He turned to help her. Once she was free of the ladder, he handed her the cover. With the rush of the sea sliding past, he strode over and sat beside the rudder.

Lathir eased down beside him, offered him a length of the coverlet. "'Tis best if we conserve our warmth."

"You should sleep by the fire below."

In the sheen of moonlight, she arched a stubborn brow.

Blast it. Rónán accepted part of the blanket, willing himself not to think of her nearness, or how her soft scent of woman and night teased him as she shivered against the breeze. Damning his decision, one sure to make him suffer, he shifted closer. "Lean against me for warmth."

She hesitated, then lay her head against his chest, pulling the spread around them.

The rush of the sea rumbled against the bow as the cog cut into an oncoming swell.

She shifted, then again. "I canna sleep."

The soft, silken sadness in her voice smothered his ire. She'd endured so much, and he suspected that although she would never admit it, was afraid. "We will do everything in our power to save your father."

Her breath feathered against his neck. "I know, but there is so much that could go wrong."

"There is. We will try our best; we canna do more."

The blanket rustled, and the play of moonlight outlined her as she angled her face toward him. "I remember him fighting his captors as he was dragged away."

"He is a warrior. If an option presents itself, he will escape."

"I pray so. I wish he knew we are alive."

"He will learn soon enough."

For long moments she stared into the night, then released a weary sigh. "How long have you been away from Ireland?"

His hand tightened on the rudder. "Sixteen years."

The cog groaned as it angled up a swell. "'Tis a long time to be away from your home."

"'Twas never a home," he stated. "I chose to leave."

"Why?"

Caught off guard, Rónán stilled an instant denial. After what she'd been through this day, if he could take her thoughts off her worries, however briefly, perhaps he should tell her. Besides, he and his torturous issues didn't mean anything except to him. Soon she'd be gone from his life.

Jaw tight, he lifted his gaze to the moon. "I was an orphan, yet fortunate to be adopted at a young age. Or so I was repeatedly told." Unable to keep the sarcasm from his voice, he closed his eyes against the blast of memories, damning each one. "Few knew that my supposed savior was little more than a vile man who spoke through his fists and drew pleasure from depriving a child of food."

At her gasp, he glanced down to find her eyes wide with distress.

"Nay one tried to stop him?"

He grunted. "Nay one looked too closely at a bruised, gangly lad. After all, I was fortunate enough to have a roof over my head." Rónán inhaled, the tang of the sea sharp as his mind tumbled to an ancient memory. "After years of living in fear, of doing whatever it took to keep alive, one night when I was seven summers, the man who'd adopted me stumbled in, well in his cups."

"W–what happened?"

The anguish of that fateful night wrenched him down dark paths he'd vowed never to recall. Yet he forced himself to continue. "I hid beneath his desk, which I had learned was the safest place. Rarely did he find me there."

"And if he did?"

"He would beat me."

She gasped. "What a detestable creature!"

"I loathed him," he spat. "However wrong it may be in the eyes of the Church, I pray he is long dead."

Eyes dark with compassion held his. "Understandably. Thank God you escaped."

"Not in time," he said grimly. "I must have made a sound, something that alerted him to my presence. In his drunken stupor, he dragged me from beneath the desk and beat me."

In the moonlight, her face paled.

"At some point, I blacked out. All I remember was waking up the next morning, the hut reeking of ale and blood. I pulled myself up to my feet." Paces away, the bastard was draped over his bed, snoring, a tilted grimace on his scarred face." He shook his head. "At that moment, I knew I had to leave. The next time I might not be fortunate enough to survive. Grabbing a stick, I hobbled into the forest and never looked back."

The night pressed on him as his words faded.

After a heavy pause, she lay a hand on his arm. Rónán pushed it away, not wanting her sympathy. He was no longer that lost and damaged child. Yet when he met her gaze, the softness in her eyes threatened to jolt something free inside him.

"I am so sorry," she whispered.

"'Twas a long time ago."

Within the shards of silvery moonlight, outrage blazed bright in her eyes. "Nay child should endure what you did."

He shook his head, unable to express what he was feeling, unsure if he should. Never had he intended to let her feel anything for him. Nobility flowed through her veins.

And who was he? A runaway orphan who'd perfected his distance from anyone or anything other than the Knights Templar. Until this boldly brash woman with beautiful eyes had burst into his life and threatened to destroy his long-held defenses.

Rónán inhaled and straightened, shrugging their shared blanket from their shoulders and dispersing her scent. He could ill afford to allow himself thoughts of her beyond the end of this mission. Once they'd rescued Lord Sionn, and he prayed that quickly came to pass, he would load the weapons needed by King Robert and depart. Then, never again would they see the other.

"You are right. No child should be subjected to such atrocity. But"—he scanned the water before turning back to her—"we both know life is not fair. 'Tis up to each of us to make the most of our opportunities, or create those to move to a better path."

"Which you did." Admiration flickered on her face. "I am proud of you, of the strength you found those many years ago."

"Dinna be," he said, his voice harsher than he'd intended. "'Twas survival, naught more."

"I disagree. Many a lad wouldna have dared to run."

His chest tightened, and he remained silent. Regardless of her belief, his actions had been far from honorable. After several moments, he frowned, for an unexplainable reason finding it important to tell her of his original intent. "When I left, I never meant to return to Ireland."

"I can understand why. You needed to remove yourself from a brutal situation." She paused. "There are so many decent people in this world. I pray that the horrendous actions of that vile scoundrel didna ruin your ability to see the good in others."

"It didna." His past may have shaped his youth, but the Knights Templar, elite warriors who were like brothers, had given him more than a way of life, but friendship. "Over the years I have witnessed much ill among people, but I have seen much good."

"I am pleased. 'Twould make me sad to think that you have lived with the cur's dastardly actions having marred your life."

With a shrug, he shifted back. Flickers of moonlight skimmed across the sea in a somber array as the bow cut through the oncoming swell. "I rarely think of him." His past was not something he lingered on.

"What is his name? Mayhap I have heard of him."

"I doubt it. Nor does it matter. 'Twas a long time ago."

She wiped strands of hair that escaped from her face. "Mayhap, but I want to know the name of the man who, if he still lives, will feel my wrath."

Moved by her fierceness, he shot her a wry smile. "Have you ever been told that you are stubborn?"

A smile touched her lips. "Often, by my father and many others." Lathir arched a brow. "The scoundrel's name, then?"

He released a slow sigh, aware she wouldn't be satisfied until she had a reply. "Feradach O'Dowd."

In the moonlight, her face blanched.

"You know him?" he forced himself to ask.

She gave a visible swallow. "Aye. Sir Feradach O'Dowd is now a powerful man in the realm of Tír Kythyr, and is the master-at-arms for the Earl of Ardgar, my father's enemy. Someone we must avoid."

# Chapter Three

Streams of silvery moonlight skimmed across the sea as if mocking the shocked outrage that pierced Rónán. It was a moment before he could speak. "In my youth," he growled, "I knew Feradach traveled often on unsavory business, and on occasion disreputable men would visit his home. Now, to learn..." He dragged in a steady breath as he adjusted the rudder. "God's truth! To learn that not only is the bastard still drawing a breath but has been elevated to a master-at-arms is intolerable!"

"I assure you, with his violent reputation, many were as outraged by the Earl of Ardgar's selection for master-at-arms. And many more wish Feradach's body was rotting beneath the ground." Lathir paused. "I doubt we will encounter Sir Feradach, much less have him pose a threat to our mission. Our time traveling afoot will be minimal, and he often resides in one of the earl's strongholds on the southeast coast of Ireland."

That he wouldn't have to face Feradach was poor consolation after the brutality he'd suffered in his youth at the cur's hands. Anger slamming through him, Rónán shoved to his feet. "Take the rudder."

Eyes wide with concern met his. "Where are you going?"

"To see if our makeshift repairs on the bow are holding." He wanted to be alone, to think. His mind a turbulent mull, Rónán strode to the front of the cog, welcomed the cold bite of wind as the vessel raised up against the incoming swell, then plunged into the trough.

As he methodically checked the repairs, the solemn cadence of wood against sea slowly brought solace. How many times had he let the freedom of the sea fill him, the sense of the wholeness one experienced when surrounded by such immense greatness?

Though many men cursed the ocean, as a lad he'd found his time underway healing. A place where he could begin again.

The soft scrape of steps had him glancing over his shoulder.

Framed within the moonlight, Lathir walked toward him, halted at his side as the ship rose up with another swell. She had forgone the blanket and wrapped her arms around herself. The wind, he couldn't help but notice, rippled the fabric of her cloak against her skin.

"This is my favorite place to go when I need to weigh my thoughts," she said.

He turned toward the sea, watched the tips of the frothy water cut away from the bow. "I told you to man the rudder."

"With the pathetic pace the *Aodh* is moving, I doubt the vessel will go astray."

The truth. Still, he was in a brooding mood, one he would prefer to keep from her. "Why are you here?"

"To let you know I am here if you need to talk."

The last thing he wished was to appear weak in her eyes. He faced her. "I am not looking for sympathy."

"And I seek naught but to offer friendship," she said, a sudden bite in her voice. "An error I willna mistake again." Shoulders stiff, she stepped back.

He cursed. "Lathir—"

Mouth tight, hair whipping in the wind with glints of gold caught within the moonbeams, she looked like an irritated fairy. If she was of the fey, no doubt she would haul him to the Otherworld and toss him into a bog.

"Your offer is appreciated," he said.

"But unwelcome."

Far from it, which was the problem. Oddly, he found himself wanting to confide in her, to let down his guard. "I deal with war, not issues that dinna pertain to my mission, nor build friendships when in but weeks I will be gone."

She frowned. "But you shared your past."

Blast it, he was making a muddle of this. "I thought to take your mind from your grief."

Her shoulders relaxed. "Which you did. For that, I thank you."

Wisps of moonlight caressing her skin lured him to meet her gaze, to see the sincerity on her face.

"There isna time for friendship?" Humor flickered in her eyes. "Or do you just avoid friendships with women?"

At the absurdity of her comment, against his intent, he chuckled, and the tension in his body eased. He liked her, more than was wise, but right now she didn't deserve a rebuff. They had been through much together since the attack. Any feelings she inspired were his to contend with. His to eventually bury beneath the weight of his mission.

"I have several close friends who are women," Rónán said, thinking of Stephan's wife, Katherine, and the spouses of his other Templar brothers. All extraordinary lasses he'd liked from the start, much as he had Lathir. An unwanted thought, given her father ruled the realm of Tír Sèitheach, while he was naught but a knight with a sword.

"Then 'tis me?" she prodded, a playful lilt to her voice.

"Why does it matter?" he asked, not wanting to be charmed.

"Because you intrigue me." The bow cut through a swell. On a soft rumble, salty spray curled into the air. "I tend to be good at evaluating people, but every time I think I know who you are, you show me a side that I didna expect."

"I am a simple warrior."

A smile curved her mouth. "Naught about you is simple. Few knights earn the trust of their king. Fewer still are assigned a mission of such importance. In truth, I expected the Bruce to choose a war-seasoned man of nobility to sail with my father to bring back the arms he needs."

If not for his and the king's Templar tie, a choice Rónán believed the Bruce would have made. "I am humbled by my sovereign's trust."

"But not surprised?"

Her intuition caught Rónán off guard. Though he'd seen Lathir in King Robert's presence, he'd believed that he'd kept any hint of a deeper relationship with his monarch hidden beyond that of a knight who served him. Yet she'd picked up on their unusual bond. What would she think if she were to learn that he, just as Scotland's king, was a Knight Templar?

On a slow exhale, she lifted her face against the soft breeze. "You didna reply."

"And what would you have me say?" he asked, curious of where her questions were leading.

"Mayhap"—her eyes danced in delight—"that in truth you are a pirate. And when the Bruce went into hiding during the winter of 1306, he hadna escaped to Ireland, or to an island off the coast of Antrim as many speculated, but that you stowed him aboard your ship, and he helped you as you marauded the English."

At the mental image, he grinned. "I have seen my sovereign wield a blade, and if he stepped into such a position, I believe he would make a fine brigand."

"But," she said, her gaze riveted on his, "not on your ship?"

"Nay." Never before had he found importance in material possessions, but for the first time, Rónán wished he indeed captained a ship, or held something of significance.

Stunned by the notion, refusing to examine the reason it'd slipped into his mind, he dismissed the unwanted thought. Nay, he was happy with his lot.

At least he had been until this moment, when the difference between their lots in life seemed glaring, at least to his eyes. "I own naught except a horse, a broadsword, and a *sgian dubh*."

"Mayhap, yet they are things one can replace, but not the caliber of a man."

"Indeed." With the cool tang of salt and the night filling the air, he gave a slow exhale, finding himself at ease in her presence, realizing he would like to learn more about her, assuring himself 'twas not due to her beauty, or how he could lose himself looking in her eyes, but to bide the time. "I have decided that we should be friends."

Lathir arched a brow. "Have you, now? And why do you think I would be interested in accepting such?"

"Because I intrigue you."

Her smile when it came reached her eyes and made his gaze linger and wish that it was within his power to keep it there. Foolish thoughts. Her life was spent in noble circles, his on the battlefield.

"There is that. You are fortunate," she teased, "I can overlook your surly nature, which I owe to your years at war."

He chuckled. "I do not believe that I have ever been called surly."

"Probably not to your face because your presence intimidated anyone from saying something so foolish."

"You arena foolish."

"Aye, as you deemed moments ago, I am your friend."

A fact that set well with him. Though he wasn't searching for a woman in his life, her strength, honor, and courage drew him. And he'd shared more of his past with her than he had with many of the Brotherhood.

With a yawn, she stepped away from the rail. "I am going to check the rudder."

"I will be there shortly." For a moment, regret weighed heavily as he watched her amble toward the stern. For a knight with a future filled with naught but wielding a blade, 'twas best to push any such thoughts of her from his mind.

\* \* \* \*

Above the thin veil of fog hanging over the sea, streaks of amber smeared the sky, framing a dance of low clouds to the west. Spearing a bit of meat on her fishhook, Lathir dropped the line over the rail. The wind of two days past had lessened to a breeze that did little more than ripple their sail and allow them to meander forward.

Still, they were headed west. For that she was thankful as it took her closer to finding her father.

Where was he now?

Please God let him be safe.

Her heart ached every time she walked over the bloodstained planks, and she said a silent prayer for the brave men's souls, knights she'd known for years, many who'd become her friends.

At the soft tap of boots, she glanced over and smiled at the sight of Rónán climbing the ladder to the main deck where she fished. Though she'd claimed he was surly, 'twas far from the truth.

In her travels with her father, she'd met many a warrior, but none like him. Aye, his attention was on war, on the mission he must accomplish, but their time together had exposed a man of great intelligence, integrity, and pride.

As well, though many knights had faith, when he'd believed her asleep, she'd caught Rónán on his knees whispering the Our Father several times over.

She grimaced. Was his devout nature inspired by his tragic youth? If so, the reason for his deep faith made sense.

A tug pulled on the line between her fingers.

She snapped the line to set the hook, then hauled up the thin twine.

Water splashed as a fish broke the surface. Satisfaction filled her as she added it to the other two on the deck.

"Seems you had more luck than I," Rónán said as he reached her. "'Twill make a fine meal."

"And be a welcome break from the oatcakes. Not that I dinna appreciate having them, or the dried beef."

He walked past the charred timber of the mast. "As you caught them, I will clean and cook them."

"An offer I shall happily accept." She glanced toward the opening to below deck, then shifted her gaze to him. "Are the rags we shoved in the new crack in the hull working?"

A frown deepened his brow. "Not as much as we had hoped. We will need to bail out water every few hours."

"A manageable amount." A gust of wind swept past and she glanced up, scanned the clouds building in the west. "It looks as if another storm is moving in."

"Aye. I had hoped to reach shore before anymore adverse weather hit." He nodded toward where they'd lashed timbers together to construct a makeshift raft. "Though we havena sighted land, we canna be far. If the *Aodh* begins to sink, we can use that."

Lathir didn't want to consider the possibility of trying to survive the frigid sea in that crude boat. With the craft tossed about in the wind, the result would be a dangerous if not miserable event. "I—" The cry of a gull had her glancing west.

In the distance, a seabird soared high in the sky, its white wings stark against the darkening skies.

Heart pounding, she scanned the thinning shroud of mist. Stilled. "I see a cliff!"

Rónán whirled, stared out a long moment, then his shoulders relaxed. "Thank God. Now, let us pray we reach shore before the storm arrives." He crossed to the rudder, steered the cog toward the distant crag. Once he'd reset their course, he looked over. "Do you recognize the area?"

As the vessel crept forward, the slap of waves steady against the hull, the vague outline grew clearer. Sheer cliffs staggered with ruddy hues of color cascaded in a fierce wall to where the surf slammed the base and erupted into violent bursts of white.

From the menacing shards of rock guarding the narrow inlet extended dark, oddly shaped stones positioned next to the other. Farther inland, the rocks lay flat like steps.

"'Tis impressive," he said.

"Aye, 'tis a causeway." As always, she was taken by the sheer beauty of the land. "Legend has it 'twas built by an Irish giant to battle his foe in Scotland."

Rónán arched a brow. "A Scottish foe?"

"Have you never heard the tale?"

He shook his head. "I had little time in my youth for such fancies."

Tenderness filled her. "For which I am sorry." She pointed toward the coast. "See that odd gathering of flat stones spread out along a portion of the shore?"

"Aye."

"'Tis all that remains of the fateful battle."

"And did the Irish giant win?"

A smile curved her lips. "I would say it depends on who you ask, but I like to believe that in the end he escaped with more than his life, but with his honor."

The lightness in his eyes faded. "'Tis irrelevant what you believe. 'Tis a story, naught but to amuse those caught within the innocence of youth." He adjusted the rudder.

On a groan, the cog struggled as it tried to turn against the strong flow of water.

He scowled at their makeshift sail. "Blast it, we are caught in the current and closing too fast. Given the ship's damaged hull, if the *Aodh* hits the rocks, 'twill split apart."

A pulse of fear jolted her. Tightening her fingers on the rail, she squinted at the shore. "From the water line on the beach, 'tis high tide."

"Aye and, God willing, it may be our saving grace." He gestured to the west of the large, flattened stones. "Though the coast is rocky, the stones are small. 'Tis where I am thinking to run the ship aground."

Icy wind thick with the scent of rain whipped past as the wind increased. Against the blustery howl, whitecaps tipped the growing waves. Dark clouds rolled overhead, smothering the sun.

She shot him a nervous glance. "Looks like we willna make it to shore before the storm arrives."

"By God, we will do our damnedest." Arms visibly straining, he shoved the rudder.

The *Aodh* shook, turned slightly to the right.

Face taut, he met her gaze. "Gather our packs below in case we are forced to abandon ship."

"Aye." Waves slammed the hull as she hurried to the ladder and scrambled down. With care, she picked her way over debris to where they'd stowed their supplies and began shoving essentials into their packs.

Wood cracked; the cog jolted.

She yelped as she was thrown back among the sodden boxes.

Steps pounded overhead. Eyes dark with worry, Rónán peered into the hull. "Are you hurt?" he bellowed against the wind.

Grimacing against the ache in her ribs where she'd hit, Lathir pushed to her feet. "Nay. What happened?"

"The *Aodh* slammed against the rocks. The rudder is broken."

As if to emphasize the danger, the next swell raised the ship, then smashed it against the stones.

Wood snapped.

Another gash opened in the hull.

Seawater flooded in.

"Lathir!"

"Coming!" With supplies in hand, she clambered over the debris. Water had risen to her knees by the time she'd reached the ladder. Fighting the wash of panic, she shoved her foot on the braided hemp, began to climb.

Wood shattered in her wake as another swell rammed the cog.

Jolted back a rung from the top, she lost her grip.

He caught her hand.

Icy wind lashed at her as, muscles screaming, she dangled above the hull.

Another wave slammed against the cog.

Teeth clenched, Rónán hauled her up.

Wind moaned as she lay against the deck, gasping for breath. "Thank God, for a moment…" Against the pain she struggled to her feet, kept her balance, refusing to further ponder her fate. "There is a huge slice in the bow!"

"And a large chunk missing in the stern." Rónán frowned. "Can you walk?"

"Aye."

"Help me shove the raft over the side before the ship sinks."

As they fought their way across the deck, another huge, white-tipped swell rammed the cog.

Lathir lurched forward.

Rónán steadied her, then holding Lathir's hand, forged through the whip of rain toward the raft, the abating wave exposing the jagged rocks below.

With his free hand, Rónán grabbed the splintered piece of the mast as the ship dropped. "Hold on!"

Timbers shattered with a violent screech as the vessel was impaled on the rocks.

Their raft broke free, slid across the deck, and plummeted into the raging seas.

The cog began to list.

"Saint's breath, we are too late!" she gasped.

"Lathir!" Rónán demanded. "Look at me!"

Wind-driven rain hurled past as gray eyes dark with fear were riveted on him.

"We can do this, but only if we work together."

She closed her eyes briefly, then gave a shaky nod.

"The cog is listing toward the rocks," he yelled above the roar of the wind, "which is to our benefit. The next wave will ground it. Then we can climb to the other side of the deck and jump to safety."

What little color in her face fled, but he saw her visually soldier herself for the challenge ahead.

The next surge of water bashed the hull, hurling the fractured vessel higher against the rocks.

Her body jerked; he tightened his grip. Once he'd secured the rope to the rail, he handed her part of the woven hemp. "Use the line to climb down to the rail."

She nodded.

Icy rain battered him as he guided her into position. "Stay close!"

"I will."

"Now!" With the cog angled sideways and slowly sinking into the churning sea, the rope taut in his hands, Rónán propelled down the incline, Lathir on his heels.

The groan of wood and splinter of timbers filled the air as another wave slammed the cog as they were halfway down.

"Hold on!" he bellowed.

"The ship canna take much more," Lathir called.

"Aye!" Braided hemp scraped his hands as he dropped and braced himself on the rickety deck. He caught her waist as she reached him.

Another large swell rose from the depths, whitecaps topping the blackened churn of water.

God's truth, they had to reach safety before the next wave hit. With the staggered rocks now but an arm's length away, Rónán guided her atop the rail. "Jump!"

Wind battered her as she leaped. Her feet hit the wet rocks; she slid, then steadied herself. She whirled back to him, eyes wide with fear as she glanced behind him. "Hurry!"

He slashed free the length of rope they'd used to climb down, held on to one side, tossed the other part to her. "Tie the end to the rock behind you."

Fingers trembling, she secured the line.

Water thundering behind him, Rónán tightened his hold on the rope, climbed atop the rail.

A swell blasted the ship.

The rail snapped beneath the force. With the roar of water rushing around him, Rónán plunged toward the violent churn.

# Chapter Four

Pain shot through Rónán as he slammed against a boulder. Icy water streamed through the rocks above, poured over him as the hull splintered to his right.

The swell retreated as he clung to the woven hemp; he gasped for breath. With a shuddered groan, wood scraped as the wreckage began sliding back, creating a gaping hole below him that was quickly filling with water.

"Rónán!"

Muscles burning, he glanced up.

Face raw with fear, holding on to the line, Lathir lay on one of the oddly flat stone leaning over the edge.

"Stay back!" Ignoring the pain, the cold wracking his body, he braced both feet against the rock. Hands fisted on the rope, he began to climb.

Another swell crashed over him.

He tightened the rope around his body seconds before he was jerked downward. Sodden, his hands numb, through sheer will he held on as he again slammed into the rocks, the large section of the broken hull splintering against the rocks paces below.

Blackness threatened. A sharp tug had him looking up.

Lathir's hair whipped around her face as she pulled on the rope.

"Get back!" Wind ripped away his warning as his body was again hurled against the stone.

The rope snapped taut. "Rónán!"

He gasped for breath, sensation in his body fading, his teeth beginning to chatter uncontrollably. Vision blurring with cold, he fought to remain awake. Another wave battered him, the icy slide of water draining his strength.

The rope lifted a degree.

"Hold on!" Lathir's voice came as if from far away, and he closed his eyes, the urgency to remain alert dwindling as he succumbed to the blackness.

\* \* \* \*

Fear tore through Lathir as Rónán's body hung limp below her. Only the line wrapped around his waist held him paces above the vicious rush of waves. "Rónán!"

Like a cloth doll, he dangled as the spray buffeted him over and again. Saint's breath, she couldn't lose him!

"Move aside, lass!"

The deep, raspy voice had her tightening her grip on the rope as she grabbed her *sgian dubh* and whirled.

A tall, rangy man with sodden brown hair and a beard framing a harsh, weather-beaten face waved her back.

Heart pounding, she angled her blade toward him. "Stay away!"

"God's teeth, lass, had I wanted to kill you, you would have long since been dead." He scowled at the taut rope. "Wasting time arguing willna help your man."

The truth. He was an imposing man, with a ragged scar slashed across his cheek and unforgiving dark eyes. She took a quick moment to make her decision. Her breathing ragged, she secured her blade, keeping her other hand tight on the rope. "Hurry, help me!"

The stranger knelt beside her, caught the line. "Pull." A swell crashed below, hurling water over them as they hauled Rónán up and onto the icy rocks.

Eyes closed, hair a sheen of icy strands, Rónán lay unmoving, water streaming from his sodden garb.

Grief tore through Lathir, and she fought the panic rising in her chest. "Oh God," she choked out. "He's dead!"

The stranger grunted. "Nay, lost consciousness due to cold." With ease, he slung Rónán's wet, limp body over his shoulder. "Follow me and take care," he yelled over the rush of water. "'Tis slick."

Shivering, Lathir scrambled up, shielding her face from the wind. "Where are you taking him?"

Shards of ice cracked beneath his boots as he picked his way along the slippery, oddly patterned rocks. "Look toward the ridge. If you see smoke through the rain, 'tis from my home."

Lathir scanned the winter-ravaged land as she hurried in his wake. Against the lash of rain, she made out steep cliffs as far as she could see, except for a steep but navigable incline to their right that narrowed at the top. She followed the upper rim, saw naught by the blurry outline of rock.

"I canna believe you made out our ship in this foul weather," she shouted as they made their way through the rocks.

"I saw the storm clouds moving in on my way back from fishing, so I went out to gather wood."

Rónán groaned as he shifted his limp form to his other shoulder.

"I was about to haul in another load when I saw your cog in the distance heading straight toward shore." He stepped gingerly over a jagged rock. "*If* you call that charred and battered ship barely afloat such."

"We were attacked at sea," she rasped, the fear for her father, and grief of losing so many good men, thickening her words. "Most of the crew died."

"I am surprised your attackers let you and your man live."

"When they sailed off, the cog was engulfed in flames. We thought…" She fought the terror still haunting her and took a moment to compose herself. "We believed we would die a horrible death. But after the enemy sailed from view, a storm drenched the ship. I assure you, had the attackers known we were alive, they wouldna have left until the last board slid into the sea."

"Who attacked the ship?"

She hesitated. Was he a champion of the English, or was his loyalty given to the Bruce?

He glanced back. "Nay, I know," he spat. "Nay doubt English scum. I have seen their ships passing by often enough. They think they can stop King Robert by severing support from Ireland, but they will fail."

Relief swept through her, and a sliver of the tension in her body eased. "'Twas."

"You were indeed fortunate." He wove along the oddly patterned stones. "Yet you managed to sail to shore."

"The rudder was undamaged, and we tied pieces of tattered sail together to make repairs. With more holes than fabric, though pathetic, it allowed us to hobble to the coast. Though 'twas ineffective once we became caught in a current that dragged our vessel to shore."

"Had the storm been upon us and visibility as 'tis now, I would have missed you."

Rain battered them as they climbed down to the beach, cluttered with small rocks. White water from crashing waves exploded in the air as they worked their way along the coastline. Regardless of his sodden state, their rescuer kept up a steady, ground-eating pace.

Fresh anxiety twisted in her chest at Rónán's face devoid of color, and the bluish tint of his lips. Please God let him live! "I would have your name, to thank you."

"Tighearnán." Ice coated his brows, lashes, and beard as he shot her a measuring look. "I need nay thanks. 'Tis the way of life to help those you can when you live near the sea."

"Not all share your way of thinking."

He grunted and started up the steep slope.

Exhausted, her entire body aching, she kept pace, refusing to allow Rónán out of her sight. "I am called Lathir. The man you carry is Rónán."

Though he'd saved Rónán's life, until she knew more about the stranger, was sure she could trust him, 'twas best to conceal Rónán's being a knight and her nobility, or correct Tighearnán's belief that they were wed.

He continued to climb.

A loud crash had her turning, squinting through the rain. In the distance, caught in an oncoming swell, the tattered pieces of the *Aodh* slammed against the rocks. Planks exploded from the remnants of the deck, and shattering wood was swept into the rush of waves.

Memories stormed her, of the times she'd sailed aboard the cog with her father, of his laughter, his sage advice and, regardless the issue, how she could always turn to him.

Emotions raw, she searched for fragments of the beloved ship upon the swell, as bits popped up, were tossed about in the rough seas.

She swallowed hard. Nay, all was not lost. 'Twas but hewn timber, which they could rebuild, and her father still lived. She refused to believe otherwise. They would find and rescue him. But how?

With a heavy heart, she continued up the steep slope, fighting against the aches in her limbs. As they topped the ridge, she glanced around.

The rolling hills beyond sprinkled with errant trees, the sweep of land pummeled within the storm's embrace.

Lathir swallowed hard, hurried toward where Tighearnán was approaching a small hut, blessed smoke belching from the chimney. Warmth Rónán desperately needed.

"What is it you do?" she asked, refusing to give in to the wash of panic.

"I am a fisherman."

"I didna see your boat."

"'Tis secured behind rocks on shore around the bend."

At the thick-hewn entry, he jerked open the door and stepped inside.

Lathir followed, pulled the door shut, thankful when the blessed heat embraced her.

He strode to where a bed haphazardly covered with blankets sat paces from the hearth, laid Rónán upon the covers, then began tugging off his sopping garb. "Remove his trews and boots."

With a nod, Lathir quickly complied, aware the wet clothes would hamper his body receiving much-needed heat. The drenched clothing slapped as it hit the aged wood floor, but her gaze was riveted on Rónán's naked body.

Though she knew his body was forged by muscle, it hadn't prepared her for Rónán's sheer magnificence, a sight forever imprinted on her mind.

"Órlaith," the fisherman snapped as he laid a blanket over Rónán, "bring over a bucket of warm water and a cloth."

"Aye, Papa."

Lathir started as a girl she gauged around eight summers hurried with a pail toward a kettle simmering near the edge of the hearth. In the rush to get Rónán inside and warm, she'd missed seeing the child.

"Lass, take this side of the cover."

Startled, she glanced up. The fisherman was holding the edge of the thick blanket toward her. Thankful for the diversion, Lathir focused on tucking in the cloth around his shoulders, then pulling another blanket atop.

The fisherman stepped back, frowned. "Once he begins shaking, 'twill be difficult to hold him still."

"Why?"

A spark popped in the hearth as he arched a brow. "Have you never been around a man near to freezing?"

She shook her head.

"Once his body begins to warm, any places that have been frostbitten can itch, swell, burn, and 'twill be very painful. Dinna fash if your man cries out, or if his body shudders God awful."

"I see." Except she didn't. Why must Rónán suffer further? Though he was alive; for that she'd be thankful.

The girl handed her the bucket and cloth.

"I thank you," she said.

Shy brown eyes held hers for a moment before she stepped behind her father.

Tighearnán nodded to the child. "Off with you, now. Finish the stew you are making. I will introduce you to the lass once she has taken care of her man."

"Aye, Papa." Eyes filled with youthful curiosity slid to Lathir, then the girl hurried to the opposite side of the hut, where a small pile of cut vegetables lay.

"We are both soaked. We need to change as well." Their host nodded to a trunk near the wall. "There are gowns that will fit you inside." He walked to another chest on the opposite wall, withdrew dry clothes.

Once he'd turned, she selected and donned a gown as fast as her shaking limbs allowed.

"'Tis best to warm him slowly," the fisherman advised her as he returned. "Rinse the cloth in hot water often and wipe it over the affected skin until 'tis warm. Let me know if you need more water heated."

She stilled and her throat clogged as the full impact of his words sank in. She was to draw the heated cloth over Rónán's body, every curve, every intimate part.

"I will return in a moment." Tighearnán departed.

Rónán's body jerked, and he began to shake.

On a steadying breath, she rinsed the woven fabric and pressed it against him, struggling to keep her attention on ensuring she warmed every part of his chilled skin, not the width or breath of his chest, or how the brown hair narrowed in a tantalizing line down the flat of his stomach to join with dark thatch to cradle his length.

"Dinna rush," Tighearnán cautioned her from near the hearth. "You must warm him slowly until the skin color returns to normal."

"Aye." She rewarmed the cloth, continued, focusing on the fact that Rónán lived. As to the intimate degree with which she'd tended him—that he would never learn.

Still, though she'd remained attentive to the task, his honed muscle, hard planes that carved his body into a man of power was one who a lass would be blind not to be drawn to.

Nor did she overlook his qualities, that of a man who'd earned her trust, his word when given, one backed by action. A knight who'd made it clear that his intent was to support their king in his endeavor to eradicate those who challenged his rightful place.

Her hand paused in its task. A potent reminder that once they'd rescued her father and the arms were delivered to the Bruce, she'd never see Rónán again.

And what of her father? Please God let him still live. Though, like their attackers, he believed her dead. After the loss of her mother, a blow that would leave him devastated.

Her hand trembled as she drew the warmed cloth slowly across Rónán's toes.

"How is he faring?" the fisherman asked as he moved to her side.

She cleared her throat, taking in the soft flush of color on his skin. "Much better. He is barely shivering, and his skin color is returning. But, from his expressions in his sleep, he is in pain."

"And will be until his body is entirely warmed. Let me help you so that you can tend to his backside." He carefully turned Rónán onto his stomach.

"I thank you." After rewarming the cloth, she slowly drew it over his shoulders.

"The stew is ready, as is the warm drink. Nay doubt you are hungry and exhausted. Go. I will do the rest."

"I will finish." She met his gaze. "'Tis important to me."

He stroked his beard as he studied her. With a nod, he walked over and sat at the table where his daughter quietly ate.

Face illuminated by the soft wash of flames, as her father settled beside her, Órlaith peered at Lathir beneath thick brown lashes.

Lathir smiled, and the child's eyes widened and turned away. She was shy. Not surprising, given her and her father's secluded location.

How far were they from a town? Had Tighearnán heard of her father's abduction? Doubtful, when but days had passed since the incident, more so considering that if anywhere, Tighearnán would have gone fishing.

She shoved her wet hair away from her face with a weary sigh and, soaking the cloth again in the warm water, she drew it across Rónán's outer thigh, paused.

A birthmark.

Intrigued, she traced her finger over the uneven brown path of skin a thumb's width to where it faded into a curl. A unique design. What did he think of its presence? As if it mattered. As an orphan, the unique mark would hold naught of significance.

A weary smile touched her mouth as she resumed her task. She needed to continue, nay linger on foolish thoughts.

A while later, after several refills of warm water, with Rónán's trembling having subsided and his skin radiating a healthy glow, she secured the covers around him and stepped away. Thankful, she rinsed out the woven fabric, hung it near the hearth to dry.

The scuff of a boot sounded as their rescuer halted beside Rónán. "Your man is going to be fine."

"Thanks to you."

"I did nay more than you would have done if the circumstance was reversed."

"Regardless, we are in your debt. I promise you will be compensated for your help."

A muscle worked in his jaw. "My help didna come with conditions."

Lathir remained silent, understanding his pride. Still, she would find a way to pay him back for his selfless aid.

With Rónán safe, she took in the simple furnishings. Besides the small bed where he lay, a bench sat near a small table, and fishing nets lay neatly folded and stacked in the corner, which lent a slight tang of the sea inside the hut. In addition to the chest where she'd retrieved the gown, several more stood against the far wall, no doubt holding spices or other valuables.

From the ceiling hung an array of dried herbs, some she'd used in preparing food in the past, others for healing, and against the opposite wall were various tools of Tighearnán's trade.

To their right, a claymore lay secured in its sheath, the pommel above the leather-wrapped grip ornately carved.

In the far corner, a ladder led to a loft. From this angle, she caught the edge of a bed. Brown hair spilled from beneath the covers, as did the stringy hair of the well-loved doll that she'd seen the child holding earlier.

Tenderness filled her heart as she met the father's gaze. "She is fortunate to have you."

He was a man who'd clearly been marked by the sea and its elements—salt, sun, and wind. Yet the taut expression on his face softened. "Órlaith means everything to me."

"Your wife?"

Pain darkened his eyes. "I...I believe she is dead."

Grief tightened in her chest. "I am sorry."

He gave a curt nod. "Sit, eat. You are hungry."

Her stomach growled as he set a tasty scented bowl and steaming drink before her. She sat, scooped up a bit as he settled opposite her, refilled his bowl, then topped off both of their goblets with ale. "If you do not mind my asking, what happened to your wife?"

Tighearnán swirled the goblet. On a rough sigh, he thumped it on the table. "Two years ago, I went to the village to sell fish. I had a grand catch and had picked out a ribbon to surprise Máire, my wife. But when I returned..." His throat worked and his eyes grew clouded with anguish. "The inside of the hut was in shambles. And the blood... The table was turned over, and cloths were strewn about. Máire had clearly put up a struggle against whoever took her. Then," he forced out, his voice but a strangled whisper, "I heard Órlaith crying in the loft."

"They didna take her," Lathir rasped.

"I still canna believe it. So young, she would have been easy to take and claim as their own. The only thing that makes sense is that she was asleep during the attack and the men didna know she was there." Grief-stricken eyes shifted to her, the devastation within breaking her heart. "Wanting to protect her, my wife would never have exposed our daughter's presence. I followed the trail, which led to the ocean. Frantic to find my wife, I left Órlaith with trusted friends and scoured every port for months. I threatened, pleaded. In the end, without a whisper of anyone having seen her, I accepted the horrific fact that she must have died from her injuries, and returned home to my daughter."

Sorrow wrapped around her heart, a cold, chilling sweep that threatened to release the tears for his pain. How he'd suffered. That he still mourned the loss of his wife after the years passed exposed the depth of his love for Máire.

How did one recover from such?

Or could they?

If, God forbid, she found her father dead, Lathir wasn't sure if she could be so strong. She prayed that she'd never have to face such a tragic circumstance.

The crackle of the fire fractured the silence, thick with heartache.

"'Tis more than you wanted to hear." He grunted. "More than I expected to share."

"I appreciate your trusting me enough to tell me. How has your daughter handled her loss?"

He glanced toward the loft, and lines of concern deepened on his brow. "Órlaith didna talk for months. Even now, she tends to be shy. I pray she can find a way to heal."

Lathir touched his shoulder; he tensed. "With your love and compassion, I have confidence you will help her overcome her grief. Your daughter is blessed to have such a caring father."

"I far from think her staying with me is a blessing. Quite the opposite." The bench scraped as he stood.

"I lost my mother during my birth," she said as he started to move away. "But like you and Órlaith, my father and I are close."

He met her gaze.

"Through his stories," she continued, needing him to understand the importance he held in Órlaith's life, "I have come to know my mother, to love her. Your daughter has memories of her mother, you to share more, and your love to help Órlaith through whatever challenges lie ahead." She thought of Rónán. "Many children dinna have even that."

He released a frustrated exhale. "I know. 'Tis selfish to want more."

"Nay. 'Tis difficult to lose those we love."

"Aye. I thank you. To sleep with you, now. You are exhausted, and your warmth will be welcomed by your man." He walked to a pile of blankets, made a pallet near the fire, then settled, his back to her.

Lathir finished her meal. As she cleaned her bowl and mug, Rónán murmured under his breath. She turned.

Rónán lay on his side, where she'd left him asleep, his breath even, errant shivers rippling across his body. The lines of pain that'd streaked across his handsome face earlier were but faint twinges. That the threat to his skin had passed was a blessing.

On the ship, she'd rested against him to share warmth, but they'd both been fully clothed. Nor could she erase the images of his body, the tempting curves, the power. What would it be like to have him hold her, want her?

Warmth crept through her, and for a moment she allowed herself to imagine his gentle touch, his kiss. She smiled at her whimsy.

Nor, with the fisherman believing they were wed, did she have another place to sleep. Assuring herself that his lying naked against her was naught she couldn't handle, Lathir walked over, lifted the cover, and climbed in bed.

As the fire snapped in the hearth, she listened to his slow, even breathing. Too aware of him, she said a silent prayer, wrapped her arm around his side, and edged her body flush against his.

His scent of man and a hint of sea filled her every breath as she rested her head within the curve of his shoulder, and a sense of peace filled her.

On a shudder, his body relaxed.

Pleased, she closed her eyes, but doubted, with her every fiber aware of him, that she'd sleep.

# Chapter Five

A deep ache pulsed through Rónán's body, invading his sleep. At the scent of charred wood, he gave a rough exhale. Another blasted night aboard the *Aodh*.

He shifted, pressed against Lathir. Through the murky haze, he awaited the creak of joints as the battered cog lumbered up another swell.

The pallet remained still, and the soft crackle of fire filled the silence. With a frown, he opened his eyes. Firelight glinted off Lathir's gold hair as she lay next to him. Tensing in realization, he shifted his gaze, took in the simple hut, a loft overhead, chests stacked against a side wall, and several bundles of dried herbs hanging nearby.

Vague memories of clinging to a rope and jumping from the ship's rail, then slamming against the icy stone rolled through his mind.

Then naught.

Where were they? Whose cabin was this?

The door scraped open.

Muscles burned as Rónán shoved to his feet. Wavering, he reached for his dagger. His hand skimmed along flesh. God's truth, he was naked!

In the doorframe, snow swirled within the morning sunlight, outlining a tall man sporting brown hair and a beard. He dwarfed the rickety opening, an armload of wood clutched in his beefy arms.

Rónán grabbed a nearby stick, determined to ignore the incessant throbbing in his head, then positioned himself between the stranger and Lathir. "Halt!"

A thick brow shot up. "I see you are awake, then."

Regardless of the man's calm demeanor, he kept his grip tight on his makeshift weapon.

"I am Tighearnán." The man nodded to the right. "Your broadsword is across the chamber on the bench. Nay doubt you would prefer using that over kindling."

"Father," a young girl's voice called from above, "'twould seem the man you found on the rocks yesterday will live."

Rónán's gaze climbed to the loft, where a child peered out, before shifting his eyes back to the man. Which answered his question of who'd helped Lathir haul him to safety.

"Aye." A smile quirked on the man's lips. "And that"—he lowered his voice—"is my daughter, who is eight summers. Though one day she will see a man naked, I prefer it not be now."

God's teeth! His grasp tight on the stick, Rónán snatched a blanket, wrapped the coverlet around his waist, then glanced toward Lathir, caught in deep sleep. The firelight exposed one shapely leg, yet a linen shift concealed the rest of her body.

His gaze darted to the large man. Wherever they were, whoever this stranger was, Lathir accepted them, and had even gone to sleep. He slowly lowered his makeshift weapon. "I am called Rónán."

The other man nodded. "'Tis good to make your acquaintance. Though I would rather have done so under less harrowing circumstance." He stepped inside, shoved the door closed with his boot. The light from the hearth illuminated the chamber in a soft glow. "Your woman explained how the Sassenach attacked your vessel. They are a nasty lot."

Sassenach, an unflattering term for the English, one he'd used many times over himself. That he and this man shared a dislike for the enemy brought a token of relief, but his attention riveted on the fact that he'd called Lathir his woman.

"They are." Rónán paused. He'd go along with the ruse of a marriage for the moment. "You found us on the rocks yesterday?"

"Of sorts. The lass was frantic when I arrived. I helped her pull you to safety, then carried you to my home." The large stranger piled the wood near the hearth, selected two chunks, and laid them upon the fire. "Your woman tended to you until your chills faded. As well, I heard her several times during the night caring for you. Nay doubt 'tis the reason she is still asleep."

An unfamiliar warmth tightened in his chest as Rónán's gaze swept over Lathir before shifting to the man. "My thanks. We are indebted to you."

A wry smile touched Tighearnán's mouth as he wiped his hands on his trews as he stood. "As I explained to the lass, 'tis the way of those who live along the sea to help those in distress and naught to repay."

Rónán nodded. A lifestyle that excluded brigands. A fact he'd learned all too well during his time sailing with the Templars.

Scuffs from above brought his gaze back to the loft. A pair of tiny feet edged over the side, followed by a fluff of fabric as a little girl stepped on the top rung of the ladder. Tangles of chestnut hair framed an angelic face. Wary brown eyes peered at him over her shoulder as she slowly made her way down. Once her foot touched the floor, she hurried to stand behind her father.

A tender smile curved Tighearnán's mouth. "Órlaith tends to be shy. That she spoke at all in your presences is a boon."

Keeping his hold tight on his cover, Rónán knelt so that he was at eye level with the girl. "'Tis nay harm in being a bit cautious. To my way of thinking, 'tis a wise lass who takes stock of a person before deciding they are someone to like, much less trust."

Unsure eyes shifted to her father.

Pride shone on Tighearnán's face. "'Sage words, lass, ones to live by."

Acceptance filled the child's eyes as she lifted her gaze to Rónán and studied him for a long moment as if gathering her courage. "Do you have a daughter I could play with?"

Her father chuckled, but the innocent question left Rónán floundering. After the hell he'd lived through, never had he contemplated having a child.

Lived? Nay, survived.

Barely.

Against the ugly memories of his youth, Rónán forced a smile. "Nay."

Her thumb wavered near her mouth in a nervous gesture. "Your woman is pretty."

He glanced toward Lathir, found her sitting up watching him, her eyes thick with sleep, lengths of golden hair tugged free of her braid.

Pretty? No, stunningly beautiful. A woman who would steal a man's breath and make him forget everything but her. Including his body's lingering aches and pains.

Lathir arched a curious brow.

Stunned by his thoughts, Rónán cleared his throat. "Aye, that she is, lass."

A blush swept Lathir's face as she wrapped the blanket around herself and stood. "I didna expect to sleep so long."

"I am surprised that you have woken up before the sun has risen high in the sky." Tighearnán set his hand on his daughter's shoulder. "Órlaith, don your traveling garb. 'Tis time to head to the market to sell our catch."

"Aye, Father." After one quick glance at Rónán, the girl scrambled up the ladder. The rustle of clothing sounded as she hurried to dress.

"You are a fisherman?" Rónán asked.

"Aye." Tighearnán withdrew a loaf of bread wrapped within a cloth, cut a few thick slabs of cheese, and laid out several oatcakes. "To break your fast." He gestured toward an aged wooden chest in the corner. "There should be enough food inside to tide you over until we return this eve. Your garb hanging near the hearth should be dry."

Lathir moved beside Rónán. "I didna realize a town was so close."

He secured his broadsword, then tugged on his cape as his daughter hurried down the ladder. "'Tis a distance away, but we are traveling on horseback. If my food stores werena low, I wouldna be going now." He smiled. "If the fish fetch a good price, in addition to restocking the larder"— he winked at his daughter—"mayhap I will purchase a few sweets."

The child's eyes danced with excitement as she donned her cloak, trimmed on the inside with fur. "I am ready!"

"So you are. On with you, then. I shall be there in a trice. And"— he handed her a broken piece of a carrot—"give this to the stubborn beast so he will take us without a fuss."

With eyes dancing in delight, carrot clutched tight, the child scampered from the hut.

Tighearnán nodded to Rónán, then Lathir. "I despise having to leave, 'tis poor manners."

"There is little to regret," Rónán said. "'Tis we who thank you for your hospitality."

Concern lined his brow as the fisherman opened the door. "I am not expecting any visitors, but I suggest keeping the door barred while we are away."

Tension slid through Rónán. "Are you expecting trouble?"

"Nay, but with the English sailing about in their effort to seize control of Ireland, 'tis prudent to remain cautious." He slid a *sgian dubh* inside his boot, another into his belt, then stepped out. Wind-tossed snow swirled inside as he tugged the door shut.

His body stiff, Rónán walked over, dropped the bar into place, turned, then stilled as Lathir's gaze rested on him. Beneath the edge of sleep lingering in her eyes, he caught awareness. Nor with how her blanket had slipped from her shoulders did he miss the slender curves of her body, the lush swell of her breasts, or how her nipples had grown taut.

He hardened, and silently swore. Onboard the *Aodh*, with their survival bound by working together and danger ripe at every turn, he had been kept too busy to think of her, of the need she inspired. With them safe and alone, the hours ahead were filled with naught but the other. Nor could he overlook that she'd tended to him while naked, lain beside him throughout the night.

Rónán drew in a steadying breath. Regardless his attraction, he was a knight with naught to offer but his sword. "I thank you for saving me." She pulled up the blanket to drape around her shoulders. "'Tis naught to thank. You would have done the same if I were in danger. Had Tighearnán not arrived when he did, I dinna know if I could have…" A shudder swept her.

"But he did. Because of your efforts, I am alive." He hesitated, deciding, given his attraction to her, the best way to broach a topic he'd rather avoid. "Tighearnán called you my woman, said that you cared for me and checked on me throughout the night."

She gave a visible swallow, nodded. "As a stranger, I thought 'twas best to allow him to believe we were—"

"'Twas." He cleared his throat. "Your body's warmth gave me great comfort."

A slight blush crept up her face.

He had to ask. "I didna do anything untoward, did I?"

Surprise widened her eyes before they twinkled with mirth. "Are you asking if you touched me inappropriately in your sleep?"

His jaw tightened. "If I did," he ground out, "I apologize."

"You did naught but sleep."

He nodded. "Do you trust him?" Rónán asked, thankful to shift the attention to their task, not her, or the way she made him feel, or the things she made him want.

She stretched. "He seems like an honorable man."

"How much does he know about us?"

"That the English attacked our ship. With the cog ablaze and believing we were dead, they departed."

"Good, but a few—"

She cleared her throat pointedly as another blush swept Lathir's cheeks. "I think it prudent to dress before we continue our discussion."

God's truth, where was his mind? "Indeed."

"Here."

She handed him his trews from the hook near the fire, then a large tunic that no doubt belonged to their host.

"My shirt?" Rónán asked.

"'Twas nay more than tatters. You are fortunate to be alive. If Tighearnán hadna arrived and helped to haul you out of the water…" Her voice broke at the last.

To give her a moment to recover herself, he took his time donning the shirt. "But he was, and we are safe. 'Tis naught to worry about now." She gave a slow exhale. "Aye."

Rónán turned his back to give her privacy, donned the remainder of his garb. "The *Aodh*?"

The splintering wood of the hull breaking against rocks as Rónán, battered by the spray of water against the rocks, hung unconscious, flashed through Lathir's mind.

Swallowing hard, she forced herself to calm. Rónán was alive; 'twas all that mattered. "The ship was crushed against the stones. Broken planks are strewn along the shoreline, with many more dragged out to sea."

Mouth grim, he rubbed the back of his neck. "Let us hope the English come upon the wreckage and believe we died."

"Aye." She secured her last tie. "Are you dressed?"

"I am."

She turned.

Rónán motioned to a bench. "Sit and break your fast."

As if after recalling his near death she could eat? "I will later."

Concern darkened his eyes as they skimmed over her. "Are you hurt?"

He didn't understand how she struggled with the fact that she'd nearly lost him. How could he when she fought to understand her intense reaction toward him herself? They had known each other less than a fortnight. It should be impossible for Rónán to matter, but something about him drew her.

Nor had she missed the tension simmering between them moments before. A dangerous awareness when, throughout the night, as she'd checked on him, heated his body with a cloth dipped in warm water, she'd found herself unable to keep from gliding her hand along the hard curve of his face, or linger on the firm tilt of his mouth.

What would it be like for a man like him to kiss her?

Heat swept her as her gaze slid to his strong jaw and rested on his lips. On an unsteady breath, she lifted her eyes to his. 'Twas best to keep her mind on their conversation and away from intimate thoughts. "A few bruises."

He rolled his shoulders, then tugged up the right leg of his trews to reveal a large patch of discolored skin.

Compassion rolled through her, and she ached to caress the harsh bruise. Rónán released the fabric. "I have suffered far worse."

No doubt, considering what he'd told her of his brutal childhood. Yet, despite the horrific beatings he'd suffered, goodness filled him.

She recalled earlier this day the way he'd knelt before Órlaith so as not to intimidate her. Given the insight he'd shared of his youth, he would understand his size could easily frighten the child.

Lathir sighed. Despite all they'd shared, she had but a glimmer into the man.

"Come and sit," Rónán said as he crossed to the table. "'Tis ungrateful to ignore the generosity of our hosts."

The thought of a new beginning lifted her spirits. At his wince of pain, she started to help him, then stopped herself. A proud man like him would not want her assistance.

He settled on the bench.

With the scent of wood and herbs filling the air, she settled beside him.

Lathir selected a wedge of cheese, took a bite, then filled their cups with ale. "I still canna believe how after the wave slammed you against the stone that naught is broken. Our host did his own confirmation of the fact while you were asleep."

"That neither of us is severely injured is a blessing." He ate for several moments, then wiped his mouth. "'Tis imperative that King Robert be alerted of the attack, and that the English have seized your father."

Lathir's hand trembled at the unwanted reminder. "I want to believe my father still lives, that, as you suggested, he is too valuable for the English to kill. What if we are wrong?"

Mouth taut, Rónán set aside the cloth. "Had the English wanted Lord Sionn dead, they would have slain him aboard the *Aodh*."

She tried to cling to his logic. "What if, after they sailed out of sight, he tried to escape and—"

"Lathir, your father is an intelligent warrior, a ruler who has planned and executed many a successful assault. Though the possibility exists that the Sassenach have killed him, it doesna make sense. Nor can I see him being foolish enough to give them reason."

"Mayhap, but"—her voice wavered despite her best intentions—"he believes that I am dead."

Eyes dark with conviction, Rónán gave her hand a gentle squeeze. "Motive for Lord Sionn to do whatever he must, use whatever resources are available, to ensure that once free, retribution is delivered to the English."

After all they'd been through, the warmth of his hand was reassuring, and the tight ball of fear inside her eased. He was right. However furious, however upset, her father wasn't a weak-kneed man who'd collapse against violence, but would use his anger to destroy those who'd caused him and his family harm.

"Now we have to find him."

She angled her jaw. "Aye."

Rónán released her hand. "After Tighearnán and his daughter return, and once Órlaith is asleep, we will discover whether he has heard any news of import while in the village. Who knows?" He took a long drink, then refilled his goblet. "We might be fortunate and our host will have heard of the Earl of Sionn's abduction."

"As much as I would like to believe such, with the attack but days past, regardless if the captain shouted they sailed to Ireland, I doubt word of the raid has reached many villages." She stilled. "What if they changed their minds and are taking my father to their king?"

He gave a quick shake of his head. "I dinna believe they will waste time bringing Lord Sionn to England. The young monarch doesna have the stomach nor interest in war as did his father."

"But King Edward II continues the attacks on King Robert to seize control of Scotland."

Rónán shifted on his bench, winced. "The monarch's interest in unseating King Robert is driven by powerful nobles who have his ear."

Something she needed to remember. "Once we reach Wynshire Castle, I will send a messenger to King Robert, alerting him to recent events, along with runners to discover my father's whereabouts."

He took a slow sip, then lowered his goblet. "Once we know Lord Sionn's location, we will devise a plan to set him free."

"Aye." Aware she needed to eat to keep up her strength, she tore off a bit of bread, then slathered butter on top.

"How long will it take us to reach your stronghold?"

"On horseback, a sennight." She took a bite, swallowed. "I am confident I can convince Tighearnán to lend us one of his mounts."

Rónán nodded. A frown settled across his brow as he started to pick up his goblet. "As we travel through Tír Kythyr, do you think anyone will recognize you?"

"Given the many times I have journeyed through Ireland, the numerous festivals I have attended with my father, 'tis possible." She brushed the crumbs from her fingers. "How many days before you think you shall be able to travel?"

"At first light."

She scoffed. "First light? Your entire body is riddled with bruises, not to mention that you almost froze to death. I have seen warriors with fewer injuries never move again."

Grayish green eyes narrowed on her. He set the goblet aside. "We leave on the morrow. Each day lost is one your father's life remains in danger."

Emotion swelled in her throat that he'd risk his life to save her father. Nor could she ignore that since Domhnall Ruadh mac Cormaic, never had another man caught her interest, much less consumed her thoughts, or made her wonder of the taste of his kiss.

After Domhnall, was it possible that he'd come to matter so much to her when they'd known each other but days? Yet the deep grief at thoughts of losing Rónán assured her that however impractical, however improbable, he'd made her care.

Deeply.

In truth, something about him had drawn her since they'd first met. She'd foolishly believed 'twas his handsomeness, but now she understood 'twas his confidence, his intelligence, and his lack of hesitation as he'd handled the dire situations during their journey.

Most men were intimidated by her self-assurance, her quick wit, but from the first, he'd treated her with respect and handled each issue that'd arisen with gallant command that didn't undermine her own abilities.

Without her wanting to, he'd come to matter to her.

Needing distance, she stood.

"Lathir," he said, his words soft, his eyes dark with sincerity. "Well I know my limitations."

A desperate laugh twisted in her throat. He spoke of his body's ability, while she struggled with her need for him. "As I know yours," she forced out, keeping her voice even, as if her growing feelings toward him hadn't tossed her off-balance. "With you all but grimacing with every step, if we depart on the morrow, even on horseback, hours out, I worry that I would be hauling you up from where you have tumbled in the snow."

Amusement glittered in his eyes. "If we ride, I assure you, if I fall unconscious, I willna let go of the withers."

"You canna make such a ridiculous claim."

"And you," he said, "dinna know my capabilities."

"True. I admit to being pleasantly surprised," she teased, "that you hadna proven to be a weak warrior as I suspected upon our first meeting, where I felled you."

Their friendly banter had strayed to a dangerous topic that had little to do with travel and everything to do with them.

He shifted closer.

Yearning rippled through her. "Risking your life is naught to make light of. You…" Emotion stormed through her as the words, *have become important to me more than 'tis wise* spilled into her mind. She stayed them, stunned by what she'd almost revealed.

He paused. "Lathir, I dinna mean to cause you dismay."

Dismay? As if 'twas so simple. Thoughts of him dying broke her heart, shattered her ability to think coherently. "You are right." Through sheer will, she kept her voice light. "For all purposes, 'tis best we depart tomorrow."

# Chapter Six

Outlined by the flames in the hearth, Lathir started to turn, and Rónán caught her upper arm.

She pulled back, her expression raw, piercing deep into his ragged soul. "Release me!"

And if he did, he'd be a fool. He eased his grip but didn't let go. Couldn't seem to let go.

The lass didn't understand that as a Knight Templar, he'd suffered many a battle wound yet fought on, faced numerous other challenges that would devastate most. Then, the Brotherhood demanded more of those who swore an oath, not only their body, but their soul pledged to God.

Nor was her concern for him alone. Understandably, she was afraid for her father, and her own life. He needed to reassure her that he well knew his physical limitations.

Although, he grimaced inwardly, his body didn't seem to be suffering from any ill effects when it came to physical attraction. He may have been weakened by the ordeal, but he wasn't dead. And her close proximity was having a potent effect on him.

He shifted to cover the evidence. "I am able to travel. If I held any doubts, I wouldna go. Lathir, I would never place your life in jeopardy."

Gray eyes narrowed. "I am not concerned about my life, but yours."

At the sincerity in her eyes, his throat tightened. Never had he experienced such comfort from a woman's worry. From the start he'd realized she was unique, unlike any lass he'd ever met. However much he tried to keep thoughts of her from his mind, he failed.

"And I yours." Beyond simply the vow to protect her. He forced himself to release her, his fingertips sliding free from her arm.

Yet, she didna step back, but peered deep into his eyes. Her gaze softened, darkened with longing.

A dangerous desire surged through his body. Bloody hell. He'd be a fool to touch her.

Yet his traitorous hand reached out, cupped her jaw.

Her lips parted as if in surprise, but her eyes flared with desire.

"'Twould be a mistake to kiss you," he said, wanting her with his every breath.

"Would it?" She moved her body against his. "Tell me that you dinna want to kiss me, and I will move away."

And if she did, he'd die. "Lathir—"

Triumph flashed in her eyes as she raised up, pressed her mouth against his.

Her taste slid through him, and need exploded in his body, roared through his veins until his every thought was of her.

Damning his weakness when it came to her, Rónán cupped her face, savored the quick gasp as he claimed her mouth, then teased, tempted, until she groaned under the onslaught.

Heat pounded through him to take, searing his every inch, scorching the warnings to leave her untouched, blaring in his head. With the last shred of will, Rónán pulled back.

"Well, then," she breathed, her voice unsteady, "'twas a bit more volatile than I expected, but it answers my question."

"Which was?" he hissed.

Her mouth quirked in a shaky smile. "How kissing you would be."

So, she'd been thinking of it as well? Meaning he hadn't imagined one whit of the ill-timed attraction between them. He stepped back before he couldn't, putting much-needed distance between them. "I am charged with your protection," he forced himself to say despite the heat pounding through his every fiber. "Until we rescue your father, we must work together as allies, naught more."

Instead of being put off by his cool tone, she evaluated him. Understanding dawned on her face, and she took a step closer. "I worry you."

Saint's breath! "'Tisna a game."

She shook her head, then lay her hand on his chest. "Rónán, I did naught but give you a simple kiss."

'Twas naught simple about what the kiss made him feel, of how his blood still slammed through his body, and how he ached to strip off her garb and drive deep. "My role here is as your protector."

"What worries you most, that I enjoyed kissing you or that you did?"

He swallowed hard. "If you are done tempting me, I need to select food for our journey." Against the thud of his heart, he strode to the food chest, shoved up the lid, and inspected the contents.

"Have you ever loved a woman?"

His fingers tightened on the aged wood. Allowing a woman in his life, one beyond that of a friend, 'twas something, as a Templar, he'd had no reason to ponder. "Nay."

"There must have been at least one lass you allowed to become close?"

He grabbed a loaf of bread, several apples, then shoved them into the sack, glanced up. "My past plays nay part in my escorting you to Wynshire Castle."

Lathir's soft scent teased him as she moved beside him. With a twinkle in her eyes, she selected several oatcakes and stacked the baked rounds atop the items he'd stowed in the bag. "Does that mean you are going to answer the question, to a friend?"

However much he didn't want to discuss the subject, during their time aboard the cog, he'd learned that with her stubborn streak, she'd pester him 'til she had an answer. And 'twould do little harm as he couldna allow more to ever grow between them, however much he desired it. There was too much at stake.

"I joined the galloglass and fled Ireland. I was often away at war." Rónán picked up a small sack, loosened the tie. The potent aroma of dried herbs spilled out. "There proved nay time for a woman, nor would I have considered placing a lass in such danger." He returned the pouch to the trunk, scoured the remaining goods. "A woman deserves a safe place. A home and a family. Not to be part of the life I live."

"I see." Her tone softened. "A safe place…that kind of life. Meaning for you that kind of life is accepted and understood?"

"I far from think of a skirmish as safe," he said, his voice dry.

"Nay for your body perhaps, but for your thoughts. And what about you? The feelings of the child of your past, the little boy who was beaten, who hid his feelings away, and shielded himself against the scars of memories. Given a lack of a foundation of trust in your youth, it makes sense that you would avoid allowing most people to become close, more so a woman."

He dropped dried meat strips, which would travel well, into the sack. "My feelings arena a topic for discussion. You asked a question, and I answered." Irritated, he focused on his task, not wanting to remember the dark years of his youth, the impact they'd had on his life. If it took him longer than most to make friends, 'twas his choice to make.

He shifted to the other knee, staring into the food chest. Was she right? Had the horrors of his youth prevented him from finding love? On a soft curse, he shoved away the questions dredging his mind. "Pick two of the blankets," he snapped.

She did as he asked.

"Once we reach your castle," he said, "I will dispatch a runner to return them, along with supplies and coin."

Lathir shot him a pointed look. "I am trying to be of help to you."

"Dinna."

"Rónán—"

"Do you always poke into other people's business?"

"I have been accused of prodding a bit."

"Well, keep your curiosity out of my life. Some problems you canna repair." Tenderness shimmered in her eyes, and he muttered a curse.

She couldn't fix a hopeless cause. He'd seen too much, suffered too long to ever believe himself worthy of any woman. He couldn't enter into a relationship without dragging dark thoughts from his past, a stain that would taint any attempt at a relationship with a lass.

'Twas best that he curb his foolish thoughts of her, or any lass, and concentrate on a life of war.

He stood. "I am going to fetch some wood." Rónán tugged on his cape, grabbed his broadsword, removed the bar on the door, and left the cabin.

He welcomed the cold slap of the wind.

The lass was naught but trouble. She made him want more; more living, more loving, more of every damned thing he'd ever denied himself.

Many of his Templar friends had found the blessing of a family, but that wasn't a life he could choose. Lathir had accused him of shielding himself against the scars of his youthful memories. The truth.

As for trusting her…

'Twas hard to give.

He'd agreed to be her friend, nothing more.

He'd lived life alone and liked it that way. With the galloglass, as a valued fighter, even after joining the Templars, it'd taken him years to allow friendships to form within the elite Christian force. But with the Brotherhood dissolved, to let a woman into his life, allow her to believe that once he laid down his sword he could be a man who could share the hidden part of himself as she would expect, nay.

He knew his limitations.

However much he was drawn to Lathir, he was broken inside. In the end, if he was foolish enough to give in, he would hurt her.

His stomach clenched at the acceptance, but it was inevitable. 'Twas best to keep her at a distance.

The tang of the sea filled the air as he headed toward a massive, dead oak perched on the rim of the slope. Its weathered roots bleached by the sun, twisted upon the frozen ground in a battle long since lost, the scarred bark a buffer against the hurl of wind as the trunk leaned at a dangerous angle toward the stone-laden beach far below.

The next storm, or mayhap the one after that, and the once grand beacon would topple to the ground and rot. Proof that naught, however strong, like the Knights Templar, lasted forever.

Rónán halted beneath the lifeless tree, wrapped his hands around a low branch, stilled.

In the distance, a cog flying the English standard sailed toward shore.

Shielding his body behind the thick trunk, he peered around. Waves curled off the bow in a roll of white as the vessel navigated to sail parallel to the coast. Several men were visible as they stood on the starboard rail.

One of the sailors shouted, motioning toward the shore.

Rónán glanced to where waves tossed the sodden, charred planks of the *Aodh* against the rocks. Farther down, stacks of splintered boards lay in awkward piles half covered in seaweed, no doubt carried to shore during high tide.

The crunch of snow behind Rónán had him whirling and withdrawing his broadsword.

Wrapped in her cape, Lathir walked toward him.

Blast it! He waved her down and sheathed his weapon.

Her face paled as she ducked, then scrambled up the incline to join him. "What do you see?"

"A ship on the horizon. Keep low and take a look."

Her breaths disappearing in fading puffs of white, she peered around the trunk. Her body tensed. "The bloody Sassenach are surveying the wreckage. Nay doubt proud of their attack."

"Aye, but the wreckage should convince them we are dead. Look, the cog's sails are filling and the ship is heading seaward. Now we can travel without worrying whether the English are on our trail."

In silence, they watched until the vessel was but a hazy dot in the distance. He stood, then scowled at her. "I told you to remain inside."

She pushed to her feet. Brushing the snow from her cape, solemn eyes held his. "I came to say that 'twas wrong of me to pry into your life."

With a grumble, he bent to gather up some wood.

"As *friends*," she said, a smile touching her mouth as she emphasized the word, "what you choose to tell me or not is up to you."

"Friendship is naught but another way to gather information," he said over his shoulder.

"'Tis."

And he knew remaining here sparring with her would offer him naught but added frustration. "Now that you are here, you can help me haul wood to the hut."

"Rónán."

At the teasing in her voice, he turned, stilled. Despite his best intentions to ignore his attraction, he was captivated by how the wind caught her hair, feathered tendrils across her cheeks, the fullness of her lips.

He swallowed hard. "Aye?"

"I willna apologize for the kiss."

Bedamned, the last thing he wanted to be reminded of was her taste, the feel of her in his arms, her body molded against his.

He snapped off several large branches, held out a couple to her. "Take these and go. I will be right behind you; then I will return for the rest."

Wrapping her hands around the thick boughs, she glanced back. "How much are we going to bring back?"

"We?"

"Aye. Like it or not, I am helping."

Fine then, let her help; 'twould give them a chore to do rather than talk about what they mean to each other. "Enough to replenish what we use and a few days' more."

The sun sank low on the horizon as they worked. Vibrant yellows and oranges smeared the sky, the sweep of errant clouds tainted with deep purple hues adding a brilliant sheen to the sunset.

Lathir loaded the final branches in her arms, then turned toward the hut and stilled. "Someone is approaching from the west."

Narrowing his eyes, Rónán dropped his bundle and withdrew his sword. In the fading light, he studied the distant movement headed toward them. In the whip of wind-hurled snow, he made out a wagon, and a child seated beside the man tending to the reins. "'Tis Tighearnán and Órlaith."

She wiped her brow with her forearm. "I didna realize so much time had passed."

"Nor I." After securing his weapon, Rónán gathered up the wood and started toward the hut, the tangle of limbs dragging through the snow. "Nay doubt they will be ready for the stew we started earlier."

"One," she said with a tired smile in his direction, "I am looking forward to as well."

"As am I."

A short time later, they stepped across the cabin's threshold and dropped their bundles near the fire. Burning wood crackled in the hearth, and the rich scent of herbs and meat filled the air as Rónán hung his cape near the fire besides Lathir's to dry.

The door creaked open and Tighearnán entered, Órlaith on his heels, humming a familiar Gaelic tune. A frown furrowed his brow as he glanced from Rónán's sheathed weapon to the wooden bar angled against the wall, which they'd used to secure the entry.

"We were out retrieving firewood when we saw you approach," Rónán said.

"You are much like me, my friend. I, too, detest lazing about." He nodded to his daughter. "Put away your goods, lass."

"Aye. Father, may I show her my surprise first, please?"

Warmth filled his expression. "If you must."

"In addition to a sweet—" She rushed over to Lathir, excitement dancing in her eyes as she unrolled the package. "My father bought me a new dress! And look—" She tugged away the remainder of the wrapping, exposing a beautiful cream gown. "It has a red sash, and I can wear it at the cèilidh this spring!"

"'Tis beautiful." Lathir stroked her fingers across the delicate Celtic design crisscrossing the decorative loops. "You will look bonny at the gathering. Why, I wouldna be surprised if a bard wrote a song about you."

A rosy flush swept the child's face as she hugged the dress, then leaned closer. "My father has already told me that he will dance with me."

"On about you, now. Be putting the fancy garb in your chest."

"Aye, Father." Half-skipping, she reached the ladder, then scurried up to the loft.

Tighearnán's gaze shifted to Lathir. "Seems the lass has taken to you, wonderful to see." Warmth touched his gaze. "Had I let her keep on, she would have shown you every seam and button."

"She is a fine lass," Lathir said.

"Aye, that she is."

"'Twould seem you made a good sale this day," Rónán said.

"Indeed."

The lightness in the fisherman's eyes faded, and unease sifted through Rónán at Tighearnán's assessing look at Lathir. "I heard an intriguing tale in the village."

Keeping his movements easy, Rónán shifted close to Lathir, as if in a show of affection, ensuring he kept his sword within easy reach. "Indeed?" "'Twould seem that after a violent sea battle, a powerful Irish earl was kidnapped by the Earl of Ardgar's master-at-arms, and they set fire to the noble's ship."

Lathir's face paled.

"They lost sight of the vessel in dense fog before it sank. Or so they believe." Tighearnán crossed his arms over his chest and spread out his feet in a firm stance. "You wouldna know anything about that, would you?"

# Chapter Seven

Rónán muttered a silent curse. With Tighearnán having seen the charred planks before the *Aodh* was swept away, he'd be a fool to claim ignorance. He risked a warning glance at Lathir.

Her hand lay readied but a breath from her dagger.

He paused to consider. The formidable man hadn't stormed inside, sword drawn, demanding answers. And he'd admitted yesterday that he despised the English.

"Aye, 'twas our ship that was attacked," Rónán stated, alert for any sign of aggression, damning the fisherman's daughter but paces away in the loft. "The *Aodh*."

Mouth grim, the fisherman nodded. "And the earl who was abducted?"

Eyes blazing, Lathir drew to her full height. "He is—"

"Lathir," Rónán cut in, wishing they'd had more time to come to know the man.

Tighearnán nodded at her. "Tell me, lass. I swear to you I am a man you can trust."

"He is my father, the Earl of Sionn."

Shock rippled across the fisherman's weathered face. He unfurled his arms. "God in heaven, the ruler of the realm of Tír Sèitheach?"

"Aye."

"Then you are…" He released an unsteady breath. "Lady Lathir McConaghy?"

"I am."

Tighearnán pushed aside his cape and bowed, his graceful movement at odds with his large, burly frame. "My lady, 'tis an honor to have you in my humble home."

Lathir's hand near her dagger relaxed. "I assure you, 'tis we who are thankful for all you have done. Once Rónán and I reach my home, you will be well rewarded for your kindness."

"As I said before, 'tis unnecessary." He lifted a brow at Rónán. "Are you nobility as well?"

"Nay, a knight and her protector. And I add my thanks." With their identities exposed, they needed to discover what the man had learned. "Did you hear any mention of where they have taken Lord Sionn?"

He rubbed the back of his neck. "A man in the village bragged that they had hauled him to the Earl of Ardgar's stronghold."

"Murchadh Castle," Lathir whispered.

"God's truth," Rónán swore under his breath.

"You are familiar with the stronghold?" Lathir asked, worry darkening her gaze.

"Aye, I passed through there during my time with the galloglass. The fortress is built on a wedge of rock below the edge of a cliff, accessible by a path the size of a cart. One would need a significant force to seize it."

"I have met a few of the galloglass in my time," the fisherman said. "The warriors are men naught but a fool would tangle with."

From the wary respect in his voice, 'twould seem he'd had more than a passing introduction. "A fact learned firsthand, mayhap?"

"I am not so reckless." Tighearnán rubbed his jaw. "Let me say I once saw a sailor foolish enough to try to steal gear from a galloglass on my ship."

"Did he live?"

"Nay."

"Nor am I surprised. The galloglass have little tolerance for thievery." Rónán paused. "Your ship?"

The pad of steps from the loft had Tighearnán glancing toward the ladder. "Órlaith, stay there and prepare for bed. I shall be up in a moment."

"But Father—"

"Now."

Illuminated within the soft glow, the little girl gave a long, reluctant sigh. "Aye, Father." She pushed back from the edge. The rustle of clothing sounded. "I am in my bed. Are you coming up now?"

A wry smile touched the fisherman's mouth. "The lass will be prodding me. 'Tis best that I see to her, then we willna be disturbed." Laugh lines crinkled on his face. "If my men could see me, aye, I would be teased no end." He headed up the ladder.

Soft murmurs sounded from above. The little girl's chuckle. Several moments later, Tighearnán descended the ladder. At the bottom, he waved them to the table. "My heart is too soft when it comes to the lass."

"She is blessed to have such a loving father," Lathir said as she took a seat. "My father couldna refuse me if I asked for a story before bed as well." The fisherman settled on a bench across from her. "He sounds like a fine man."

"He is." Her lower lip trembled. "He must be saved."

"Aye." Rónán sat next to Lathir, assessing their host. "You mentioned that you had a ship?"

"Several years ago." A grin touched his mouth as he filled three mugs with ale, set one before each of them. "Let us say that my crew and I tended to be a bit unorthodox in our methods to raise coin, for the most part from the Sassenach, I might add."

Unorthodox? Lathir frowned at the odd description. At the twinkle in his eyes, realization dawned. "You were a pirate?" Given his frank and confident manner, and the way he'd stepped in to help Rónán without hesitation, it was a fact she found easy to believe.

It required little imagination to see him barking orders on a deck, or standing at the helm as a ship cut through storm-fed seas after leaving English ships lighter, and the Sassenach quivering with fear in his wake.

"Let us say, 'twas my way to support King Robert. Neither do I abide by the scoundrel Lord Comyn." His expression darkened with distaste. "I will tell you right now, I dinna hide behind practiced words."

"Nor do I," Lathir said, appreciating Tighearnán's forthright manner. Her father had taught her to trust her gut, and the fisherman had been nothing but honest and helpful. "Sir Rónán and I support King Robert as well."

The muscles in the large man's shoulders eased.

She met Rónán's gaze, pleased to find his body relaxed. 'Twould seem they'd come to the same conclusion about the man. Still, she would take appropriate precautions.

"Before I continue," Lathir said, "you will swear not to tell anyone what I am about to disclose."

The mug scraped on the wooden table as he set it down and raised his hand. "I swear it, my lady."

"Several days ago, after a meeting with the Bruce, my father, Sir Rónán, and I departed St Andrews Cathedral for my home. The English attack was for more than to abduct my father for ransom, but to stay our king's hand."

Sharp brown eyes narrowed. "How so?"

"Lord Sionn holds a secret cache of weapons," Rónán explained. "Arms needed by our sovereign to push back the English along with supporters of Comyn."

She nodded. "Now that we know where my father is, 'tis imperative that we reach Wynshire Castle, where I can raise a large contingent to free him."

"If I can be of help, my lady, I am at your service."

"I thank you. Rónán and I seek to borrow your steed."

Sparks popped in the hearth as Tighearnán frowned. "My steed is yours, but traveling through Tír Kythyr to reach your realm is not only dangerous, but will cost valuable time when you must act with haste."

Alarm streaked up her spine. "What do you mean?"

"The braggart boasted that Lord Sionn was to be held at Murchadh Castle until they had received word of where he was to be taken, but he never revealed from whom or where."

Fear thickened in a tight ball in her throat. "Saint's breath, we must reach my father before they move him."

Tighearnán stroked his beard as he gave a slow nod. "My thinking as well. My lady, my friend owns a cog. He and his men will help you, though their ways might be a wee bit unorthodox."

"You mean they are pirates as well?"

Pride flickered in his eyes. "They were part of my crew. I would trust each one with my life."

Rónán took a sip, then set down his mug. "Will you sail with us as well?"

"I will."

Although the response relieved her, Lathir glanced toward the loft, frowned. "What of your daughter?"

"Órlaith will travel with me."

"Only if you agree that once we reach Wynshire Castle, she will remain there while we rescue my father. And," Lathir said, too aware of the multitude of things that could go wrong, "God forbid if anything should happen to you, I swear I will see to raising her myself."

Appreciation darkened his gaze. "I thank you for your generous offer, my lady, but I will be back." He shot her a roguish wink. "I have been known to be a bit stubborn about dying."

Her chest tightened at the mere thought of his child without a father. "'Tis naught to make light of."

"My lady," he said, his voice somber, "our days are too short to walk in fear."

"Indeed," Rónán said. "When can we depart?"

"At first light. 'Tis dark by now and too dangerous to travel." Tighearnán took a sip from his goblet. "Once we reach town and have gathered a crew, 'twill take naught but hours before we set sail."

Relief swept through her. "Can I ask you a question?"

He cradled his cup in his hands. "Indeed."

"I can hear the fondness in your voice when you talk about the sea. Why did you give it up?"

He cast a glance toward the loft. "For Órlaith," he whispered. "The lass is all I have left of my wife, Máire."

Lathir's heart went out to him.

"A part of me wants to believe that somehow, miraculously, she is alive." For a long moment he studied the flames in the hearth, then he shook his head. "Foolish I know, but Máire was everything to me." Face ruddy with emotion, he shoved to his feet. "'Tis growing late. Try to get some rest. I have a few errands to take care of before we depart."

The faint hoot of an owl sounded from outside as Rónán stood. "I will help you."

"Nay, 'tis something I need to take care of alone." The door closed with a firm snap as Tighearnán exited the hut.

Tears Lathir had fought to hold back spilled down her cheeks. She understood his anguish-laden request. Tighearnán wanted to be alone with his grief, with the heartache that haunted him still.

"Nay man has the right to abduct another's family," she hissed, fury pouring into every word. "Once we have rescued my father, I will send a contingent to see if they can discover where his wife was taken."

Gaze somber, Rónán lay his hand over hers. "However much you wish to help, as I, many years have passed."

"There must be some trace of where she was taken."

"Given Tighearnán's extensive and unconventional resources," he said quietly, "dinna you think if any evidence of her being alive existed, he would have found it by now?"

The anger inside eroded to sadness. "Aye, but 'tis hard to accept."

"I know. Regardless of what Tighearnán says, with the depth that he loves Máire, I doubt he has ever stopped looking."

A belief she shared. God help her, if she discovered something had happened to her father, she wouldna rest until every single person responsible lay dead.

At the slow pounding building in her head, she rubbed her brow.

With a grimace, Rónán stood. "Come, we are both tired. 'Twill be a long day on the morrow."

Exhausted yet still on edge, Lathir yearned to lay beside him this night, to feel his strength, to have him hold her. Nor, given the situation, a wise action. "With Tighearnán aware we arena married, we canna sleep together again. A fact I am thankful he didna mention."

Broken yellow light from the flicker of flames in the hearth wavered over Rónán's face as he looked back at her, and she remembered their kiss, one he'd ended too soon. For a moment she caught the awareness in his grayish-green eyes, a need that surged through her as well.

"Once Tighearnán learned the truth of our situation, he understood your action. Nor—" Favoring his leg, he walked toward the bed. "did I expect to sleep beside you. I will make a pallet on the floor, between you and the door."

Irritated, she shoved to her feet. "I think I have well demonstrated that if a need arises, I can fend for myself."

"Indeed, but until we have reached your home, I will ensure your safety to the best of my ability."

"Always the protector?"

"I swore to my king that I would see to your safety. A vow I intend to keep."

And what if she wanted their relationship to be more? After the nights they'd slept together aboard the *Aodh* out of sheer survival, after the way he'd comforted her, and the moments when they'd become close, more so than either had planned, why was she caught off-balance by the thought?

Nor should she be surprised to be wanting more after their passionate kiss earlier, one that'd ended all too soon. Though she'd been curious of what his kiss would be like, never had she expected it to sear her every inch, to leave her shaken and wanting more.

Look at her, musing like a woman with naught but thoughts to keep her company when her father's life, as their king, depended on them. She cleared her throat. "With your body healing, I think 'tis best if you take the bed."

"'Tisna a decision that is up for debate." His eyes warning her that he wouldna tolerate further discussion, he began spreading a blanket on the floor.

Nor did she miss the humor of the situation. His stubbornness matched hers.

Tiredness swept Lathir. Stifling a yawn, she crossed to the bed she'd slept in the night before. The soft pop of the fire filled the silence as she slipped beneath the covers and closed her eyes.

The haze of sleep sifted over her, a soft calm that seemed to absorb her every thought, to steal the tension sliding through her.

The whisper of prayers filtered through the haze.

Through her lashes, she peered out.

A pace away, on his knees, Rónán was whispering the Our Father. As on the ship, once he completed the prayer, he started again. After several Paternosters, he made the sign of the cross, then turned.

Surprise flickered in his gaze when he found her watching him; then his expression grew guarded. "I thought you were asleep."

"I heard you praying." She shifted to her side and pillowed her head on her hands. "When you pray, why do you repeat the Lord's Prayer several times?"

With a grimace, he glanced toward the door. "Tighearnán will be back any time."

"Which," she pointed out, "doesna answer my question."

He lifted his blanket, settled on the floor near her, then tugged the cover atop him. "I am a devout man."

"Which explains why you pray often, but not the reason why you took a spiritual path."

Silence.

"Did you want to become a monk?"

He turned his back to her.

An ache built in her heart as she surmised the reason was tied to his past. She shifted closer to the edge. "After your tragic childhood, it makes sense you found yourself wanting to join a monastery. You disclosed so much while we were stranded on the *Aodh*. Is it too much to share this?"

The blanket rustled as Rónán gave an irritated sigh and pulled it higher.

Though her life had been dramatically different, needing him to comprehend that to a degree she understood, her thoughts drifted back to her youth. "When my father was at battle, or on a journey that would take him away for months, I found solace in the chapel at Wynshire Castle."

Silence.

"At times our priest would find me alone, praying in the pews," she continued as she lay back on the bed, far from dissuaded, "with but a single candle lit in the middle of the night."

Rónán shifted noisily.

Sensing he was looking at her, Lathir didn't turn his way.

"Why were you in the church at such a late hour?"

Memories of wisps of frankincense and myrrh sifted through her mind, of sitting on the wooden pews, embraced by the waver of candlelight, the solitude, and Him.

"I found a sense of peace there. Within the cast of the single flame spilling upon the cross before me, however afraid, however alone, He was near me." A smile touched her face. "Whenever the priest would find me there, instead of chastening me to return to bed, he would sit beside me and listen to my worries, or share passages from the Bible. But..." Emotion swept her, and she stilled.

"But what?"

She looked over, found him indeed watching her, his gaze intense, as if her answer mattered.

"But when he found me crying, he would hold me. And when I had finally calmed, he would kneel beside me, and we would pray."

"I am glad the priest was there for you, that in times of hardship you turned to Him." Eyes dark with sincerity studied her, as if coming to a decision. "What I tell you isna to be shared."

The gravity of his voice had her pausing. "I swear it."

"As to your question, I never wanted to be a monk. The reason for my deep faith is that I became a Knight Templar."

Humbled he'd trusted her with such an admission, Lathir sat; then her brow furrowed with another thought. "Your time with the Templars may have intensified your faith, but I think it never brought you true peace."

Rónán tensed, stunned by her insight. "I loved being a Knight Templar."

"But you left. Why?"

"Left? The demands of the Brotherhood, of those traveling to the Holy Land, gave me a sense of purpose," he rasped. Painful memories of the way, beneath the cover of darkness, he and many of the Brotherhood escaped, ripped through his soul. "Never would I abandon my brothers or the service I loved."

Any color on her face fled. "Saint's breath, you were in France when King Philip ordered the arrests of the Knights Templar on charges of heresy."

"Aye, I was there, and his claims were all lies," he spat, unable to contain his fury. "Nor were his accusations frivolous, but chosen to enflame those envious of the Templars' wealth and power." His nostrils flared. "But unknown to King Philip, before the charges were publicly disclosed, word of the monarch's despicable intent was secretly delivered to the grand master."

She lay on the side of the bed, resting her head on her folded hands, but her expression remained intent. "How did you escape?"

"By the grand master's orders, prior to the day of the arrests, beneath the cover of night, a significant portion of the Templars boarded our galleys at the port of La Rochelle and fled."

"But not all the Brotherhood left," she said, a waver in her voice.

A lump built in his throat. "Had the grand master warned the entire Templar force, 'twould have alerted King Philip that his plan had been exposed."

"But the Brotherhood's ability to fight, their brilliance in strategy are well known. Instead of fleeing, why didna the grand master rally the Brotherhood and confront the king against his treachery?"

"With the growing dissent of those jealous of the favor given to the Brotherhood over the years, even if we had wanted to, we wouldna have found enough support to confront France's sovereign." He shook his head. "Nor with Templars scattered in several countries did we have the luxury of time to contact everyone, and for them to sail to France, much less organize a formal denial." Rónán clasped his hands into fists against the surge of despair. "So, until October, Friday the thirteenth, when the decree was revealed, many Templars remained ignorant of King Philip's barbaric intent."

Tears slipped down her cheeks.

"Though devastating to sail from port without all of the Templars aware of our plan," he forced out, the grief still raw in his heart, "all within the Brotherhood understood our first priority was to ensure that the secrets beneath Templar guard were kept safe."

Hand trembling, Lathir wiped away her tears. "What secrets did you abscond with that outweighed the lives of the Brotherhood who were left behind?"

He closed his eyes against the horrific thought, understanding that because of the French king's greed, men he'd fought alongside had been imprisoned, tortured, or killed. Yet there was some consolation in knowing the crew he'd escaped with had captured Avalon Castle and hidden the Templar goods in the catacombs beneath, a fact known by few.

He met her gaze. "I canna tell you. Know that their lives were not given in vain."

Somber gray eyes held his with steadfast sincerity. As she reached out to him; he took her hand, appreciating her touch, the bond that however much he tried to fight, grew stronger each day.

"I am so sorry for you, for what all within the Brotherhood have suffered, have lost."

Breaths unsteady, he pressed her hand against his heart. "I–I thank you."

"Your being a Templar explains much. Your skill with weapons, your knowledge of sailing, and your confidence." Gray eyes with a hint of lavender darkened in a thoughtful frown.

"What?"

"How is it that you are working for King Robert?"

"Because Robert the Bruce is a Knight Templar."

Her mouth dropped open in the same way that his had upon learning of the Templar connection. "I never knew," she murmured in wonder, "never heard a wisp of rumor."

"Nor would you. God help the Brotherhood if King Philip ever learned the fact, more so with France's sovereign having recognized King Robert in a letter as the 'king of Scots.'" He paused, the complexity of events since they'd sailed from La Rochelle amazing him still. "King Robert's religious exclusion, and the Scottish clergy's refusal to acknowledge his excommunication, allowed the Bruce to offer all Knights Templar entry into his realm with impunity. So, the night we sailed from France beneath the cover of darkness, five ships sailed to Scotland, the remainder headed to Portugal."

"'Tis much to take in."

He gave her hand a gentle squeeze, pressed a kiss upon her knuckles, then set it upon the bed. "'Tis."

The scuff of steps outside alerted them of Tighearnán's return.

Rónán held his finger to his lips in a request that they remain silent.

She nodded.

*Go to sleep*, he mouthed.

Lathir lay down and closed her eyes.

As the door began to scrape open, Rónán followed suit.

# Chapter Eight

The first rays of light filtered through the clear skies with the promise of a cold but beautiful day as Lathir rode in the back of the cart with Órlaith. Tenderness filled her as she glanced at the sleeping child, bundled in several heavy blankets, beside her. To sleep so soundly without worries; the wonders of the innocence of youth.

Another wash of tenderness swept her as she glanced at Rónán seated beside Tighearnán as he guided the horse through the thick weave of trees.

Rónán's revelation of being a Knight Templar the night before explained his deep faith. In addition to his vows, she believed that his abusive youth, one that had left the lad yearning for hope and belonging, played a part in his deep spirituality.

The ramshackle wagon jolted as it lumbered over a mound on their snow-filled path. Faint tracks lingered in the newly fallen snow no doubt left yesterday by Tighearnán during his and Órlaith's trek to the village.

A gust of snow-laden wind hurled past as they broke from the woods. Sturdy huts with stone walls and thatched roofs similar in design came into view.

The village stood situated along a cleared angle of ground backing up to a sharp rise of land. Clever. Whoever designed the settlement did so with intent. With the sheer rock behind them, no one could sneak into town without being seen.

As they neared, several people waved or called out to Tighearnán as they rode past. Part of his former crew? If so, the secure design of the town made sense. No doubt ships raided by Tighearnán and his men were sought with a vengeance. A smile tugged at her mouth at his admission that, for the most part, his targets had been the English.

"Whoa," Tighearnán called, as he drew his horse to a halt. The wagon rolled to a stop. He glanced back. "The lass is still asleep?" Lathir brushed away a swath of brown hair that'd fallen across the girl's cherubic cheek. "She is."

"Nay doubt from staying up too late with the excitement of having you both here." He climbed down, walked to the back, and lifted his sleeping daughter into his arms. "Wait here while I take her to stay with a friend until we depart." With an easy stride, he walked along the line of huts.

The rich scent of peat fires filled the air as Lathir stood. Muscles stiff from travel, she moved to the back of the wagon.

Rónán stepped before her as she reached the edge. Though his limp was gone, from the taut lines on his face when he moved, he was still in pain. Not that he would admit such.

"How did you fare?" he asked.

"Not as well as Órlaith." She rubbed her back. "Mayhap I should have tried to sleep."

"Do you think you could have?" he teased.

"With all the shifting and bumping during the journey, nay." She started to step down, but he caught her by the waist and lifted her to the ground. "We are here now, and soon will be at sea."

"For which I will be thankful."

She waited for him to release her and step away, but the humor in his eyes faded, and her breath caught as his gaze darkened with desire and lowered to her mouth. Her heart pounded as an answering flash of need shot through her.

His throat worked. "Lathir—"

At the sound of distant voices, he released her.

Suppressing a sigh of disappointment, she looked around. Near the edge of the village, Tighearnán was heading toward them with a tall, burly man garbed in a thick fur cloak at his side.

She looked at Rónán; his gaze had shifted to the approaching men, the longing of moments before shielded. What had he been about to say? Blast it, why was she torturing herself? He'd made it clear that his life was dedicated to war, not to settling down with a wife or family.

Despite what she may have wished, after their covert conversation the night before, she understood his reasoning. His account of what he and his fellow Templars had endured would leave anyone with a heart in despair.

Although she believed that, like his profound faith, his life as a warrior had evolved out of self-preservation, and there was more to him than being a weapon at the king's command.

As for his being a good father, she recalled how he'd knelt before Órlaith so as not to intimidate her with his size. How many men would do something so thoughtful for a child? Aye, regardless of the doubts he held in regard to a family, he would make a fine father. With the passion that he applied to his life, he would make a wonderful lover as well. Heat crept through her, and for a moment she embraced the need Rónán inspired, confident his passionate kiss was but a wisp of how tender and fierce he would be in bed. Then she sighed and dismissed her wayward thoughts. It wasn't meant to be.

Two children carrying bundles glanced curiously at them before darting into a home at the end of the village.

The crunch of steps on snow sounded as Tighearnán and his friend neared. Several paces away, they halted. "I would like to introduce you to Bran."

No surname, she noted. Nor, as no doubt he'd been part of Tighearnán's illustrious crew, did she expect one.

Thick brows salted with gray lifted and sharp eyes took her in. "Lady Lathir McConaghy."

She nodded. "Bran."

"And," Tighearnán continued, "Sir Rónán."

The burly man gave Rónán a nod, then crossed his arms over his chest. "The captain said you would be needing my help, and that of my crew."

His crew. 'Twould seem that the other man had stepped into Tighearnán's shoes. "Aye," she replied. "Sir Feradach O'Dowd has abducted my father, the Earl of Sionn. Sir Rónán and I must reach Wynshire Castle to raise a force to find and rescue my father."

Before they killed him. Lathir shuddered at the terrifying thought.

Bran gestured toward the hut paces away. "Most of my men are inside, as we recently returned from a"—he cleared his throat—"from seeing to an important matter."

In other words, a raid. "I hope the ship was English."

Humor twinkled in his eyes, and Bran gave a hearty laugh. "Indeed. Their cog is limping toward England as we speak. They were none too pleased with our *visit*, but I assured them that my allowing their vessel to leave with them alive was a boon."

Tighearnán grunted. "You are a better man than I."

A combination of sympathy and anger flashed on his friend's face. "Nay, had the Sassenach killed the woman I loved as I sailed away, the cog would have been naught but kindling in my wake."

Tension singed the air. Face taut, Tighearnán stepped back. "Let us go inside and speak to your men."

They started toward the hut, and Lathir shot Rónán a glance, caught the anger in his eyes, fury she empathized with. To tear a woman from her home, murder her, was despicable.

A scrape sounded as Bran tugged the door open. Billows of grayish smoke belched from the entry. He stepped inside, and they followed.

Welcoming the warmth, Lathir halted as Rónán pulled the door closed behind her. The tang of ale competed with smoke as her eyes slowly adjusted to the murky interior.

A massive stone hearth stood against the back wall, two swords, one crossed upon the other hanging above. Inside, fire raged, bursts of yellow and orange flames consuming the large chunks of wood as smoke rolled into the chimney.

Thick, round posts flush against the walls supported the thatched roof. Casks of brew, no doubt acquired on one of their exploits, lay stacked against the left wall.

A large trencher table in the middle took up a sizable portion of the remaining space. Rough-looking men half-filled the benches on either side; men who, with their entrance, had shifted their attention toward them.

With a confident swagger, Tighearnán strode across the room, Bran at his side.

The men shouted out their welcome.

A man sporting a long, scraggly beard and a scar down the entire side of his face lifted a brow toward Tighearnán. "You were here yesterday. I didna expect to see you for another month or more."

"Had not the reason been dire, I wouldna have returned," Tighearnán said.

Wary eyes narrowed on Rónán, before shifting to Lathir. "Ye bring strangers."

The others around the table scanned them with shrewd eyes.

"Their ship was attacked by the English," Tighearnán said. "They were fortunate enough to reach shore before their vessel was smashed against the rocks."

"Bloody scoundrels," a fierce-looking man near the end spat. "And the English?"

"Dinna know we are alive," Lathir said.

Thick eyebrows pressed together from a man several paces away. "And who be you, lass?"

"Lady Lathir McConaghy," Tighearnán said. "The Sassenach abducted her father, Lord Sionn."

The man's eyes widened in surprise. "Lord of the realm of Tír Sèitheach?"

"Aye," she said, "and this is my guard, Sir Rónán."

"Guard?" Tighearnán scoffed. "Sir Rónán served with the galloglass."

Impressed grunts erupted from the crew, along with respect in their eyes. Rónán remained silent beneath their scrutiny.

Another man near the center of the group wiped his mouth with his arm and nodded at her. "Are the galloglass searching for your father?"

"Nay," Tighearnán said. "As of now, we are."

Rumbles of surprise passed through the crew.

Bran gestured to Lathir, Rónán, and Tighearnán, and bellowed an order for their drinks over his shoulder. "Sit. We have much to discuss."

Though the group appeared an unsavory lot, Lathir quickly discovered they were intelligent, knowledgeable, and loyal. In addition, they knew the surrounding sea and currents of Ireland and beyond. No doubt cultured by their dealing in illicit goods.

She shifted in her chair, the incredibility of the situation not lost on her. Who would have believed that one day she would seek aid from pirates? If it saved her father, she'd seek help from whoever necessary.

"God's teeth," a man she'd learned was called Senach growled, a stocky, hard-edged man who bluntly said what was on his mind. A trait she'd quickly discovered was common among the entire crew. "The earl is the man that braggart who was passing through yesterday was talking about, then?"

Tighearnán nodded. "Aye."

Senach's face settled into a hard expression. "Sir Feradach O'Dowd is a crafty rogue who knows what he is about. There will be naught simple about freeing the earl."

The crew rumbled their agreement.

Still outraged the treacherous cur who'd abused him in his youth had earned the title of master-at-arms for the earl of Ardgar, Rónán shoved his own mug on the table. Nor did stewing over the fact help them save Lord Sionn.

"Feradach deserves to pay," Rónán said. "Which is why we must sail to Wynshire Castle."

"Aye," Lathir agreed. "Once home, I will raise a force to find and rescue my father."

Rónán glanced toward her. Despite the dark emotion seething within him, he couldn't help but be impressed by her daring, appreciating her strength to face a challenge head-on. Any man would be proud to have her at his side.

Rónán glanced at the crew. "Your captain said you can be convinced to help us."

Senach's eyes lit up. "For the right price, we can set sail in but hours." He chuckled, and the men surrounding the table laughed, but Rónán caught the serious undertone.

"Name it," Lathir said.

The men's laughter fell away. The lure of fortune glittered in their eyes. Sparks popped in the hearth as Bran studied her for a long moment, the haze of smoke within the sturdy building rich with the tang of mead.

"Ten bits of gold."

Fists pounded on the table in agreement.

"Done," she stated. "Once we reach Wynshire Castle, you will be paid."

"Which is naught located on the coast," a large man seated in the back pointed out.

"It isna," Lathir agreed, "but a shielded river few know of runs from the coast to a loch near the stronghold."

Surprise flickered in the men's eyes.

"I know of nay waterway there," a short man to the right blustered.

"You have sailed but a few months with us," Senach scoffed. "You have just found the crow's nest."

Men's laughter filled the chamber, and relief swept Rónán. They had a ship and a crew. "You said we could leave in but hours?"

Bran's face twisted into a thoughtful frown as he glanced at his men. "Aye, the only thing we unloaded from our last rai"—he cleared his throat—"foray, was goods we had procured. As there is plenty of food and drink still aboard, we can carry the few provisions necessary to the ship. If you wish, my lady, we can leave at midday."

Relief filled her gaze. She raised her as-yet-untouched mug and downed it swiftly, to the rousing humor of the rabble of men. "Aye, the sooner the better."

\* \* \* \*

The cog's bow angled up the swell, then dove into the oncoming trough. Hewn timbers shuddered beneath the force, and white water blasted from both sides of the hull as if a cannon fired.

Legs braced, the sail full, strained beneath the lash of wind, Rónán savored the potent force of nature, the fresh whip of salty air as he scanned the horizon.

Naught met his view but the dangerous roll of blackened waves as far as he could see. Nor with storms seeming to pile upon the other during the winter in Ireland did he expect different. Naught but those seasoned aboard ship dared brave the tempest-fed waters.

Paces away, Lathir stood. Like him, she'd braced her feet in an easy gesture of one who has sailed often. Her hand shielding her eyes from the spray, they both searched for any sign of enemy ships.

Since their departure a day past, they'd been fortunate not to see any. Nor did the turbulent seas cause complications. The crew handled the wind-tossed whitecaps with the ease of reaching for a tankard. A smile touched his mouth. He'd swear that the rougher the sea grew, the happier the crew became.

Regardless if the skies had grown dark with the threat of a storm as they'd prepared to depart and the wind had risen, Tighearnán, as Bran and his men, had set sail without hesitation. 'Twas as if they shook their fists at the incoming squalls, anticipated the challenge of defeating whatever nature hurled their way.

Though Rónán loved sailing, having navigated the waters surrounding Ireland, England, and the Mediterranean many times over with the Templars, he was impressed with the sheer defiance and incredible skill of the crew.

Water rumbled against the hull as it carved through a large wave slamming against the bow. The vessel groaned as it was again tossed up.

"We are making good time," Lathir shouted above the roar of wind.

After one last scan of the horizon, he glanced toward the sun overhead, then stepped closer.

"As long as there are nay delays," she said, "we may reach my home by late tomorrow."

"Aye."

"God forbid if we dinna rescue my father before 'tis too late." She turned her face toward the wind, but not before he caught the lines of concern on her face.

Too aware of Feradach O'Dowd's preference for violence, neither did he add that in the scoundrel's control, Lord Sionn may have already suffered a beating or worse. Rónán prayed the noble's powerful position as the ruler of the realm of Tír Sèitheach would keep him safe as long as he was the Irishman's captive.

Hard curls of white water blasted from the sides of the cog as it dropped into an oncoming trough. Spray pummeled him. After he wiped his eyes, his gaze found Lathir.

Face misted, droplets clung to tendrils of her hair tugged free. Except to him, she'd never looked so beautiful.

Memories poured through him of her asleep in his arms last night aboard the ship. How without hesitation, she'd leaned her face against the curve of his neck, her soft breaths feathering against his skin like a wish. Foolishly, a part of him had wished they were alone. A dangerous thought when there could never be more between them than he as her protector. But that didn't lessen the want.

Blast it.

Rónán gave a rough exhale, fighting the desire growing stronger for her every day, the taste of her kiss, the feel of her mouth pressed against his, etched in his mind. Nor did it help that several times since they'd set sail, he'd seen her watching him, caught the desire in her eyes.

"Lady Lathir?"

At the youthful voice, Rónán glanced down, impressed as Órlaith moved about the deck without hesitation. An ease no doubt culled by numerous voyages with her father.

Though Tighearnán would leave his daughter on land during his pirating days, 'twould seem she'd sailed with him often when he sold goods. He grunted. Stolen goods. At least they once belonged to the English.

A smile on her face, Lathir knelt as the girl reached them. "Aye?"

She held out a sack. "My father said 'tis for you"—she glanced at Rónán—"both to eat."

"I thank you." Lathir accepted the cloth sack, untied it. She withdrew a wedge of bread and cheese, held them out to the child. "Here."

Surprise flickered in the girl's eyes. "I shouldna eat until I have finished my task."

A smile touched Rónán's mouth as he watched the struggle in the child's eyes. In the meager time they'd known Órlaith, she'd stolen both his and Lathir's hearts. Who could resist those innocent brown eyes filled with curiosity and wonder, her unchecked enthusiasm at everything? And her questions. Since she'd moved passed her shyness, she'd had many. But her sweet manner made him anticipate each and every visit.

Her father had teased Lathir that she would be asking for a princess crown, and Lathir had laughingly replied that mayhap 'twas a wish that could be granted.

He enjoyed watching Lathir with the child. Their growing bond made him think of what it would be like to have a child of his own, more, to have a child with Lathir.

An ache built inside for what never could be. Aye, 'twas best to focus on reaching Wynshire Castle, to raise a force to rescue her father. But—

"Ship on the horizon!" Bran bellowed from the bow.

Jaw tight, Rónán scoured the dark roll of wind-whipped waves. Atop a distant swell, a large cog cut through the rough seas, its white sail full, straining against the harsh winds. His gaze narrowed on the banner waving from the mast. 'Twas an English warship.

# Chapter Nine

"The bloody Sassenach are closing fast!" Bran shouted, his words ripped away by the howl of the wind.

Salty spray whipped Lathir as, heart pounding, she turned toward their pursuers.

Large waves battered the English warship as it cut through the rough seas. On a muttered curse, Bran spun toward the stern of the ship. "Senach, trim the sail. Everyone else, keep emptying water from the hull. By God, we can outrun these scoundrels!"

"Aye, Captain." Brow furrowed with determination, Senach worked with the lines, finally securing the rope.

Lathir joined the crew around her, filling buckets of water that'd washed over the bow, then passing them along to sailors who emptied the contents overboard.

The cog shuddered as another large swell crashed against the hull. A plume of water exploded upward, washed over the bow. The violent slide of frothy white stormed the deck, invading every nook, surrounding each crate as the cog was again shoved upward.

Wood scraped as Lathir slid her bucket along the fast flow, handed it to Rónán.

Jaw set, he passed the pail to Tighearnán, who emptied it over the rail.

Tighearnán's gaze cut toward the enemy cog before shifting to his daughter, hidden beneath a shelter. "I had hoped to avoid a confrontation with the English. But the lass must learn never to fear a life of pursuing what she believes in."

Eyes wide, the girl watched her father, but she didn't move from where he'd ordered her to remain.

Lathir fought her fear on the child's behalf, but Tighearnán was right. A belief her father had shared, and one, however dangerous, she understood. Naught about life was safe, there were no assurances, and 'twas those who took the risks who carved their own destinies.

And allowed others to dare to hope.

To dream.

Nor would the Sassenach deter her. Her hand settled on her dagger. Whatever it took, they'd rescue her father.

The pounding of water filled the air as Lathir bent over to scoop up the next bucket, then turned to the captain. "Are we pulling away?"

Thick brows salted with gray narrowed as Bran scowled at the large warship cresting the next swell. "Nay." He turned toward his crew. "Man the oars!"

Boots thudded on the slick deck as his crew ran to take their places.

Salty spray from the next swell filled the air, again drenching Lathir as she slid onto the bench beside Rónán. She curled her fingers around the smoothed handle of the oars, barely registering the surprise and admiration of several men in the crew, then leaned forward as the men shoved the tips of the paddles into the water.

Bran strode before them and braced his feet, his weathered face taut with determination. "Row!"

In unison, they drew the oars through the water.

The cog surged forward with each sweep of the oars driving through the churn of the sea.

Muscles bunched and burned as Lathir pulled on the next command. On a deep inhale, she leaned forward at the captain's next call.

Rónán's powerful body flexed as he worked in unison beside her, hauling the oars through the churn of water.

A grim smile creased Bran's face. "We are pulling away!"

Cheers rang out from the crew as they again leaned back, plunged the oars into the churn of white.

The slap of smoothed wood was lost against the hurl of wind, but Lathir focused on each pull, blood pumping as they slowly but steadily continued to put distance between them and their enemy.

A shadow had her glancing up. They were sailing near a cliff. "We are too close to shore!"

Excitement sparked in Bran's eyes. "Nay, lass. We are approaching the shadow of the wolf."

Beside her, a grim smile curved Rónán's mouth. "Serve the bastards right."

Confused, she shook her head. "What is the shadow of the wolf?"

"Look through the porthole," Rónán said.

Along the shore, a shadow fractured the thick line of firs tangled with large oaks, their limbs barren except for a few stout leaves that whipped in the wind. Lathir frowned. "An entry to a waterway?"

"Aye," Rónán replied.

She stared in disbelief. "'Tis none I have ever heard of."

"Most have not." Droplets clinging to his harsh, weather-beaten face, Tighearnán studied Rónán. "I admit my astonishment that he is aware of this hidden inlet. 'Tis known mostly by those who sail outside the law, and, 'twould seem, the galloglass."

"Helmsman," Bran called, "guide us in."

"Aye, Captain," the sailor manning the rudder called.

Wood groaned as the vessel made a hard right, the large waves battering the craft. Wind filling the ship's sail, they raced shoreward, the banks narrowing dangerously.

"Saint's breath," Lathir breathed. "We will be trapped!"

Tighearnán winked. "Which is what the English will be thinking when they follow. Nor are they aware that this vessel has a shallow draft."

"What do you mean?" Lathir asked.

"That," Rónán said, "whoever is captaining the warship isna familiar with this part of the coast."

"Why do you say that?" Lathir asked.

"From the angle they are approaching," Rónán replied.

In the slash of frothing white, eddies curled around the tip of the oars as she, along with the others manning them, pulled forward. "You are not making sense."

Tighearnán gave a mock salute to Rónán. "Aye, he is, my lady. Large rocks are shielded below water during high tide along this portion of the coastline."

She scanned the rough seas as the enemy cog closed, finding naught irregular about the incoming swells. "I dinna see any sign of boulders below."

"Which, if unfamiliar with this area," Bran said, "is what the English will think until 'tis too late."

The distant crunch and snap of wood sounded.

Lathir, as the crew, hurried to the rail for a better view.

A large swell slammed against the warship wedged within the hidden rocks. Wood screamed and planks snapped as the cog twisted beneath the force.

Tighearnán chuckled. "Looks as if they have discovered the stones."

The crew cheered as swells continued to bash the English cog. With each crash, groans and squeals of tormented wood spewed into the air. Large chunks of the vessel broke away, and the cog began to list, then sink into the dark churn.

"Come about," Bran yelled, "and sail for open water."

"Aye, Captain," the man at the rudder called.

More cheers sounded as the crew patted one another on the back, then returned to their posts.

As if in celebration, streams of sunlight broke through the clouds and shimmered upon the storm-tossed seas.

With the number of fathoms below them increasing, the tension pounding Lathir's body eased. Thank God they'd escaped.

Bran scanned the horizon, then walked over to his friend. "It looks as though the wind is beginning to calm."

"Aye, the storm is moving out." Tighearnán rolled his shoulders, glanced toward the stern. "Órlaith!"

The girl scrambled from her hiding place. Brown hair dancing in the wind, she ran to her father.

"There is a lass!" Her squeal of laughter filled the air as Tighearnán caught her and whirled her around, then propped her upon his hip.

Cheeks rosy, she lifted her gaze to his. "Did you stop the bad Englishmen, Da?"

"Aye, lass," her father replied with a soft, lighthearted growl. "They be scrambling for shore now."

Lathir glanced back. Large, wind-whipped swells rocked the small boat as crew frantically piled in. As the final man struggled to climb in, with a violent twist, the craft broke away. The sailor lost his balance, tumbled into the water, and disappeared.

The next swell rolled the remnants of the damaged hull. Planks flew, and the fragments of the once majestic cog disappeared beneath the blackened depths.

Amid the rush of wind, with a grunt of satisfaction, Rónán stepped beside her. "Their ship willna present a threat to anyone again."

She met his gaze. "Indeed, but those who escaped will sail again. Neither is the danger over. If not build another ship, they will commandeer one."

"Mayhap," Rónán said, "but for now we are safe."

"We are." For that, she would be thankful. With the immediate threat past, exhaustion wove through her. Lathir rubbed the low ache in her shoulder. "I havena manned an oar in many a year."

Rónán grimaced. "Dinna be surprised if you are sore on the morrow."

"An unimportant fact given our goal." Restless, Lathir stood, leaned on the rail, and angled her face, the salt-laden breeze cool on her skin. Within the clearing skies, shades of deep, rich, gold slowly smothered the wash of blue. "'Twill be dark soon." The rumble of water slid against the hull as Rónán rested on the smooth wood beside her. "'Twill. I look forward to the warmer days of spring and the long hours of daylight."

"As I."

"With the seas abating, as long as we dinna encounter any further threat, by this time tomorrow we could reach Wynshire Castle."

Elation filled her, dissolved as quickly. Without her father. Heart heavy, she watched the large swells roll shoreward. On a sigh, she closed her eyes, sent up a prayer for his safety.

"You are thinking of your father."

At the compassion in his voice, she opened her eyes. Emotion tightened in her throat. "How can I not? He should be here with me, not in enemy hands, with me unsure if he is alive or dead."

He gave her hand a gentle squeeze.

Regardless of the turmoil inside, of the dread filling her every breath, his touch brought much-needed comfort. Tempted by his nearness, by the calm he'd brought to her life, Lathir yearned to move closer, to rest her head on his chest, to allow his strength to fill her. Not that she was weak, but because the confidence Rónán exuded allowed her to lower her guard.

The cry of gulls sounded overhead as, beneath thick lashes, she studied the hard cut of his jaw, the way he stood beside her in stoic silence. Though he didn't comment further, understanding rolled from him in waves.

With the hardships they'd shared, she'd learned he was not only her protector, but a friend, a solid force who would treat her as an equal and encourage her when she held doubts.

The passion of their previous kiss made it clear he'd wanted her. But he'd kept himself at a distance ever since. She lowered her gaze to where his hand lay upon hers—a gesture given in comfort and support, no more. If she moved into his arms, would he embrace her or push her away?

Rónán had made it clear that his future was one of war, of fighting for King Robert. But with each passing day, at thoughts of his departure, an emptiness built inside her.

What if he remained?

As if she could convince him to stay in Ireland.

Or could she?

Intense, grayish-green eyes studied her. "What is it?"

She hesitated. Should she admit the truth? With him determined to return to Scotland and her destiny within her realm, she had little left to lose. Beyond her fear of his leaving was that once he did, he would never return. But what was it that Tighearnán had told his daughter, not to be afraid to pursue one's dreams?

Pulse racing, Lathir moved 'til she was a hand's width away, the rush of the sea, the tang of salty air a potent backdrop. "Once you have delivered the arms to your king, I ask that you return to Wynshire Castle."

Desire sifted through his eyes. As quickly, his expression grew unreadable, and he withdrew his hand. "If King Robert bids me to return, I shall."

She moved and lay her palm against his chest. "Not for duty, but for me."

Wind ruffled his brown hair as he studied her for a long moment. His gaze dropped briefly to her mouth. On a hard swallow, his hand lifted to the side of her face, then he curled his hands into fists at his sides. "Regardless of what I may wish, I am but a knight. 'Tis best that I remain away."

Anger ignited that he would deny what they both wanted. "As if I give a damn about your status?" she hissed, keeping her voice low. "Few ever find someone who matters deeply to them. I dinna want to lose that."

The thud of steps sounded upon the weathered deck as three sailors moved by carrying buckets.

Once the crew had strode out of earshot, he shook his head. "Regardless of your wish, or mine, you have the responsibility of a realm that one day will be yours to rule. You dinna have the freedom to seek a man who turns your head, but a man of nobility to stand by your side."

"Nobility," she stated, "that can be easily given. Once we rescue my father, he can—"

"Lathir," Rónán rasped, cutting her off. The visions her words drew forth were too tempting, a mirage yet enticing all the same. With her by his side, the bleak years ahead of wielding a sword for his king vanished, replaced with time when they could be together.

And a family?

Children's laughter trickled though his mind, and a haze of warmth, of fulfillment, swept him. With ease he could envision a little girl running toward him with Lathir's golden hair and gray eyes.

Lathir was so beautiful, even with eyes weary from the countless exhausting days they'd been struggling through together. She truly was a future queen. 'Twould be so easy to agree, to take her into his arms, to allow himself to believe 'twas possible.

The dream of her in his life shattered in his mind. For the best. They each had other destinies.

Aching inside, he stowed the bitter fragments deep in his mind, focused on now and damned the words he must say. "However much I feel for you, I am not a man who will be bound to a woman, now or ever."

She tilted up her chin. "And why not?"

"You deserve better than a knight. My future lies with restoring the Bruce to the throne."

The hurt on her face sliced his heart.

His heart?

Rónán stared at her in disbelief. He'd thought when the mission was over and he left her it would hurt and he'd miss her. But now he realized 'twould be as if tearing away a piece of his soul.

Nor, however much the words tangled on his tongue, could he ever reveal his true feelings. She deserved a man whose past wasn't tainted by brutal memories of a shattered youth, one confident in his ability to raise a family. He wasn't made for the softer side of life.

He understood war.

Rónán clung to his logic as his every breath ached with what he wanted to tell her, to give her.

"Damn you," she whispered through clenched teeth, "I know you care for me."

Care? A paltry word for the emotions storming through him. "How could I not?" he rasped. "You are beautiful, a woman to admire, one my king has bid me to protect."

Gray eyes narrowed, but he saw her confusion and despised himself over and again for hurting her, but 'twas for the best. After a time, she would forget him and find a man who could satisfy her and wholly love her as she deserved.

The ache in his chest grew at thoughts of Lathir in the arms of another man. Blast it! Needing to put distance between them, he turned on his heel and strode away. The whip of the cool sea breeze battered his face as he reached the bow.

The quick tap of steps sounded a moment before her hand caught his arm. "Rónán."

He didn't turn. "'Tis best that I go."

"Best for who?"

The fury in her voice had him turning.

Tears backed by passion and determination glittered in her eyes. "I love you, damn you, and I willna let a chance for us pass."

# Chapter Ten

Of all the words Rónán had expected Lathir to say, never had he imagined her to admit that she loved him. His thoughts floundered, as did his incredulous heart. "Lathir, you dinna understand—"

"Nay?" She jabbed her finger against his chest. "What have I missed, that never before has a man made me want him, that regardless of how you avoid the topic, there is something between us, a passion when we kiss that canna be denied?"

A dangerous desire skewed his thoughts. He resisted the urge to gaze at her mouth. "'Tisna so simple."

Wind feathered through her golden hair as she stared at him in defiance. "Aye, 'tis. Tell me, do you want me?"

He clenched his jaw painfully tight.

She angled her jaw. "Do you?"

"God's truth!" he hissed

Satisfaction darkened her gaze. "I will take that for an aye. And do you care for me beyond any other woman you have ever met?"

To admit that would be to give her too much power beyond what she already had over him. "I am unsure if I am irritated or flattered by your perseverance."

She laughed, and the tension on her face eased. When he thought she might choose aggression to pursue her quest, it turned to quiet fact, yet was no less powerful.

"Rónán, I love you, 'tis that simple."

Had she railed at him, that he could have defied, but with laughter in her eyes, and his feelings for her tumbling upon the other forces railing him, his defenses faded. "Lathir, this, us, isna what I had planned."

Her eyes softened with tenderness. "The best things are not, are they?" Caught within the turmoil in his heart, he cupped her face. "Never did I set out to find you, much less fall in love with you."

The humor on her face faded first to shock, then elation. "You love me?"

"Aye," he rasped, still in shock from her admission, but unable to deny it to her any longer, "with my every breath. I am a fool to admit it."

"Nay, you are the man I love. Kiss me, Rónán."

With his last inkling of resistance, he glanced around, frowned. "'Tis unwise before the crew."

A smile curving her mouth, she lifted on her tiptoes. "Take the risk if you dare."

With happiness in her eyes and need pounding through him, he was lost. He claimed her mouth, and desire surged through him, stoking every dream he hadn't dared believe could be real.

For years he'd focused on duty, never considering a home or a family. Yet Lathir made him think, believe anything was possible.

Rónán angled her head, took the kiss deeper, allowing the depth of his passion to infuse the kiss, needing her to understand that for her, he'd risk everything.

At shouts of approval, Rónán lifted his head, pleased by the flush on Lathir's face as he scanned the grinning faces of the crew, having paused in their duties. He skimmed his thumb across her lower lip, still slick from their kiss. "'Twould seem that for what I wish to do with you, discretion is necessary."

The redness on her face deepened. "Privacy we will find upon our arrival in Wynshire Castle."

As the cog cut through a swell, with deliberation, he set her a step away. "However much I want you, I willna take you to my bed until we are married."

She swallowed a visible gasp, watching him with her fierce yet gentle eyes.

Ignoring the members of the crew still watching them, Rónán knelt before her, took her hand. He cleared his throat. "'Tisna the way I would plan such, but marry me, Lathir. Stand beside me for the rest of my life, share my dreams, build a home and a family with me."

Tears of joy spilled down her cheeks. "Aye, I will."

The crew roared.

Amid the cheers, Rónán stood and kissed her thoroughly, never wanting to let her go, wishing they were alone, their vows behind them so he could take her to his bed and show her how she made him feel.

On an unsteady breath, he drew her to him, savored the feel of her body against his. Time for intimacy would come.

"However much I would enjoy spending the day alone with you—" Rónán gave her one last kiss—"our time would be best served preparing for our arrival."

With a twinkle in her eyes, she stepped back. "Aye. And I need to retrieve the map I drew of the river for the captain."

He nodded. "I will meet you where Bran is working at the stern."

She hurried toward the bow, where he'd seen her sketching on the parchment earlier in the day.

That, he mused as he watched her comely figure depart with a fight-worthy step, is my future wife.

Lighthearted despite the lingering niggles at the back of his mind, Rónán strode toward the stern as the cog carved its way westward. He savored the mist of the salty spray upon his face, understanding the demanding life aboard a ship. The sea held its own code, one that didn't allow for emotions, but hard work, a quick wit, and at times a little luck.

White water curled from the bow as Rónán halted beside the captain. A smile curved Bran's mouth. "'Twould seem congratulations are in order."

"I thank you," Rónán said, unsure if he was more stunned by his proposal or that Lathir had accepted it.

"Lady Lathir is a fine lass."

"She is. Time and again, our journey together to this point has proven her character. As I hope she has learned mine." Nerves bunched inside. "Now to find and rescue Lord Sionn, and to convince him to allow me to wed his daughter."

Even without having voiced the words, he knew how difficult that was going to be. Despite how Lathir and he had saved each other time and again, and regardless of the way their feelings had grown, it was a mismatch from the start.

Neither could he forget that once he'd brought the arms to King Robert, his sovereign would send him on his next assignment and they would again be apart. Still, after all of Scotland was beneath the Bruce's rule, he would return to Lathir.

The thought comforting him, Rónán turned to scan the shoreline, recognizing the twists and turns after having sailed here several years before.

"I have never navigated the river," Bran said, "but Lady Lathir assured me that, along with a detailed map she is crafting for when I depart, if there are any questions en route, she can guide me as we sail."

"With her experience at sea, that I have nay doubt."

The captain motioned for a man near the stern to help another sailor, then turned back to Rónán. "The lass has sailed often, then?"

"Aye, with her father since her youth."

"Which explains why she has held her own." The captain gave his chin a thoughtful rub. "I have seen many a young man green at the gills with the rough seas we have navigated. Your lass never flinched."

The hull cut through the oncoming swell as they sailed, the rush of water rumbling past in a frothy churn, the calmer seas welcome after the hours of punishing waves a short time before.

A pad of footsteps had Rónán turning.

With a smile, Lathir halted beside him, held out a rolled parchment to the captain. "The drawing of the coast and river we will navigate on the morrow, as promised."

"I thank you, my lady." Bran accepted the map. "I offer my congratulations to you as well. Sir Rónán is a fine man."

Her smile widened. "I feel the same."

Mayhap, but Rónán caught the hint of strain in her expression, suspecting she thought of her father. Worries he shared, but he settled for giving her hand a squeeze 'til they could speak in private.

Parchment scraped as the captain unrolled the paper. A bushy brow lifted. "I am familiar with the tree line marked with an $X$, but I had always believed there were sandbars about at the mouth of the river and stayed away."

The cool, salty breeze played with Lathir's blond locks as she nodded. "Given the thick line of trees, most who pass are ignorant of the waterway's presence, fewer who realize the river is deep enough to sail up, or that it winds past Wynshire Castle into a loch." She quirked her lips. "That you noticed the inlet at all is impressive."

A wry smile settled on his mouth. "When your life hangs on venues of escape, 'tis best to be aware of any site you might need in the future."

Lathir laughed. "An excellent point."

The pirate's expression grew serious. "When we sail up the inlet, my lady, though your map is detailed, I ask that you are at my side."

"Of course."

Bran nodded. "I have a few things to tend to before it grows too dark."

"I will help you," Rónán said.

The captain shook his head. "Stay with the lass. Nay doubt there are many things you and she need to discuss." With an ambling gait, he moved through the throng of his men working on deck.

Rónán inhaled the tang of salt-rich air as he looked westward. Across the calming sea, the tip of the sun glowed on the cloud-smeared horizon, the sky a blur of angry purples entangled within a mixture of orange and red. Another day lost.

Nay, another day closer to saving Lord Sionn.

Shoving aside his troubling thoughts, he turned to Lathir, who was watching him. "Aye, there is much we need to discuss, but first"—he cupped her chin with reverence—"I need this." He claimed her mouth, savored her potent taste, allowed himself to drown in their kiss, and, for a moment, help them both forget the dangers ahead.

* * * *

Overcast skies smothered the landscape in a desolate wash, casting the winter-scarred land in a pitiful gray. Thick, leafless oaks, ash, and alder lay entwined with gnarled shrubs along the river's banks.

The distant rush of water sounded ahead.

As they sailed around the bend, a small stream tumbling down a hillside came into view. Large boulders tipped with icicles framed the gurgling spill as it splashed down the awkward landscape until it poured into the river.

A snow-laden gust swept past. Excitement rushing through her, Lathir tugged her cape tighter as she scanned the familiar banks. Soon they would reach her home.

A tangle of long grass and sticks floated by as they rounded the next bend. She drew a deep breath, savored the unique scent of earth and water in Ireland. Regardless of where she'd traveled, the air was fresher here.

Tenderness filled her as she glanced at Rónán at her side. That he loved her still seemed as if a dream. Throughout the night, they'd made plans for their life together.

Bran shouted orders to his men.

A smile touched her mouth. She'd offered the stubborn leader and his men shelter within the castle this night, or for the next several days if they chose. He'd declined, but a sense of victory had filled her as in addition to the agreed upon payment, he'd acceded to allowing her to replenish their supplies.

'Twould take but a few hours to restock their goods. Once the cog sailed away, she and Rónán would meet with her trusted advisers and begin plans for raising an army to free her father.

Please God, let him be alive, not sprawled deep within a pit on a cold, dank earthen floor, tortured and fighting to survive, or...

Nay, she wouldna think of him gone. He was alive, she knew it with every beat of her heart.

A dove landed on a branch along the shore, and she took the peaceful bird's appearance as a sign she was right. She faced Rónán, and the turmoil twisting in her gut eased. Equally important, regardless of the challenges ahead, she was no longer alone.

A hawk soared overhead as they made their way around the next bend. Anticipation speared Lathir as she scoured the shore. Gray stones flickered within the break of leafless trees tangled with fir and brush. The sail snapped as a gust filled the stretched canvas, and the craft surged forward.

The clouds parted. Golden rays severed the bleak skies, and the tips of the waves shimmered as if coated with fairy dust tossed. The river widened, the flow spilling into a large loch embraced by the curve of land.

Memories of playing along the shore filled her. Of the soft press of grass beneath her feet as her father had walked beside her at sunset, told her stories of the fey, and helped her look for the wee folk rumored to be seen as the last flicker of sunlight slipped through the evening sky.

"Wynshire Castle lays ahead," a rangy sailor at the bow called.

Throat tight with pride, she took in the fortress boasting four towers, one at each corner, built by her ancestors hundreds of years before. A legacy she would one day inherit. Movement on the wall walk caught Lathir's gaze.

A bell rang out.

Weapons drawn, armed guards took their stations on the wall walk.

"Bloody hell," Bran grumbled as he strode up beside her, "they are preparing for an attack."

"They are." The bow easily cut through the water as Rónán stepped to Lathir's other side. She met the captain's gaze. "Once they recognize me, they will secure their arms. Until then, I would expect nay less than fierce defense of the stronghold." She chuckled. "Nor does it help that you are flying a pirate flag."

With a muttered curse, Bran ordered a man to lower the banner. He shook his head. "I should have bloody—" He cleared his throat. "A task I should have seen to earlier."

After having sailed too many times with her father and overhearing his crew, she was far from slighted by his salty tongue. "When an unfamiliar vessel enters our waters, my guards prepare in case of attack."

The clank of iron sounded.

Stunned, Lathir stared in disbelief at the gatehouse. "Why are they raising the portcullis?"

Face taut, Rónán glanced over. "'Tis possible that it has something to do with your father's capture."

"How? It has been less than a fortnight since his abduction, far from time for any of his friends to have been alerted."

"Mayhap, they arena his friends?"

Horror filled her. "You believe Sir Feradach O'Dowd has seized Wynshire Castle?"

"I dinna know," Rónán said, his expression grim, "but whatever is about, 'tis best to prepare for the worst."

"Indeed." Bran turned to his men. "Ready arms!"

Sailors ran to their stations, withdrew their swords.

The rumble of hooves sounded moments before armed riders began to pour out.

"Your men?" Rónán asked.

A stately man led the knights, a rider nearby holding a banner bearing a burgundy standard emblazoned with a silver lion rampant gueules wielding a sword.

"Saint's breath!" Lathir gasped, grabbing his arm. "'Tis Éogan McKelan, Earl of Torridan."

\* \* \* \*

Rónán stilled. A staunch enemy of Lord Sionn. Or was he? Much could have changed over the years, and he prayed somehow the fierce leaders had found peace. He met her worried gaze. "Is Lord Torridan still your enemy?"

Eyes dark with strife met his. "I am unsure. About a year ago, due to the rise of clashes between our realms, my father sent the Earl of Torridan a runner with a missive seeking peace."

"And his answer?"

She released a shaky breath. "I am unsure; all I know is that my father was furious at the lord's first reply. After, several missives were passed back and forth between my father and Lord Torridan, but I was never informed whether they had reached an agreement, but I pray so."

Blast it! He scoured the armed contingent, damning the entire situation. "Until we know for sure, you willna go ashore. Alone."

"My father—"

"I refuse risking your capture. What if they havena reached an agreement?" Rónán asked. "What if Lord Torridan had guards watching your father's every move and, during your absence, the noble, one who could be in league with the Earl of Ardgar, laid siege and seized Wynshire Castle? Is that a risk you wish to take? Your father's life is lost if that is the case."

Any remaining color in her face fled. Determination flashed in her eyes. "I have little choice."

"Bedamned you do!" Rónán snapped, furious she'd endanger her life. "We will find out, but I will go."

"Nay!"

The distant thud of hooves upon turf reached them as the column neared the shore.

"Well?" demanded Bran as he joined them.

"We will do this my way," Rónán snarled to her, on this point refusing to cede, "or we sail away."

Bran grimaced. "I would be listening to him, my lady."

Fury blazed in Lathir's eyes.

"Aye," Tighearnán said as he stepped up to join them. "From the stern looks on their faces, it doesna appear to be a welcoming party."

Despite the conflict in her eyes, Rónán held Lathir's gaze as he continued. "Captain, dinna bring the cog any closer. I will row a small boat ashore and discover what they are about."

Bran nodded, then shouted orders to the crew.

Rónán met the captain's gaze. "Once I reach shore, if they seize me, take Lathir to King Robert."

"Saint's breath, I willna be shuffled about as if a helpless maiden!"

"I know a place to bring her," Tighearnán said, "and I swear that she will be kept safe."

"My father—"

Tighearnán gave a grim nod. "Regardless of what happens, I will help you find your father."

Eyes narrowed, she glared at Rónán. "I dinna like the risk. What if..."

From her voice, he knew she thought of the worst. He'd faced many conflicts before, but never had one mattered so much.

He drew her to him. "'Tis a necessary risk. If indeed Lord Torridan has made peace with your father, he will agree to help us free him."

Her lower lip trembled, but Lathir gave a rough exhale. "Be safe."

"Lower the boat," Bran called to his crew.

Rónán cupped her face. "I love you, Lathir. I will be back."

"You had better," she said fiercely, "or I will come ashore after you."

A promise no doubt she'd try to keep, though Tighearnán and Bran would prevent her from doing something so dangerous. Lathir strode to the rail, where a sailor unfurled a rope ladder over the side.

"I love you, Rónán," she called.

After accepting a white strip of cloth from Tighearnán, Rónán shot her a wink, then climbed to the small craft bobbing in the water.

Water splashed as he dipped in his oars and rowed shoreward. Out of arrow range but close enough to be heard, Rónán turned the craft sideways before the man astride his black steed on the grass.

He paused as he saw a younger man bearing a striking resemblance to the earl, his fine garb and extraordinary mail declaring him of noble birth. No doubt a relation. A son, perhaps?

Rónán waved a white strip of cloth. "Lord Torridan, my name is Sir Rónán. Before I come ashore, I seek your assurance that I willna be seized."

The noble's lean face drew tight. "I dinna make deals with brigands!"

"I am not an outlaw. I come to speak in the name of Lord Sionn."

Lines of doubt creased the earl's brow.

The younger noble leaned close to Lord Torridan and spoke in tones too low for Rónán to hear.

The elder shook his head, then lifted his hand. "I order you to come ashore."

"And your promise that I willna be captured?" Rónán called.

The earl shook his head. "Once I learn your reason, I will decide."

Bedamned, there was no easy way do this. Nor would he reveal that Lathir was on board. If they apprehended him, Bran would be able to escape and take her to safety.

With a prayer that Lord Torridan had indeed found peace with Lord Sionn, Rónán rowed to shore. A short while later, ice crunched beneath his steps as he climbed up the half-frozen bank and strode toward the ruler of the realm of Tír Connail. Paces away, he halted.

Gray sprinkled the fierce leader's dark brown hair, which was secured in a tie behind his neck. His slate-gray eyes were piercing, those of a man used to wielding power, a warrior unafraid regardless the challenge.

He glanced at the noble at the daunting man's side. Not a lad, but a year or two younger than himself. Though lean, the cut of his muscles along with his shrewd, unapologetic green eyes assured Rónán that he, too, was a man seasoned in war.

Rónán faced the powerful leader. He'd dealt with men of their ilk many times over. The formidable lord would appreciate a direct approach, so he would tell him, and deal with whatever repercussions followed. "Lord Torridan, as I stated before, I come to speak in the name of Lord Sionn."

Mouth tight, he glanced toward the cog before his gaze turned back to Rónán. "Why does he not come ashore?"

"Because he isna aboard." Images of the attack poured through Rónán. "He was abducted from the *Aodh* almost a fortnight ago by Sir Feradach O'Dowd, who led a crew of Irishmen and Englishmen under King Edward II's flag."

A ruddy hue darkened the man's face. "Are you sure 'twas Lord Ardgar's master-at-arms?"

The image of the cur was burned in Rónán's mind. Regardless of the years that'd passed, if the miscreant had grown haggard and walked with a stoop, he would still recognize him. "Aye. If Lord Sionn is still alive, we need your help to rescue him."

Lord Torridan took his measure before replying. "'Twill be done."

The tense muscles in Rónán's body relaxed a bit.

Wary eyes of the younger noble held his. "How is it that you were sailing with Lord Sionn?"

"Before I reply, due to the nature of my mission, I must know two things. First, whether you and Lord Sionn have made peace."

The powerful leader studied him briefly, then gave him a curt nod. "We have. The second?"

After his reaction to what he had said of Sir Feradach's crew, Rónán felt confident of the noble's reply to his next question. "Whether you support King Robert."

"I swore an oath to the Bruce when we met several months ago."

A fact, Rónán mused, Lathir's father hadn't shared with her.

The noble nodded to the younger lord. "As did my son, Kieran, Earl of Craigshyre."

Which explained the similarities between the two. Rónán explained his allegiance to King Robert, and the reason their sovereign had sent him with Lord Sionn.

Both nobles stared at him in disbelief. "'Tis why we are here," the elder said.

Confused, Rónán frowned. "My lord?"

"Several weeks ago, I received a missive from Lord Sionn, informing me he was sailing to speak with King Robert. He requested that I meet him at Wynshire Castle upon his return. His reason, to assist in retrieving weapons to send the king to help squelch the lingering resistance." The earl paused. "That the king sent you as his envoy leads me to believe you are charged with ensuring the arms reach Scotland."

Rónán nodded. "I am."

Lord Torridan glanced toward the loch. "And the pirate ship?"

"After Sir Feradach's men seized Lord Sionn, believing everyone remaining on board dead, they set the *Aodh* afire."

Concern lined the Earl of Craigshyre's brow. "Lady Lathir?"

At the anxiousness of the younger man, unease sifted through Rónán. He dismissed his disquiet. No doubt they had met in the past. Only a fool wouldn't be attracted to her. "She is safe."

The young lord relaxed. "Where is she?"

"Safe," Rónán replied.

Craigshyre's brows slammed together. "Tell me where she is!"

Rónán stiffened, then forced himself to relax. The nobles presented no threat. Once he'd returned to the ship, he'd bring her ashore. "Lady Lathir is aboard the cog."

The young lord's shoulders eased, and he gave a brief nod. "Then all is set. As in the agreement for peace between Lord Sionn and my father, and by her father's consent in the last missive, Lady Lathir and I will seal our betrothal this night."

# Chapter Eleven

The deep clang of the bell rang out from Wynshire Castle, barely piercing Rónán's consciousness as he stared at Lord Craigshyre, struggling to accept the earl's claim. The pending betrothal to Lathir couldna be.

Not when he'd found her, loved her, had begun building a future with her.

Nor could he forget her in his arms, the love shining in her eyes when she'd accepted his proposal, or the dreams they'd shared.

Fury slammed through him, and his fingers dropped to the hilt of his sword.

The nobles' hands moved to their own weapons as he struggled for control. By God, he wouldn't take her. He'd fight for her, force Craigshyre to realize he had no claim on her.

He dragged a rough breath. He would... He would...

Cold reality cut through him. Her betrothal to Lord Torridan's son was part of the peace agreement between powerful lords.

A condition Lord Sionn had not disclosed to his daughter.

That her father would want her protected made sense. That he hadn't pushed her into a marriage after the loss of the man she'd loved two years before was a convenience few would have allowed their daughters. Nor was Lord Sionn's action rash, but wise. Many nobles over the centuries had found peace as strength through marriage.

Though Rónán wanted to despise her betrothed, he'd done naught but agree to his father's wishes to wed an intelligent, beautiful, and strong woman any man would want as his wife.

However much he wished otherwise, he would do naught.

On a hard swallow, Rónán lowered his hand; the nobles followed suit. "Lathir is unaware of this betrothal."

"Lord Sionn's decision of when to disclose it to his daughter isna my concern," Lord Torridan said, watching him closely, as if he didn't quite trust Ronan's calm. "The promise has been made."

One that would enrage Lathir. Yet, with the vow made, a disruption of the betrothal could not only interfere in rescuing her father and bringing much-needed arms to King Robert, but might cast their realms into war.

However much he loved her, wanted her forever, he couldn't jeopardize his mission.

Rónán nodded to the nobles. "I will return with Lady Lathir posthaste."

The breeze picked up as he walked to shore. Wood scraped against rocks as he shoved the boat into the building waves and stepped inside. He sank onto the bench, caught the oars. Heart aching, he started toward the cog.

"Thank God you are safe!" Lathir ran up to him as he climbed on board, and his chest squeezed tight. When he'd departed earlier, he'd believed they'd share the rest of their lives together. An incredible dream with a woman who'd stolen his heart, lost.

With the cog shifted so those onshore couldn't see them, Rónán drew her against him. She smelled of salt and woman, a scent he would forever remember. He wanted to hold her forever, aware that any hope of her being his was lost. "I love you," he rasped. "Never forget that."

She stiffened in his arms and lifted her head. Gray eyes narrowed as she stared at him. "What happened?"

Before he could answer, boots thudded upon the weathered wood as the captain strode toward them. "I see you returned safe and sound."

"Aye." Never wanting to let her go, Rónán forced himself to step back. "As you suspected, Lathir, two years ago the Earl of Torridan and your father made peace. He is here at your father's request."

"Thank God." Even as her shoulders relaxed, a frown creased her brow. "Why would my father seek his aid?"

"He traveled here to help retrieve the arms that your father promised the Bruce."

Surprise flickered on her face, then a smile curved her mouth. "He supports King Robert?"

Rónán nodded. "Aye."

Hope ignited in her beautiful eyes. "A prayer answered. Nay doubt when he learned of my father's capture, he agreed to help us rescue him."

"He did."

Sunlight shimmered upon the loose blond strands fluttering on her cheek as the joy on Lathir's face faded. "Except you dinna seem pleased. Why?"

Grief gathered in Rónán's heart, a hurt so fierce, 'twas as if his every fiber, everything he'd ever cared for was being ripped apart. Nor would he divulge such devastating news before the captain and the crew. "I will explain as we row to shore."

At his tone, apprehension trickled through Lathir. Whatever had happened during his visit with the earl had left him shaken. Exhausted, her nerves awry, mayhap she was reading more into Rónán's request for privacy than was there?

She should focus on the fact that Lord Torridan had agreed to help free her father, that by sheer fortune, her father had requested the noble's presence. With the size of their combined forces, in addition to finding her father more quickly, regardless of the size of Lord Ardgar's guard, they would free Lord Sionn.

Her mind racing at the many things they needed to do in the days ahead, she hurried to collect her few belongings. Once she'd stowed them aboard the dinghy, she returned to Bran. After an assurance that supplies would be sent back with this craft and the one used by Tighearnán and his daughter Órlaith after they rowed to shore, Lathir climbed down the rope ladder into the small boat. The gentle rocking of the vessel soothed her as she settled upon the back seat.

After placing the few items he'd brought next to her, Rónán untied the rope, sat on the middle bench, then grasped each oar. Instead of beginning to row, Rónán lifted his gaze to hers.

The sheer torment filling his eyes stole her breath. "Tell me what is wrong."

The light wind rich with a mix of the water and earth pushed the small boat away from the cog, the soft slap of the waves but a whisper upon the side of the craft.

On a muttered curse, he looked away and dragged the oars through the water, which splashed from the bow as the boat sliced forward.

Her fingers bit into the weathered wooden seat. "Could the news be so terrible?"

For a moment, he didn't speak. "The Earl of Torridan arrived for more than aiding your father." Face taut, he leaned forward, then drew the oars back. "His son, Kieran McKelan, Earl of Craigshyre, accompanies him."

Lathir recalled having met the earl's son briefly, not that she had had any interest in him at the time, as she'd been grieving, and then only at her father's bidding. A handsome and intelligent man with a wonderful sense of humor. Many a woman had tried to catch his eye, but she had not heard that any had succeeded.

"We have met," she said.

"Indeed."

At the coolness of his tone, she surmised the reason for Rónán's upset. Regardless if she'd told him that she loved him, he struggled with his rank as a knight against her nobility. More, he was worried she would be attracted to the son of a powerful noble, a man who held significant rank in his own right.

The foolish man. Hadn't he learned by now that she wasn't swayed by titles?

"Rónán—" With a smile she leaned forward and touched his arm. "I care not about Lord Torridan's son, or any other man bearing a title or holding a position of power. 'Tis you that I love, you that I want for the rest of my life. Naught will ever change that."

Instead of relief, his eyes darkened with regret. "You dinna understand what we are facing."

She begged to differ. There was little he could say to dissuade her from their life together. "Understand what?"

Oars splashed as they cut through the water, sending vicious eddies into the wake. He looked away for a long moment, then faced her. If possible, his expression had grown more desperate.

A chill trickled through her, and she tugged her cloak tighter.

Hands trembling, he pushed the oars back. Swirls of water spun off the tip as the small craft sliced through the building waves. "Lord Torridan explained that his journey to Wynshire Castle was for more than aiding Lord Sionn to retrieve arms for the Bruce, but—" He muttered a curse. "It was to solidify the betrothal he and your father agreed upon between you and his son."

Air rushed from her lungs as her father's warning during their journey that 'twas time to marry flickered to mind.

"I…" Tears burned her eyes as she fought against realization, the hurt, the sense of betrayal. "I never believed my father was serious."

Rónán jerked the oars back, slammed them through the water. "You knew of your betrothal?" he demanded.

Fury rumbled in his voice, but she refused to look away as she struggled to accept this terrible situation. "Nay. As we sailed to Scotland, Father stated that enough time had passed since Domhnall Ruadh mac Cormaic's death, and he insisted 'twas time for me to marry. I swear to you, I never knew of the betrothal, but…" She closed her eyes, then forced herself to meet his tortured gaze. "On the *Aodh*," she continued, battling for calm, "my father proclaimed that before we arrived home, he had important information to share." She shook her head in despair. "It must have been this."

Emotions rippled across his face: grief, sadness, then acceptance. "You never knew."

"Nay," she whispered. Waves buffeted the bow as, with each row, they grew closer to shore.

He opened his mouth as if to say something, then closed it.

She swallowed hard. "I swear, never would I hurt you."

"I know," he said simply.

Somehow, his acceptance roused her own ire. Bedamned, her life wouldn't be dictated to by her father. "Nor have I given my consent to this arrangement. I shall refuse to marry Lord Craigshyre, and you and I shall wed as planned."

A muscle worked in his jaw as he continued to row. "If you refuse to wed Lord Craigshyre, the hard-won peace between your realms will cease."

Her knuckles whitened as she clasped the edged of her seat. "Is that what Lord Torridan threatened?"

"Nay, but Lord Torridan is a proud man, one only a fool would cross."

She shook her head in silent despair. Rónán was wrong. He had to be. "There must be a way to settle this without violence returning to our realms."

Eddies swirled away from the honed wood as he again pulled the oars in an aggressive stroke through the water, now tipped with white caps. "There is no way to change the promise your father made. If you refuse to wed, 'twill be viewed as a slight. Both he and his son will be outraged. Indignation will spill into Lord Torridan's decision regarding more than whether to go to war against your realm, but in refusing to help rescue Lord Sionn. The plan to rescue your father will be over before it begins."

Overwhelmed by the sense of impending doom, Lathir sagged back, watched as a hawk screeched as it soared overhead, disappeared beyond the shield of winter-blanched trees.

"Nor, with his troops ensconced within Wynshire Castle," Rónán continued, his voice grim, "furious at the shun, he might seize the stronghold and force you to wed against your will."

Saint's breath. Never had she considered the repercussions. "But you dinna know for sure."

He arched a brow. "I dinna, but with Lord Torridan's reputation as not a man to cross, and after having met him, with everything at stake, 'twould be unwise to risk offending him."

Heart aching, she damned each row that brought them closer to shore. "But 'tis you I love, you I want."

"I love and want you as well, Lathir," he forced out in a strangled whisper, "but our feelings for each other dinna outweigh the peace between your realms, or your father's life."

The last wisp of hope inside faded. Emptiness clawed through her as she sat back, deep, dark gouges that left her floundering for choices, found none. Tears burned her eyes as Lathir wanted to scream her denial, but she forced both back. Neither would help, and the last thing she wanted was to make this terrible situation more so on Rónán.

Though she didn't want to marry Lord Craigshyre, despised contemplating a life without Rónán, to save her father, maintain peace within her realm, and keep control of her castle, 'twould seem her choice was made.

At the hopelessness on Lathir's face, Rónán damned the situation. With a curse, he dragged the oars through the water. Nor as a knight could he challenge the earl's son for Lathir. With naught but his sword, the noble would order him banished from the castle under the threat of being hanged if ever he tried to contact Lathir.

Who could blame the lord? If she was his intended, he would do whatever necessary to keep her.

The bow scraped the sand as they reached shore.

"Wait here." Each breath burning like bile in his throat, Rónán climbed out, lifted the bow, and pulled the dinghy another step up the beach. His boots crunched on the icy ground as he walked over and offered Lathir his hand.

Her breaths falling out in fragmented puffs of white, she lay her fingers within his palm, and he gave a gentle squeeze that drew her gaze to his.

"I will love you forever," he whispered, the devastation in her eyes matching his. Nor, however much he wished to keep her, could he change fate now. Heart crumbling, on a shaky breath, he stepped back.

She let her hand fall to her side. "I will never love another." Her pallor having faded to a bloodless white, she straightened her shoulders and walked past him, as regal as a queen.

At the distant creak of wood and splash of water, Rónán glanced back.

Tighearnán and his daughter, along with two crew, were rowing toward the shore.

Muttering a curse, Rónán, started up the incline. As if either he, or Lathir, had a choice? He fought the heartache, doubted he'd ever get over losing her. If there was but a hope, a chance to salvage the love they'd found, he'd take it.

But none existed.

Resigned to an empty life ahead, he focused on duty. Nor was all dismal. As promised by Lathir, Tighearnán and Órlaith would begin a new life at Wynshire Castle. As well, peace would exist between the realms of Tír Sèitheach and Tír Connail. At least King Robert had support from both formidable nobles. In time, any foothold against the Bruce in Scotland, as in Ireland, would be destroyed.

His legs heavy, as if filled with lead, Rónán fell in step beside Lathir as she headed toward the men who'd gathered to greet her. The younger noble's gaze was fierce as he watched her approach, the older's stalwart. She continued up the incline without hesitation.

Though she was promised to another, for a time they were together. He would have that memory, if not her.

The crunch of their steps upon the frozen grass filled the silence. As if there was anything left to say. Their love, hope of ever being together, was lost.

\* \* \* \*

The scent of roast boar, herbs, and several delicacies that were served during the betrothal celebration lingered in the great hall as Lathir stepped from the dais, exhausted and more than ready for this night to end.

Though her betrothed's mouth had tightened at her request to allow Rónán to sit at the table on the dais with them, she'd held firm. Regardless that she wouldn't marry Rónán, he'd saved her life and deserved a place of honor.

The meal, one filled with naught but cordial pleasantries, was over. In the morning, once everyone had broken their fast, Lord Torridan, her betrothed, Rónán, and the master-at-arms would meet in the war chamber to discuss plans to find and save her father.

It was what she desperately wanted, yet her heart still ached at the way she and Ronan had deliberately avoided each other's gaze throughout the evening.

As for her betrothed, regardless of his looks and solid reputation, she felt nothing for him but duty.

En route to the turret, she glanced around the large chamber at her father's arms hanging above the hearth, the colorful banners displayed on either side, then toward the hewn arches that had fascinated her as a child.

Along the wall hung paintings of her ancestors. Emotions storming her, she took in her father's portrait. Sandy hair framed a striking face. Clear blue eyes like the depths of the sea held hers, that of a man confident of his abilities, a man who ruled with a fair but firm hand, a man who'd sentenced her to a life with a man she didn't love.

Nor could she cling to her grief. Her father had made his decision out of concern. Aware of the heartache he'd suffered at the loss of her mother, she believed he hadn't wanted Lathir to remain alone as he had, holding on to naught but a memory.

The soft slide of her slippers upon the curved stair echoed within the turret as she started up. Torchlight wavered upon the walls ahead, and she recalled being afraid of what lay beyond the fall of light in her youth, of how her father would take her hand and walk beside her to ward off the unknown.

Her throat tightened and she sent up a silent prayer for his safety.

Lathir reached the corridor leading to her chamber, started down. As she entered her room, she paused. With the strife crowding her mind, she doubted she'd sleep.

Throughout her life, when she needed to be alone, to think, to ponder a problem, she'd gone to the wall walk. There was something soul cleansing about standing upon the battlements and looking out.

On a clear night, she could lose herself as she stared up. The stars in the heavens shimmered so bright, 'twas as if she could reach up and touch them. 'Twas as if for a moment her problems disappeared.

But she was no longer a child who could lose herself in the wonder of the sweep of land or beauty above, but a woman with responsibilities, duties she must uphold.

The image of her signing the betrothal to marry Lord Torridan's eldest son but hours before slipped through her mind.

Regardless of her desire for a life with Rónán, she must focus on the peace her agreement to marry brought to their realms, and the fact that united, the odds of finding and saving her father greatly improved.

Footsteps heavy, she retrieved her cape and hurried to the wall walk. If only for a moment, she wanted peace.

At the top of the steps, she shoved open the carved door. A light wind brushed her face as she went out into the night. A full moon rising in the east illuminated the land, casting silver shimmers on the snow as if magic dust had been tossed by the fey.

Magic, she scoffed. A foolish notion to enchant a child.

Lathir again looked around, saw naught but the night severed by the brutal sheen of the moon, molding shadows where danger could hide.

Her breath misted before her. With a shiver, she tugged the cloak tighter, walked to the corner, peered out.

In the distance, the hoot of an owl faded, replaced by the soft slide of cold wind through the trees.

"'Tis unwise to be without a guard at your side."

At Rónán's voice, joy swept her. Out of sheer reaction, she whirled and ran to him. He drew her into his arms and pressed his cheek against hers. Within the silvery sheen of moonlight, sadness darkened his gaze as he stroked his finger against her cheek. "I didna expect to see you alone again."

"Luck," she said on a shaky smile, wishing for the thousandth time that a realm's peace and her father's life didn't depend upon her marrying Lord Craigshyre. Then she and Rónán could wed, as they wished.

After a long embrace, he set her away from him. "'Tisna wise. 'Twould bode ill if we were seen."

The ache in her chest intensified. He was right. Damning that he was now forbidden and, ignoring her body's need, she took another step back, turned toward the loch. Shimmers of moonlight played upon the smooth surface in a macabre dance.

"I always used to love the night," she whispered, her voice rough, "but now all I see are shadows."

His boots scraped as he stepped beside her. "Aye, there will always be shadows, but regardless the danger, the unknown, beauty still exists. All you have to do is look."

The distant hoot of an owl filled the strained silence. "Where will you go once my father is rescued?"

He scanned the stars overhead. "To fight for King Robert."

"And after our sovereign has eliminated the last of the resistance against his reign in Scotland?"

Rónán shrugged but didn't look at her, as if it was too painful. "'Tis too far away to think of, or worry about." He stepped back, offered Lathir his arm. "Come, 'tis time to leave. I will escort you below."

The grief she struggled against threatened to overwhelm her. This was all so unfair; could they not linger a while longer? "Hold me again, Rónán, if only for a moment more."

On a muttered curse, his expression wrought with heartache, he reached for her.

"Lathir!"

At Lord Craigshyre's terse voice, she whirled to face him.

# Chapter Twelve

Heart pounding, Lathir turned, damned herself for placing Rónán in a suspicious light to her betrothed. Rónán had behaved as a gentleman. Any impropriety came from her. "Lord Craigshyre." She faced Rónán again. "I thank you for informing me that you have spoken with the master-at-arms to arrange tomorrow morning's meeting in the war room. That is all I shall need from you this night."

"Aye, my lady." Rónán's eyes, dark with concern, held hers. "If you need me to remain—"

"I willna." Any anger from her betrothed was hers to deal with.

"As you wish." Mouth tight, he nodded to the noble. "Lord Craigshyre." The soft crunch of snow filled the silence as Rónán departed. The door to the turret closed on a soft thud, leaving them alone.

Torchlight wavered upon the snow-dusted wall walk as her betrothed eyed her. "Be warned, regardless of your feelings for Sir Rónán, I willna be cuckolded."

She stiffened. "I have done naught improper, nor will I tolerate your slander." She started to walk away, and he caught her arm. Lathir rounded on him. "Release me!"

He did, then stared at her for a long moment in a way she couldn't decipher. "You love him." It wasn't a question.

Emotion balled in her chest, the pain, the loss of never being with Rónán breaking her heart. "My feelings for him are irrelevant," she said, her voice cool. "My vow to wed you has been given. 'Tisna one I will break or taint with misdeeds."

"Nor was I pleased by our betrothal." On a sigh, he crossed his arms over his chest. "Not because you arena a lass I admire."

"Then what?"

"Like you, I love another."

She blinked, shocked. Yet at the anguish in his voice, the bleakness of his expression, her anger faded. Saint's breath, he was suffering with heartbreak, just as she.

Impulsively, she touched his arm. "'Tis not too late. We can speak with your father. Then, once we free my—"

"Nay. I tried, I assure you. My father made it clear that he, as yours, wants a tie between our realms. Neither will be swayed."

Wind feathered across her face as the last wisp of hope faded to a blackened mar across her heart. Like Craigshyre, she was bound by a duty that would sever any possibility of their being with those they truly loved.

"Now what?" Lathir rasped, wanting to scream her frustration.

"I…" He lowered his arm. "We become friends?"

Friends? In some ways, he reminded her of Rónán. His confidence and forthright manner. An alliance of friendship was a wise decision. Lathir doubted she'd ever come to love the man, but 'twould make the years ahead easier to bear.

"Aye, though 'tis best that you know that I am my own woman and willna be someone to command, now or ever. As my mother and father did, once you and I wed, we will rule together."

She awaited his anger at her bold words; instead, a smile tugged at his mouth. "Nor would I have it any other way. My mother was a strong and spirited woman as well, who ruled alongside my father."

Her body relaxed. She'd prepared herself for a confrontation. In truth, though a formidable man, since they'd first met, he'd been naught but respectful and kind.

Nor could she deny he was handsome. No doubt many a lass had tried to win his attention. If she hadn't met Rónán and fallen in love, she could have accepted their match and believed they would have lived if not in love, then in peace.

"Lord Craigshyre, I believe I would have liked your mother."

"As we are betrothed, call me Kieran. As for my mother, she would have enjoyed your forthright manner as well."

Another hoot of an owl sounded from the distant trees.

He turned toward the shore, gave a slow exhale that tumbled out in misty white. She wondered if he was thinking of his lost love.

"'Tis beautiful," he finally murmured.

Shimmers of light danced upon the loch, glinted off the bits of ice clinging to the edge. "Being here has always brought me peace." At least she would have this place to return to.

She stilled.

Or, once they'd wed, would he insist on returning to his castle? She fisted her hands at the thought of leaving her home. And her father; if they didna rescue him, then what?

Kieran leaned upon the carved stone, glanced over. "'Tis foolish to think about, but our upcoming marriage wouldna be an issue if I wasna the only surviving son."

Caught off-balance by his words, she frowned. She'd never heard that Lord Craigshyre had a sibling. "I am so sorry for your loss. Did your older brother die in battle?"

"Nay, during birth. 'Twas something I overheard as a child, when my mother and father were speaking and didna realize I was nearby." He paused. "Do you have any sisters?"

"Nay, I have nay siblings."

"Which brings us back to our predicament. Worry naught, I assure you, I am thankful you are a strong and wise lass unafraid to speak your mind. And"—he said with a hint of a smile—"beautiful."

His words held naught but camaraderie, and she relaxed. "And I that you arena a weak-willed man."

"I have never," he said, his voice dry, "been accused of such."

The annoyance in his reply sounding so much the way Rónán would say it, she chuckled. "That I can believe."

Kieran pushed away from the stone. 'Come, 'tis growing late. Allow me to escort you to your chamber."

After one last glance over the land she loved, Lathir nodded.

"Though we are bound by duty," he said as he walked toward the turret, "for the first time since my arrival, I feel relief in that, though ours will not be a marriage of love, 'twill be one of respect."

"I feel the same." Though she doubted she'd ever recover from the pain of losing Rónán.

They walked in silence for several moments, their shadows blending into the night.

Another gust whispered past, tossing flakes of snow in a delicate swirl. They spun in the star-laden night in a graceful spiral, swaying softly to land upon the wall walk. She was glad for the thick fur cape that kept the cold at bay.

"My lady—"

"Lathir."

He nodded at the invited intimacy as they strolled. "Lathir, I wanted to inform you that runners were dispatched shortly after your arrival to learn any details of where Lord Sionn may be held."

"I thank you, but why did you not tell me earlier?" she asked, irritation sliding into her voice.

"Until we have a solid idea of where he is being held, I didna want to give you false hope. After our conversation just now, in the future I will be forthright with you." He paused. "Rest assured, my father and I will do all within our power to ensure Lord Sionn is freed."

Shame filled her at her terse manner. He knew so little about her; his actions were born from caution. And she'd reacted instead of appreciating his consideration. "Forgive me for sounding so harsh. I am tired and on edge, and you were being naught but thoughtful."

"'Tis naught to apologize for. If my father was in danger, I would be the devil to deal with."

"I thank you for understanding. My father and I are very close."

"As are my father and I."

Their both holding strong ties with their parents was important. That they'd both lost one of their parents, however devastating, was another bond. Then there was the fact that each of them loved another.

They may not have chosen the other, but the more she came to know Kieran, the more she tried to convince herself that their union would be more than peaceful, but close.

Though she'd never lost a sibling. Did he ever think of his brother? Something she would not ask until their relationship was more secure.

Moments later, torchlight wavered in the turret as he closed the door behind them. The chill of the fresh night air melded with the scent of tallow and rushes as they made their way to her chamber.

Outside her room, she paused. "Thank you."

Thoughtfulness chiseled his features as Kieran lifted her hand, pressed a chaste kiss upon the back of her fingers. She felt nothing, but gave him a smile nonetheless. His lips quirked in silent understanding.

"'Til we break our fast, my lady."

Her mind spinning, Lathir entered her chamber, closed the door, and leaned back against the thick, carved wood. He seemed like a good man, one she could depend on. She struggled to be thankful that although her life ahead wouldna be the one she'd chosen, their union wouldn't be one laden with strife, a fate that could have all too easily occurred.

In a twisted sense, 'twas a gift that Kieran loved another, that they were both bound by duty. He was gracious in his understanding, and from his manner tonight, Lathir suspected he wouldn't press marital obligations until she was ready.

Nor would she ponder further familial duties their marriage directed. The time for that would come soon enough.

But she couldn't banish thoughts of Rónán, of the emptiness in her heart, a place he would hold until she drew her last breath.

Emotions storming her, she crossed to her bed and climbed beneath the thick covers. Restless, she stared at the flames. Though exhausted, she doubted she'd sleep this night.

* * * *

Sunlight streamed through the leaded glass window, illuminating the crafted image of a biblical scene as Rónán settled in an empty chair at the table in the war chamber. He glanced at Lord Torridan, Lord Craigshyre, Lathir, and the master-at-arms, who were taking their seats as well.

Rónán ignored the luxuriously crafted tapestry depicting a battle scene, the formidable display of swords, daggers, and other weaponry hanging on the wall, and remained silent. His head pounded from lack of sleep, a common occurrence since he'd learned of Lathir's betrothal.

He'd ordered himself to push thoughts of the life they'd planned aside, but like a thorn that festered, he ached for what they'd lost. Watching her was painful, her strong and graceful beauty that of a true noble. And the spare seat to her side, clearly saved for him, was like a dart of poison. Had his relationship with God not been strong, he would have suspected the chair was meant for him to endure the torture of her company.

He'd wanted to hate her betrothed. But after almost a fortnight, time to come to know the noble, Craigshyre was proving to be a man he could admire. He was even-tempered and clearly a man who had earned authority. Even though he heeded his father's wishes for a wife, he did not live in his elder's shadow. His own opinions were well-thought-out and spoke of a stalwart character.

Nor, if he was being purely logical, could Rónán fault Lord Sionn. Lathir's father's intention was to erase tensions between the two realms.

In truth, if he didn't love Lathir, he would have agreed that she and Kieran made a fine match.

The chair scraped as Lord Torridan stood, met each person's gaze. "I received word from the first of the runners."

Lathir straightened. "Have they found him?"

"Nay," he replied.

At the devastation on her face, Rónán's gut twisted. Blast it, by now he'd expected to have heard where her father had been taken.

On several occasions he'd strode to the stable, wanting to take a mount and search himself. But too many years had passed since he'd traveled in Ireland, and he no longer had contacts he could turn to for help.

"The runner," the noble continued in a quieter tone, seemingly in response to Lathir's distress, "departs tomorrow to search in southeastern Ireland, where the English have control." His gaze rested on her. "We will find him, my lady."

She gave a shaky nod.

Though the questions of when and if he would still be alive burned in Rónán's mind. Bedamned this waiting!

The rapid tap of steps had them glancing toward the corridor moments before a knock sounded.

"Enter," Lord Torridan commanded.

A guard stepped inside. "Lord Torridan, the pirate ship has returned. Their captain requests to speak with you. He states 'tis of grave importance."

Hope flickered in Lathir's gaze as it met Rónán's a second before shifting to Lord Torridan. "My lord, there can be only one reason Bran would return. He has word of my father's location."

Lines of strain settled across the noble's brow. "I pray you are right." He nodded to the guard. "Escort the captain here immediately."

"Aye, my lord." The guard hurried away.

Rónán leaned back in his chair and took a moment to collect himself as he reached for the glass of wine.

As much as he wished 'twas the reason for the pirate's visit, he despised the chance of seeing Lathir's hopes crushed. Many things could have guided Bran's hasty return, including that English ships had spotted him and were giving chase. His arrival here may be naught but a frantic search for protection.

He longed to lay his hand over hers. With her betrothed seated beside her, not a possibility. God's truth, he despised being unable to touch her, to hold her.

Tense silence filled the chamber, broken by the errant crackle of the fire in the hearth.

"More wine, my lady?" her betrothed asked.

She shook her head. "I doubt I can drink anything until I learn Bran's news." The steady tap of leather boots echoed from the corridor. Moments later, Bran entered, followed by Tighearnán.

Rónán nodded to the man, far from surprised to see the previous captain accompanying Bran. No doubt after the pirate ship had been sighted, Tighearnán had hurried to meet his friend.

Nor had Rónán missed, during their time here, how Tighearnán, and one of Lathir's maids had shown interest in each other. Given that he'd seen the pair talking in a quiet corner of the bailey, 'twould seem that Tighearnán would find more than a wife, but a mother for Órlaith.

Bran took another step forward.

Tighearnán halted beside his friend.

"Lord Torridan, Lord Craigshyre, Lady Lathir, Sir Rónán," the captain said. "I come with news of import regarding Lord Sionn."

Lathir rose to her feet. "You have found him?"

"Aye," Bran replied, his voice gruff. "He was alive when I saw him taken—"

At the dread in the pirate's voice, she clenched her fists at her sides. "To where?"

Bran's jaw tightened. "He is imprisoned at Murchadh Castle."

Lathir gasped.

Kieran lay his hand upon hers.

She withdrew from his touch, struggling against the fear at this news of her father incarcerated within the earl of Ardgar's stronghold. All knew of the powerful lord's brutality. Over the years, she'd never heard of any who'd entered his dungeon emerging alive.

"Was he hurt?" she asked in a voice that trembled despite her best efforts to contain it.

The captain cleared his throat. "He had a few bruises, my lady. For the most part, he was able to walk on his own."

For the most part? Nausea welled in her throat. No, he was alive, she would concentrate on that.

"Captain," Lord Torridan began, "what challenges do we face in freeing Lord Sionn?"

After a look of regret at Lathir, Bran nodded to the noble. In detail, the pirate explained the defenses they'd have to overcome at Murchadh Castle, fortifications that included the arrival of a fresh contingent of English troops.

Face flushed with anger, Lord Torridan pounded his fist on the table. "Bloody upstarts. Any Irishman who joins the Sassenach is naught but a traitor! Nor will their forces joining the English help our cause." The snap of the fire filled the silence as he scanned those within the chamber.

"Given the stronghold's cliffside location, a frontal assault could devastate our combined forces, and a siege could last months, time we dinna have. If only we knew of a secret tunnel."

"Lord Torridan," Rónán said, "if I can find any galloglass to speak with, as I once served within their ranks, they will inform me if any of their warriors has detailed knowledge of Murchadh Castle's layout."

A fresh surge of hope shot through Lathir as the room erupted into thoughtful murmurs.

"We passed an encampment of galloglass en route to Wynshire Castle," Lord Craigshyre said.

Rónán's gaze cut to Lathir's betrothed. "How far?"

"A few hours' ride, if they are still there," Craigshyre replied.

Rónán's chair scraped as he stood. "There are still several hours of daylight. I will leave immediately."

Lord Torridan nodded. "While you are away, I will prepare the men to sail. Upon your return, we will depart."

Bran cleared his throat. "My lord, we have another problem."

Lord Torridan's gaze cut to him. "Which is?"

"En route, I was informed by a *friend* that the English and Irish are gathering a fleet of ships off the northeast coast of Ireland filled with troops who are planning to halt northeastward along the coast, then move overland to attack Wynshire Castle. To make it here without delay, I was forced to sail past them in the dark."

Knuckles white on her chair, Lathir leaned forward. "How many ships did you see?"

"At least eight," the pirate replied, "but 'twas a cloudy night. There could very well have been many more."

Terror filled Lathir as she struggled to think of a way to rescue her father as well as save her home from being seized. None came. "I canna leave Wynshire Castle unprotected."

"Aye," Lord Torridan agreed. "With our combined troops, we have more than enough men to defend the stronghold and send a contingent by land to rescue your father."

Her head was whirling, yet on some level, she was strangely calm. She'd damned her pending marriage, but now 'twould seem a blessing. Lathir met Rónán's gaze.

"I willna fail you," Rónán whispered as he passed her, and she prayed he was right.

After the door closed behind Rónán, Lord Torridan glanced at his son. "Once Sir Rónán returns, he will ride with you as you lead a force to

Murchadh Castle. I will prepare our men for the aggressor's arrival." He nodded to her. "Lady Lathir, you will remain here and protect your home."

Fury sliced through her. "I will travel to rescue my father!"

The man's mouth tightened with disapproval.

"I am skilled with weapons," she snapped. "If I believed, even for a moment, that I would hinder the rescue of my father, I would remain here."

Eyes hard, Lord Torridan studied her. After a long moment, he nodded. "You will ride with Kieran. My son will protect you."

As would Rónán, though trained in weapons, she would need neither's safeguard.

Bran cleared his throat. "Lord Torridan—"

Sage eyes turned to the pirate. "Aye?"

"I believe 'twould be a mistake to wait for them to reach Wynshire Castle."

The noble's eyes narrowed. "A mistake?"

Confused, Lathir stared at Bran.

"Aye." Bran folded his arms across his chest. "The place for us to attack them is at sea."

# Chapter Thirteen

Lathir arched a brow as Lord Torridan said, "Us?"

"Aye. I need little prodding to go after the Sassenach. More so when their warships are overloaded with crew, supplies, and weapons." A devious glint sparkled in the captain's eyes. "With their cogs slower than pigs stranded in muck, we could surround them and attack at our leisure."

With a satisfied nod, Lord Torridan leaned back. "Aye, 'tis a fine plan. We will depart at dawn. Ensure your crew is ready."

"Aye, my lord." Bran paused. "One last thing."

Lathir stilled. Saint's breath, now what?

Bran lowered his arms to his sides. "I thought 'twas be best to send a messenger to King Robert to inform him of the situation." He winked at Lathir. "I might have indicated the news came from you."

"Brilliant," she said as she stood and gave the pirate a hug. His face flushed, but she didn't care. If word reached the king in time, he could send men to aid them in rescuing her father.

Lord Torridan stood. "Does anyone else have anything to add?"

Silence filled the war chamber.

The noble nodded. "There is much to attend to. I will see you when we sup." Footsteps firm, he departed.

Her mind filled with the details she needed to attend to prior to departing at first light, she started toward the door.

"Lathir."

At Kieran's voice, she turned. The solemn expression on his face had her guard up.

"As your betrothed, I ask that you wait here."

"Like a defenseless woman needing tending?"

Anger flashed in his eyes. "There is naught weak about defending your home."

"Nor in leaving my castle in competent hands and riding to war. I believe," she stated, her voice like ice, "I made it clear that once wed, we shall rule together."

Face taut, he stepped before her. "Aye, but this is not the same."

"Far from it."

"Blast it, if I didna give a damn about you, I wouldna care."

Her brow knitted. "But you love another!"

"I do, but in the time we have spent together, I have come to care about you, to want you safe, or as safe as possible."

She should be happy, but the heartache of not having Rónán in her life lingered. Nor, however much she and Kieran became close, would that change. "I doubt there is anywhere truly safe," she said, the anger of moments before waning. "I will go, with or without your blessing. 'Tis who I am."

A wry smile touched his mouth. "Tighearnán warned me that you were stubborn."

The last of her anger faded. "I am, nor will that change."

He chuckled. "I think I would be disappointed if it did."

"Come," she said with a smile, "let us prepare our troops to depart on the morrow." In silence, they strode down the corridor side by side.

* * * *

The crash of waves sounded from far below the steep incline as large, thick flakes of snow drifted down, the rich scent of pine and chilly sea air filling Rónán's every breath as he crawled to the cliff's edge.

On any other day he'd find beauty in the shimmers of white, of how they coated the rough landscape within their gentle embrace. Now, with his entire focus on the upcoming rescuing of Lord Sionn, naught about this day invited whimsy.

He pushed aside the limb of a dense fir. Clumps of snow splatted on his head. With a muttered curse, he wiped the icy mess from his neck, then crawled under. Thankful for the cover from this vantage, he studied Murchadh Castle. The crunch of snow had him glancing back.

On his belly, Lord Craigshyre edged up beside him. Lathir moved to his other side.

She stared down the cliff. "Thank God you were able to learn of a secret passage into Murchadh Castle."

"Aye," agreed the earl. "I pray we can free Lord Sionn with the small contingent we will lead inside."

Rónán nodded. The massive fortress situated on the rock-laden peninsula angled up with merciless disregard. On three sides, steep slopes cut away to where large swells pounded the coastline, an unforgiving mix of jutting, angled rock and sheer cliff.

Between a break in the crag and in view of the guard on the wall walk, a single road wound down the rough patch of land to the stronghold. The narrowed path forced anyone who sought entry to ride no more than two abreast. Three quarters of the way down, the track branched off to the small inlet, where the castle could receive replenishments from the sea.

Rónán grimaced. Whoever built Murchadh Castle had considered every angle to ensure that once it stood, the fortress was nearly impenetrable. Had he not spoken with a galloglass who knew of a secret entry to the castle, little hope would have existed that they could reach, much less free, Lord Sionn.

Regardless, before they could slip inside, he, Lathir, Craigshyre, and the handful of warriors chosen for this task must reach the inlet unobserved.

Thankful for the map drawn by a galloglass rolled in his pocket, he grimaced at the sun sinking in the west. When they reached the cove, he prayed enough light remained to find the hidden passage. God help them if they were discovered. Given the solitary location of the castle and the stronghold's formidable defense, if their plan was thwarted, all in their party could die.

A fact that had pushed him to speak with Lathir alone before he'd shared his plan with the others. Her refusal was expected, but he damned placing her life in great danger when they had the choice to leave her protected by the remainder of their combined contingent.

If only they were sure Lathir's father still lived.

Jaw tight, Rónán glanced over. "Ready?"

Expressions grim, Lathir and Craigshyre nodded.

Rónán waved forward the remaining men chosen to accompany them.

Snow began to fall at a steady rate as they made their way down a break in the rocks. Though the thick wash of white made the trek dangerous, 'twould provide cover from the guards on the wall walk.

A snow-filled gust blustered past, then another. Rónán tugged up the hood of his cape, glanced at Lathir. "I was hoping we would be inside the tunnel before the wind picked up."

"As I." She stepped onto the stone he'd vacated. "The weather is beginning to worsen."

Teeth clenched, Rónán reached out, caught the ledge. He used the fragment to steady himself as he wedged his boot onto a jagged rock. The thunder of waves below pounding the sheer rock grew as they neared the bottom.

With care, Rónán stepped down. His boot slipped on the foothold. With a curse, he tightened his hold on a wedge of stone, steadied himself. "Take care. Ice is forming on the rocks and 'twill be slick the rest of the way down." A complication they didn't need. Rónán again lowered his leg, this time bracing his boot against the damp rock.

The heavy scent of sea filled each breath, and the muted thud and errant clack of shifting rock clattered in the wind as they continued. By the time he reached the bottom, the sun was a ball of orange on the horizon.

In the waning light, Lathir's betrothed reached the cove, his face flushed with effort, but satisfaction as well. Craigshyre glanced up the cliff, frowned. "In truth, I had my doubts 'twas passable."

"Which is why none in the stronghold will expect us," Rónán said. "If only we didna have to climb back up, more so as even if all goes as planned, we will scale the break in the cliff at night."

Eyes dark with concern, Lathir stepped over a jagged rock and paused a pace away. "I pray my father is able to walk."

"As I." After Bran's report of Lord Sionn's condition, doubts plagued Rónán. He suspected if he was still alive, they'd have to carry him out. Given the icy rocks, the steep climb, a dangerous challenge.

A gust howled past, blinding him for a moment. The soft, fluffy flakes had hardened to frozen barbs that pelted his face and fought to slip beneath any crevice in his garb.

Once all the men had reached the slick, rocky shore, Rónán stepped inside a worn indentation in the large rock, waved everyone to follow.

With the small contingent crowded inside the shelter, Rónán withdrew the map. He shifted the drawing to catch the last of the fading light. "Look for a large boulder that is angled on its side."

Craigshyre scanned the area, scowled. "That could be several."

"Aye." Rónán again glanced at the map, tapped the parchment. "The entry will be marked by three small stones at the base. Come." He exited their shelter; all following, then they began spreading out.

"There," Lathir said, excitement filling her voice. "To the left."

The others hurried over, and after several tries, in the last rays of sunset, they pried open the half-frozen entry. After a quick glance around to ensure they hadn't alerted the guard, he led them into the tunnel.

Inside, Rónán noted the clever design that after breaking the icy bond, allowed them to push the large rock open with minimal effort. One used by the Templars.

Unease filtered through him. Had the Brotherhood been involved with crafting this stronghold? 'Twould explain why the fortress had been built in such a strategic location, though neither King Robert nor Stephan MacQuistan had mentioned Murchadh Castle as a previous Templar stronghold.

Though over a year and a half had passed, thoughts of the way the French king had sacrificed men who'd protected him over the years for power and greed, fury still burned through Rónán. Nor could he allow his anger to overshadow the need to free Lathir's father.

In the wisps of gray coming from the opening, Rónán turned. "Wait while I locate the flint, candles, and dry tinder." Once he'd retrieved these items, after a few strikes of his knife on the flint, a cascade of sparks ignited a flame on the dry shavings. He lit one of the tapers.

Stone scraped as two knights near the entry moved the stone back into place.

Once each person had lit a candle, Rónán raised his taper. Golden light wavered upon the damp walls. "Let us find Lord Sionn."

* * * *

Lathir kept her hand near her dagger as they worked their way through the narrow passage. She wrinkled her nose at the growing stench as they neared the dungeon. A soft glow from a hidden opening allowed her a peek into the dank confines.

Torchlight exposed narrow cells, many with prisoners inside, sprawled upon the cold stone floor. Errant groans sifted within the muted howl of wind and the roar of the sea outside. Fury ignited that in addition to the brutality her father had suffered, he endured such filth.

Had she not despised Earl of Ardgar before, out of contempt that he permitted anyone to live in such squalor, she would do so now.

Throat tight with fear, she scanned the foul confines. Please God, let him be alive!

"Lord Sionn is in the cell next to the end," Rónán whispered.

She shifted her gaze. Sprawled on the floor, her father's right leg lay at an unnatural angle, and blood smeared his torn garb. Her body shook with fury. "I will kill Lord Ardgar for what he has done to my father!"

"He will pay for his foul deed," Kieran hissed. "That I swear."

"As I. Nay doubt Sir Feradach played a part in your father's suffering as well." A muscle worked in Rónán's jaw, the outrage matching her own. "Once Lord Sionn is safe, he will taste my blade."

At the reminder of Rónán's horrific past, of the man who'd served him with such cruelty, another surge of anger shot through her. "Aye, all involved will regret their misdeeds."

Drips of water plopped in the distance as she started forward.

At the wall adjacent to her father's cell, she peered through the hidden slit. This close, she could make out the bruises atop the swelling on his face.

Tears burned her eyes. "Saint's breath."

"I dinna see any guard," Rónán said.

"Nor I." Kieran grunted. "Given the location of the fortress, neither am I surprised."

After one last glance around the dungeon, Rónán knelt, ran his fingers along the chiseled stone as the galloglass he'd spoken to had described. After a gentle push, the hewn stone scraped open.

"I know you are anxious to see your father," her betrothed said, "but I will go first." Hand on his sword, Kieran crept inside the cell. After looking around, he pressed his finger over his lips, then waved her forward.

Pulse racing, she hurried over and knelt beside him. "Father, 'tis Lathir."

On a groan, swollen lids flickered open. Confusion lined his brow, softened to joy. "Lathir?" he rasped.

Tears burning her throat, she nodded. "We are taking you home."

Lord Sionn glanced at the men moving into the cell; his gaze settled on Rónán. His throat worked. "You shouldna have allowed Lathir to come."

"My lord, have you ever tried to dissuade your daughter?" Rónán asked, his voice dry.

A pain-filled smile flickered on the man's face. "Aye, she is a stubborn lass."

"I had to see you, ensure you were…" Her voice almost broke. She took a deep, steadying breath. "You are alive, Father. 'Tis all that matters."

Groans from nearby cells echoed in the dank space as her betrothed stepped to her side. "My lord, thank God we found you in time."

"Lord Craigshyre." Her father shot him a questioning look. "I didna expect to see you."

"Nor did I upon my arrival home," Lathir said, hurt that her father had arranged her betrothal without so much as a by your leave. Nor was this the time to discuss it. "There will be time to talk later. We must leave before a guard comes on rounds."

Pain contorted her father's face as he braced his hands on the floor and tried to stand. On a hiss, he slumped to the floor. "Blast it, I canna stand."

Rónán accepted a length of wood from another knight, lay it flush against Lord Sionn's injury. "Once we bind your leg so it remains still, we can carry you out." In quick, efficient movements born of tending many an injured man, he wrapped strips of cloth around the makeshift splint. After he secured the last tie, he glanced at Craigshyre, kneeling near Lord Sionn's other shoulder. "Ready?"

"Aye."

Together they lifted her father. Rónán searched the dungeon's entry, thankful it remained closed, then scanned the men locked within. If any of the others noticed them, they said naught, or didn't care.

How many within were wrongfully imprisoned? Too familiar with Sir Feradach O'Dowd's love of violence, Rónán would guess most. However much he wished to help them, they could not linger. After he'd delivered the arms to King Robert, he could seek Lord Sionn's aid in freeing the innocent.

Rónán motioned the knights they'd brought toward the tunnel. "Go ahead; keep watch for any sign of trouble."

A broad-shouldered man nodded, then departed. The other warriors fell in behind him.

"Lathir, stay near the knights. Lord Craigshyre and I and your father will be right behind you."

She slipped into the secret tunnel.

Shimmers of candlelight wavered on the walls as they made their way along the dank confines. In the distance, the pounding of wave upon rock grew.

Worry lining her brow, Lathir glanced back. "We are nearing the exit."

"Aye." Nor did he relax. Somehow, in the black of night, they had to carry the earl to where the rest of their contingent was camped.

The scrape of stone grated down the passageway as the guards opened the entry, and the tangy rush of salt-laden air swirled within the musty stench.

Once they reached the opening, all extinguished their tapers.

Smothered in blackness, after a few moments, Rónán's eyes adjusted to the night. Against the roar of the sea and batter of wind, he scanned the night.

A full moon was rising in the east. The silvery light illuminated the white caps tipping the swells as they crashed ashore.

Blast it, he'd hoped by the time they started their climb the wind would have died down. Nor was he pleased by the clearing skies. However dangerous, the falling snow would have shielded their movements as they scaled the break in the cliff.

"Lathir," Rónán said. "When the guards begin the climb, stay between them."

She hesitated.

"If there is trouble and we need to move quickly," Rónán said, "'tis best if you are ahead, where you could help offer protection."

"A solid plan," Craigshyre said.

"How do you fare, Father?"

"I am well enough," Lord Sionn forced out. "Dinna worry."

Well enough? Rónán remained silent. Several times during their journey to the exit, the earl had stumbled and nearly fallen. That however slow he was able to walk with their aid was imperative. With the steep climb ahead of them, one littered with danger, God help them if he fainted.

"Let us go." Lowering his head against the blast of icy wind, Rónán and Craigshyre helped Lord Sionn out of the tunnel. While he leaned upon Lathir's betrothed, Rónán sealed the secret passage, then they started after the knights making their way to the steep trail.

Against the slap of the cold, Rónán kept his movements precise as they climbed, each step achieved against the noble's injuries and weakened state a victory.

Paces from the top, the man collapsed.

Rónán caught him. "Lord Sionn."

Gasping for air, his body began to shudder. "Blast it." He struggled and finally stood.

"What is wrong?" Lathir called back, her voice fragmented on an icy gust.

"Keep going," Craigshyre called.

She hesitated a moment, then continued.

Rónán kept his grip firm on the lord's shoulder. "Do you need to rest?"

"Nay," he forced out.

"Lord Sionn," Craigshyre said, "I am going to climb to the next ledge. Once there, Sir Rónán will help you while I pull you up."

"Aye," he forced out, pain raw in his voice.

In the silvery light, his steps taken with care, Lathir's betrothed moved onto the jutting rock. Breath coming fast, Craigshyre lay on his stomach, reached down. "Take my hand."

Body trembling, Lord Sionn reached up.

A bell tolled from Murchadh Castle.

"Lord Sionn has escaped!" a deep voice from the wall walk boomed. "Raise the gates!"

Clanks of the heavy forged steel rattled into the night.

Panic slammed Rónán. God's truth, the guards were leaving the stronghold!

# Chapter Fourteen

The distant shouts of men and the clatter of hooves rang out from Murchadh Castle. With Lord Sionn's unconscious body slumped against him, and the sky flooded with moonlight, Rónán glared at the knights riding from the castle. God's truth! Though the icy, winding path would slow the guard, they had to get Lord Sionn to safety before the enemy reached the top.

Rónán gave the noble a firm shake. "Lord Sionn, wake up!"

On a groan, his eyes flickered open.

"The Earl of Ardgar's men are coming," Rónán snapped. "We must hurry."

Teetering, the noble lodged his foot against a rock jutting out, pushed. Thank God!

Feet braced on the snow-covered ledge above, Craigshyre reached down, caught the noble's hands. Teeth clenched, he lifted Lord Sionn as Rónán aided him up the slick, makeshift steps.

The whinny of a horse had Rónán glancing over.

From the top of the cliff a short distance above, Lathir peered over the edge. "Father, thank God you are here!"

Relief flickered on Lord Sionn's face as he raised his eyes. "Lathir." He started to slump.

Rónán tightened his hold.

Strain lining her face, she moved from sight. Seconds later she reappeared, a rope clutched in her fist and several knights at her side. She tossed down most of the line. "Tie this around my father's waist, then we will lift him out."

Wind-tossed snow hurled past as Rónán helped Lord Sionn secure the woven hemp. He met the noble's pain-filled gaze. "As you are pulled up, I am going to climb out alongside you." The noble sucked in a steadying breath. "Aye." Once Rónán had shifted into position, he noted that Craigshyre had joined her. He nodded to Lathir. "Pull!"

The line grew taut. Lord Sionn's face paled, but thankfully, he didn't faint. At the top, tears in her eyes, Lathir hugged her father as the others moved back. "I love you so much!"

His body trembling from exertion, he returned the embrace. "I love you too, lass." On wobbly legs, he stepped back.

Loose strands of hair lashed against Lathir's face as eyes dark with emotion shifted to Rónán, then Craigshyre. "I thank you both."

Rónán frowned at the riders making their way up. "The Earl of Ardgar's men will be here soon."

Lines of worry on her face, she lay her hand upon her father's shoulder. "Come." Her betrothed helped Lathir guide her father onto a steed, where several mounted riders waited. "The knights will take you to Wynshire Castle."

The man's face darkened to a fierce scowl. "By God you will ride with me!"

She angled her jaw in a stubborn tilt. "I will stay and fight."

"B–blast it," her father snapped, "I—"

"The enemy is nearing the top!" a watch at the ledge called down.

Steel hissed against leather as Craigshyre withdrew his sword. He whirled toward their knights. "Prepare to fight!"

Lathir nodded to the lead guard. "Go!"

The warrior scooped up her father's reins. With Lord Sionn's face twisted in pain and frustration, the small contingent cantered into the woods.

The slide of steel against leather hissed as Lathir withdrew her sword. "The Earl of Ardgar will pay for his cruelty." Eyes burning with fury, she stormed toward where their combined forces were preparing a defense.

Blade in hand, Rónán kept pace. "I understand your anger, but to allow emotion to guide you gives your opponent the edge."

Cool eyes shifted to him. White knuckles on her hilt relaxed to a degree. "He almost killed my father."

"He did, but Lord Sionn is alive and free." Rónán caught her wrist, drew her to a halt.

"Release me!"

"However much you wish to decimate the enemy, our mission to free Lord Sionn is done. If we want to seize the stronghold, to make those who harmed your father pay, with them now having learned that we know a secret way into the castle, we will need to return with at least three times the force. To stay and challenge their attack will do naught but leave many warriors willing to risk their lives to protect you dead."

The outrage in her eyes faded. "You are right. Though I despise Lord Ardgar for what he has done, the time to confront him will come, but not this day."

Relief swept Rónán. "Before we depart, we must hold Ardgar's men back to give your father's guard time to take him a safe distance away; then we will join him."

\* \* \* \*

The cacophony of blades rang out, melding with the screams of men as the battle raged around Rónán. Another spray of blood streaked his mail as he drove his sword deep into the next aggressor. Breathing hard, he glanced toward Lathir. Pride filled him as she quickly defeated her attacker.

Their having shoved boulders to seal off the incline, along with archers raining arrows on the advancing fighters, were preventing many of the assailants from reaching the top of the cliff. Though the fighting was fierce from those who'd managed to slip past, their tactics were keeping the main force trapped on the road.

With a deft slash, Rónán took out a charging knight, then glanced around. Enough time had passed. Lord Sionn should be a safe distance away. "We can begin pulling back."

Sweat mixed with blood on her garb, Lathir downed her next attacker. With a nod, she edged toward the forest.

His mail bloodied, Craigshyre battled two assailants. With impressive skill, he killed the first, whirled to deliver a lethal blow to the second, yelled to their guard to withdraw, then backed toward the woods.

Boulders scraped.

In midstep, Rónán glanced toward the top of the road.

Horses pulling ropes lashed around the large rocks, hauled them aside.

"Charge!" a large Englishman boomed.

Swords raised, their faces masks of violence, a stream of knights flooded Rónán's view. "The guard have opened the castle road!"

"God's teeth!" Craigshyre clashed with the next assailant, then continued to move back.

Lathir slashed her attacker across the neck; he collapsed. "We will have to fight our way out."

Screams of steel and cries of pain rang out over and again as Rónán and the others worked their way into the woods. He searched the violent scene, cursed the number of knights they'd lost.

Craigshyre shouted.

After a final blow to his opponent, Rónán glanced over. The noble lay sprawled upon the snow, blood streaming from his gut.

"Kieran!" Lathir drove her sword into Craigshyre's attacker, then raised her weapon as the next foe charged.

Blast it! Rónán bolted over, helped her fend off several guards as her knights surrounded them, creating a barrier between them and the attackers.

Breath coming fast, Lathir knelt beside her betrothed. "Kieran."

Face ashen, eyes dark with pain, he took in the blood streaming from his wound. "Leave me," he rasped. "Go before you die."

Like Hades! Rónán grabbed the reins of a nearby steed, shoved them at Lathir. "Take Lord Craigshyre to Wynshire Castle!"

Her mouth tightened. "I willna leave you."

"If your betrothed stays here, he will bleed to death." If the enemy didn't kill him first, a fact Rónán refused to mention. "Your father needs you as he recovers as well. Nor can you disregard the fact that the arms Lord Sionn holds along with his support, as Craigshyre's, are imperative to King Robert's success."

Snow-laced wind whipped Lathir's face as she hesitated. "But—"

"I have a plan to hold off the enemy while you escape," Rónán rushed out as he struggled to devise a way to stall Lord Ardgar's men. He gestured to several guards before she dug in her heels to stay. "Place Lord Craigshyre on his steed. Lady Lathir will be riding with him."

Her eyes narrowed.

"Go!" Rónán shouted. "I will follow shortly."

"Swear it!" she demanded.

Well aware, regardless of any plan he invented that would buy him and his men time, 'twould leave little hope for their escape. Rónán nodded. Though she would despise him for never returning, 'twas a small price to pay for her life. "You have my vow."

Her breathing unsteady, her face strained with worry, for a moment he thought she'd run to him.

Two warriors lifted Lord Craigshyre up on his mount, while another held her steed.

Tears glittered in her eyes. *I love you, Rónán,* she mouthed.

His heart ached and he longed to confess his love, to hold her, to kiss her, but the time for such luxuries was past. He prayed that if not in love, Lathir would have a good life. With a nod, gusts of wind picking up, Rónán pressed his fingers against his mouth, touched his heart, then stepped back. Face a mask of grief, she swung up on her destrier. Turning, she dug her heels into her mount and led her betrothed on his steed, along with a significant portion of their force into the dense woods.

Against the increasing wind, Rónán and the remaining men battled their way deep into the forest. Within the trees, Rónán guided his men in tactics learned as a Templar. Strategies designed to stall their foes and allow them to continue to withdraw.

The pounding of waves below echoed like thunder as, with the sun slowly rising in the sky, he kept his small group within the dense forest, but near the cliffs.

The morning passed.

After numerous small skirmishes, the number of guards he led had dwindled to a handful. He took in the sun's position. By now Lathir, Craigshyre, Lord Sionn, and their contingent were well en route to her home.

Rónán drove his sword into the next aggressor. As the man tumbled down the snow-covered incline, he led his guard along the edge of the cliffs to a dense swath of trees.

He waved them down, motioned for them to crawl deep beneath the tangle of limbs.

Shouts and frustrated curses rang out behind them as the castle guard started hacking their way through the dense thicket.

As he and his men continued working their way beneath the dense weave of branches, the ground angled up, and the limbs overhead gave away to the edge of a crag.

Though steep, the broken rocks littering the face offered a way to climb down to shore and escape. Rónán shoved to his feet, waved his men forward. "Hurry!"

As the last of his guard began descending the steep incline, Rónán sheathed his sword, caught hold of a jagged shard, and took a step down.

The slash of a blade to branches paces away had Rónán glancing up.

Eyes wild, a large warrior charged.

To his left, fury in their eyes, two more knights came into view and rushed in.

Rónán glanced to where his men were making their way down the dangerous cliff. Bedamned. They needed to be farther away to avoid rocks tossed by their enemies.

"Stop him!" the closest man yelled.

Nay, they wouldna win. Body tense, Rónán made the sign of the cross, stepped back up to the snow-laden ground, and withdrew his sword. If he were to die, 'twould be in giving his men a chance to live.

# Chapter Fifteen

The fire in the hearth crackled cheerfully, the soft scent of wood and fresh rushes filling the air in her father's richly adorned chamber. Tension humming through her, Lathir touched his brow as he slept in his large, ornately framed bed.

Cool.

Thank God. A shudder ripped through her at the memory of his right leg in an unnatural position and blood smearing his torn garb in Murchadh Castle's dungeon. Had they not arrived when they had... She shoved aside the horrific thought. But they had. For that she was thankful.

Though two days had passed, her father, like her betrothed in a room down the corridor, still slept.

Lathir brushed an errant lock from her father's weathered face, willing him to awaken. However thankful to have brought him and Kieran home, she damned leaving Rónán and a small force behind.

Blast it, where were they?

Nerves twisting in her gut, she shoved to her feet and walked to the hearth. She took in a portrait of her father and mother hanging above. The love in their eyes made her heart ache. She wished the years back, that her mother still lived and her father was well.

A soft groan had her turning.

Pain-filled blue eyes lifted to hers. "Thank God you are alive, lass. I thought 'twas but a dream."

"Father!" Tears blurred her eyes as she hurried to his side.

His covers tumbled back as he tried to sit up.

On a sniff, she caught the edge of the quilt. "'Tis best if you rest."

Lines marred his brow as he shoved her hand away. "Help me. I willna lie here like an invalid."

Frustrated by his stubbornness and aware he wouldn't change his mind, once she'd aided him to sit, she filled, then handed him a goblet of ale. He downed the cup after several slow but long swallows.

She set the empty mug on the table. "Nor with your leg broken will you be walking unaided."

He tried to raise his leg, winced. "Bloody hell. Tell the steward I need a walking stick. Despise the confounded things, but I willna be condemned to this blasted bed."

His grumbling raised her spirits. He may be injured, but 'twas proof he was well on his way to healing. "Aye."

"When did I arrive?"

"Two days ago."

"Kieran, Sir Rónán, and our men?"

Her breath caught, and she glanced toward the window, yearning to hear the tower bell ringing of their arrival. "Kieran arrived with me hours after you. Rónán and the small contingent that remained behind so we could escape havena returned yet."

Fighting back the worry, in brief, she explained the events that occurred after his capture, of the perilous journey as she and Rónán had sailed the half-burned *Aodh* ashore, and of how pirates had helped them reach home, where Lord Torridan and his son had awaited them. Then, of Lord Torridan's having sailed with the pirates to attack the English fleet while she, Rónán, and Kieran had led a combined contingent to free him from Murchadh Castle. Last, of Kieran's injury and how, when they'd reached a safe distance away, Lord Torridan's healer, Imag, had cauterized Kieran's wound, an act that left him unconscious. A godsend in that he hadna stirred for the remainder of their journey to Wynshire Castle.

Her father dragged in a slow breath, exhaled. "'Tis an amazing chain of events. Thank God you are safe, and I pray Craigshyre awakens soon. Once Sir Rónán arrives, I will laud him for his bravery." Wincing, he pushed his body to a more comfortable position. "And Lord Torridan?"

"We have heard naught from him." And she prayed Kieran's father's forces, as Bran's, had been successful in driving away the English fleet.

She lifted a basket near the bed packed with several pouches, placed it on a chair. "The healer left herbs to aid with any discomfort once you woke."

Mouth twisted in a frown, he eyed them as if a curse, then glanced at his leg.

That he hadn't refused to take them outright assured Lathir he was in pain. She remained silent. He abhorred appearing weak in any way and would despise admitting that he needed even a little.

"They will help me sleep?" he finally asked.

Tenderness filled her. "Aye."

He grunted. "A wee bit, then."

She convinced him to eat first, and after he'd finished the mixture, her father lay back. Pain-filled eyes shifted to the painting above the hearth, softened. "She was a beautiful woman. You look like her."

Emotion tightened in her throat as Lathir packed the herbs and set the basket aside. "Though I never met her, I miss her. Odd, is it not?"

Amid the scent of fresh rushes and herbs and the faint wisp of smoke, a smile touched his face. "Nay. You have her tender heart as well." His lids started to droop.

The valerian root was taking effect. "Father..." With him safe and healing, she needed to broach a topic that still troubled her.

Tired eyes held hers. "Aye?"

"You arranged my betrothal without informing me," she said, her voice curt. Nor would she apologize. He'd breeched their trust by agreeing to it without her knowledge.

"I was to be here when Lord Torridan and his son arrived," he stated.

Lathir rose to her feet. "And that makes your action acceptable?"

"'Tis time for you to wed, an issue I raised a year after Domhnall Ruadh mac Cormaic's death."

She swallowed hard. "I wasna ready."

"Nor would you ever be." Tiredness glazing his eyes, he adjusted his position on the bed. "However well trained with weapons or intelligent you are, neither brings you warmth in the night."

"Or an heir?" she added, frustrated by the entire situation.

"An heir is necessary. I willna apologize for doing what I believe is right."

"Saint's breath, to not even ask me—"

"And if I had," he snapped, his words thick, "would you have agreed?"

"Nay."

"Which is why I arranged the betrothal with Lord Torridan, one with which you *will* comply."

Chills prickled Lathir's arms and she shook her head, unsure if she was angrier or sadder that her father hadn't spoken with her first. "I have already agreed to wed Kieran."

Surprise flickered in his eyes. "When?"

"Upon my reaching Wynshire Castle. Before Lord Torridan would help rescue you, he demanded I accept the union you and he had negotiated." Her father gave a tired exhale. "As for the betrothal, I only wanted to protect you."

The anger inside faded. Fatigue at worrying about her father, Kieran, Lord Torridan, Rónán, and the others had her collapsing in the chair beside his bed. She didn't want to fight, nor, regardless of her wishes, could she change the pending marriage now. Her father was alive. For that she would be thankful.

Lathir rubbed her brow. "I know."

Her father shot her a hesitant glance. "The Earl of Craigshyre is a fine man."

"He is."

The chapel bell began to ring.

Hope surged through her, and she ran to the window. The stone sill cool on her palms, she searched the gatehouse for Rónán leading his small force entering the bailey.

Naught but women carrying buckets of water, food, and other goods moved about while men practiced in the lists.

"Who is arriving?" her father asked.

"I—" The ripple of a sail upon the loch caught her attention. "Lord Torridan has returned!"

Eyes drooping with sleep, her father nodded. "He has been successful, then."

She fisted her hands. "How do you know?"

"He wouldna have given up, but fought until his ship went down."

After meeting the fierce nobleman, that she could believe. She studied the majestic cog cutting through the whitecaps toward shore. "After we talk, I will inform you of what I learn."

A soft snore rumbled in the chamber.

She glanced back.

Propped on his bed, face pale, the lines of strain easing on his face, her father slept.

On a hard swallow, she walked over and gave him a hug. However upset at his making arrangements for her betrothal, he'd done so out of love. Never could she hate him for that.

\* \* \* \*

Hours later, Lathir stared at Kieran, prone on the bed. Face pale, his eyes closed, his breathing remained steady.

The soft scuff of leather sounded as Lord Torridan stepped beside her. Since his return, after checking on her father's progress, he'd remained by Kieran's side. "Your father is speaking with the steward, but he asked me to inform you that once finished, he will be here."

"I thank you. I thought he would sleep longer when I gave him the herbs." She shook his head. "You wouldna know that, but mere days ago my father was critically wounded."

"Lord Sionn is strong-willed, a trait," he said with pride, "his daughter carries as well."

A smile touched her mouth, faded as she took in her betrothed. "I am pleased that you and our men returned so quickly."

A satisfied grimace touched the noble's face. "We caught the Sassenach moored on the coast. With the fog beginning to thicken, they believed they were safe. Before most could haul up their anchors, our ships attacked."

"Most?"

"Aye, though we sank most of their ships, one cog escaped."

A chill swept her. "Then the English will be warned of the attack."

"They will. I sent a runner with Bran to inform King Robert of what has happened, and to ask for support."

Which explained the absence of Bran's ship. "The English will be seeking vengeance."

"Let them try. With many Scottish and Irish forces combined, they will achieve naught but failure."

Aware most of the ships that attacked the *Aodh* once they'd departed Scotland were destroyed brought a wisp of relief, but far from eased her worry. "Mayhap, but until the English are brought to heel, they will continue their destruction upon both Scottish and Irish soil."

"Indeed, but King Edward II doesna have a burr up his arse to conquer Scotland and Ireland, as did his father."

A burst of sparks swirled up the smoke in the hearth.

She looked at Kieran, frowned. "Two days have passed since we arrived at Wynshire Castle, yet he hasna woke."

"His body will take the time it needs to heal," his father said, his voice somber.

"But he hasna moved, not even grimaced, as Aíbinn, my healer, tended to him," she said, damning the tremor in her voice. "I would think by now he would have done something."

Face drawn with worry, Torridan stared at his son. "I have seen warriors in this deep state of sleep before," he admitted.

At the despair in his voice, she met his gaze, cursed the fear lingering there. "For how long?"

"A fortnight, a month at times," he said, his voice tight, "a year or more. The waiting is always the hardest part."

Heart pounding, she met his stricken gaze. "But they do recover?" she whispered.

Anguish ridden eyes met hers. "Nay always."

Nay! Please God, let him live. Though she didn't love Kieran, he was a fine man. Nor did she wish to see Lord Torridan lose his son.

The noble rubbed his brow, then cleared his throat. "I, as your father, am pleased that you and my son have become close. 'Twill make the years ahead easier."

Understanding his need to shift to a less troubling subject, she nodded. "Your son is a man to admire." But he wasna Rónán. Frustrated, she pushed thoughts of a life with him from her mind. "I was surprised to learn Kieran was the younger of your two sons."

The earl arched a surprised brow, then understanding shimmered in his eyes. "So Kieran told you of the woman he loves."

"He did." Why was she surprised the earl had deduced the reason so quickly? Since they'd met, he'd proven over and again to be an astute man, one only a fool would cross. Qualities his son held, as well as Rónán.

"Though we havena spoken of the son lost at birth in many a year, I know Kieran wishes his brother had lived so he could marry the woman who has stolen his heart." He leaned back. "'Tis a poor topic to raise to your betrothed. I will speak to him once he awakens."

"Lord Torridan, I ask that you dinna broach the subject with your son. Our conversation was naught that spoke ill of his betrothal to me."

In the flicker of firelight, sage eyes softened. "Kieran would be a fool to dismiss your beauty, your intelligence, or your loyalty."

"He is an impressive and clever man, one who looks up to you, and recognizes the need to place duty before personal desire."

He inclined his head. "As do you."

Nor would she pretend she didn't comprehend his subtle intimation that he understood she loved another. "Aye."

Lathir rubbed her arms. Where was Rónán now? From their time at sea, he had proven himself capable of overcoming the most difficult challenge. Nor could she forget that he was a Templar. Still, until he arrived, she'd remain on edge.

The noble shifted, released a rough exhale. "My wife was devastated by the loss of our firstborn," he said, his voice laden with lingering hurt. "She, nor I, ever held Dáire."

Compassion filled her, and Lathir stepped closer. "What happened?" He shook his head. "One would think after all these years losing a babe wouldna affect me."

An ache built in her heart. "I doubt one ever gets over the loss of a child."

"Aye," he breathed, "'tis terrible. A tragedy I wish no one to ever experience. You never forget." His throat worked. "Oh, there are times when other thoughts fill your mind, but in the dark of the night, when you are unable to sleep, memories haunt you."

The church bell rang.

"Nones," he said.

She glanced toward the window. Hints of darkness stained the winter sky. "Aye, another day almost gone."

The noble crossed to the hearth and selected several sticks. He knelt and placed them within the flames. On a weary sigh, he stood, turned.

"My wife and I had looked forward to our first child. She was so sure 'twas a son, she selected the name Dáire and wouldna discuss another." Hurt stormed his gaze. "After the birthing, you can imagine our joy to learn we had a son. But in tears, Imag, our healer, told us the child had died at birth." His fists clenched. "My wife was inconsolable, and I…was broken. Months passed before either of us broached the topic."

"I am so sorry."

"I thank you." He stared at the flicker of the flames for a long moment. "Two years later, when Kieran was born, 'twas as if a miracle. More so as after, we were not blessed with any more children."

Warmth filled her. "You raised a fine son, one who will make you naught but proud."

Pleasure smothered the sadness on his face. "He has already done that and more. I—" He glanced toward the bed. Determination filled his gaze. "I look forward to the day I hold the son your union will bring."

Moved by his strength, his love for Kieran, she vowed that never would she fail him. "And our child will wrap you around his finger."

"He will."

"He?" she teased, pleased when she caught the hint of a smile creasing his mouth.

"Aye, and one day he will be the heir to the realm of Tír Connail."

"And the realm of Tír Sèitheach," Lathir said, "both of which, by Irish custom, can be led by a man or a woman."

Respect glistened in his eyes, and he gave a solemn nod. "So it can, lass. Whatever child your union brings will rule with a fair hand, but most of all, they will be loved."

"They will."

A companionable silence fell between them, the first since she'd met the powerful lord. That he'd trusted her enough to share such personal suffering left her humbled. Regardless that she hadn't wanted this marriage, she was blessed that Kieran, as his father, were men to respect.

Lord Torridan walked over, lay his hand upon his son's shoulder.

Kieran didn't move.

Sadness filled Lathir at the father's helplessness over his son's condition. She yearned to do something to alleviate his worry. Mayhap she could distract him with a thought that haunted her.

"I thought Sir Rónán and the men fighting with him would have returned by now."

A frown dipped his brow. "As I. Upon entering the stronghold, I had expected to find them here. Depending on what tactic he used to delay the Earl of Ardgar's forces, or lead them on a false trail, it could be days yet."

Something she hadn't considered. "If Rónán has led the Earl of Ardgar's forces into the bens, the journey will be slow and dangerous, which explains their delay." She paused. "Though in the rough terrain they could lose the earl's men, 'twill take twice as many days to reach Wynshire Castle, if not longer, considering the icy conditions, along with Ardgar's men searching for them."

"Indeed."

Lathir stilled. "What if they have been caught?" she whispered, voicing her worst fear. "We would never know."

"Aye, we would know fast enough. The Earl of Ardgar and I are longtime foes." Lord Torridan grunted. "He would like nothing more than to cast Sir Rónán's dead body, or anyone loyal to me, at my feet."

"Yet you allowed your son to ride to free my father."

Sage eyes narrowed. "Neither I nor my son will live in fear. Nor will I teach my son to be a coward."

She nodded. A belief she shared.

"Nor do I like Lord Ardgar's master-at-arms," the earl ground out. "Sir Feradach O'Dowd is an evil man, one with a vile reputation for enjoying bringing misery to others, brutality he served to your father."

She nodded. "Aye, he is a despicable man. Sir Rónán loathes Sir Feradach as well."

Lord Torridan paused. "I didna realize Sir Rónán knew him."

In brief, she explained how the ruthless man had adopted Rónán, not out of love but to do his bidding, and of his abusive treatment.

"The cur! I had already planned to lay siege to Murchadh Castle and end the Earl of Ardgar's support of the English. Once your father has fully recovered, 'twill be a pleasure to join forces with him to serve just punishment to Lord Ardgar as well as Sir Feradach."

"My lord, I ask that you dinna inform Rónán that you know of his past."

"Nay, lass, and I thank you for explaining. Sir Rónán seems like a stalwart man."

"He is."

The uneven tap of steps sounded from the hallway, mixed with the clack of wood. Warmth touched her heart. Her father.

A soft scrape sounded as the door opened. Face grim, Lord Sionn shuffled his way across the chamber.

At the seriousness in her father's expression, she tensed. "What is wrong?"

"Several knights who stayed behind with Sir Rónán have arrived."

Lord Torridan stepped forward. "How many?"

Her father's mouth tightened. "Four."

Why hadn't he said Rónán's name? Lathir fought against a burst of fear. No, she was wrong. Rónán had come back with the men, a fact her father was about to share. "Sir Rónán?"

Her father shook his head. "One of the knights in his small contingent explained that Sir Rónán ordered them to leave, and that after he'd created a diversion, he would join them. So, they departed."

Tense silence filled the chamber.

Panic clawed through Lathir. She didn't want to ask, prayed she was wrong, but needed to know. "And Rónán?" she rasped, her entire body trembling.

Regret filled her father's eyes. "I am sorry, lass. They believe he is dead."

# Chapter Sixteen

Lathir's body began to shudder, and tears burned her eyes as she fought to breath. Rónán was dead?

Nay, he'd promised to return.

Sworn to come back to her.

Vowed to—

"Lathir." Her father's voice seemed to come from faraway as the room blurred around her. Strong hands caught her, helped her to a chair.

"I am so sorry," Lord Torridan rasped.

Her heart lay cold and heavy in her chest as she stared at the flicker of flames in the hearth. A spark popped into the lazy stream of smoke, faded to a smear of black. A sob came forth, then another.

Her father drew her into his arms. "Let the grief come, lass."

How long she cried she wasn't sure, but when no more tears would come, and her heart-wrenching sobs grew silent, she rested against her father, thankful for his presence, that as she faced this horrendous loss of a man she would love forever, she wouldn't be alone.

\* \* \* \*

Rónán wiped the blood from a cut above his brow, struggled to see through the smear of red and hurl of snow as two of the Earl of Ardgar's knights climbed down to the jut of rock he'd retreated to moments before. The stone, flattened on the top, provided him with stable footing; the width, enough to hold five men at most, limited his movements.

Arms trembling with exhaustion, he again swung his sword, took out the nearest man, waited for the second to move close enough to attack, dispensed with him as well.

The pounding surf far below seemed to taunt him, the rhythmic slam as each wave pummeled the base of the cliff as if chanting that his plan would fail.

Nay.

After he'd left the remainder of the guard, for the past two days he'd led Lord Ardgar's men on a merry chase. He'd used the cliffs and dense woods as a foil, several times having set up false points of resistance, diversions that would fool the guards into believing he was accompanied by several men and had given him a chance to move to a new location to position more decoys.

This afternoon, confident by now Lord Sionn, Lathir, Craigshyre, and any remaining knights in company would be close, if not have reached Wynshire Castle, he'd planned to slip deep into the forest, then head back. Except Feradach had split his troops and sent a significant portion of his force ahead, who'd doubled back and sealed off his avenue of escape.

Like a harbinger of death, the afternoon sun illuminated the enemy lining the cliff above. The formation shifted, and a tall, stocky figure stepped into view.

His sword smeared with the enemy's blood trembled in Rónán's hand. Years may have passed, but never would he forget Feradach O'Dowd.

Memories of his childhood, of the brutality endured surged through him. Somewhere over the years, the miscreant had slithered his way into becoming a knight, then a master-at-arms for Lord Ardgar. A blemish upon the brave men who rightfully earned the honor.

Outrage flushed the warrior's face as he glared at his men. "'Tis naught but one man. Where are the others!"

He hadn't recognized him? Rónán scoffed. Why would he? When he'd fled many years ago, he was a lad. "Go to Hades!" he shouted up.

An evil glint flickered in Feradach's eyes. "You will regret daring to abduct Lord Sionn!"

"Abduct?" he yelled. As if he should be surprised the scoundrel would dare lie. "You mean rescue the man from your attack on the *Aodh*!"

The formidable warrior's face darkened. "Who are you that you dare speak to me so?"

He angled his jaw. "Rónán O'Connor."

Confusion, then surprise widened his eyes, then a satisfied grimace curved his mouth. "I see that you havena learned your place since you ran away like a coward many years ago. A lesson I will ensure you receive now." Face smug, he turned to his men. "Everyone, stay back; he is mine!" He began to climb down the steps.

Rónán was tempted to engage the warrior, like the others, before they reached the flat stone. But the child who had suffered beneath the cur's hand, who had lived in fear, the lad who'd almost tasted death beneath his brutality, demanded vengeance.

Blade readied, he stepped back, waited until the formidable knight reached the flat rock where he stood.

Weapon drawn, Sir Feradach turned, his lip curling into a sneer. "You think you are man enough to take me, lad?"

"Lad?" Rónán circled him; the knight shadowed his moves. "You have never been a man, but a tyrant who intimidates the weak for your own twisted pleasure."

Red infused his face, and the veins in his face popped out. He charged.

Metal scraped as their blades locked. Icy, snow-filled wind slapped Rónán's face, but he focused on the man he despised with his every breath. "I think," he said with deadly calm, "'twill be you meeting his maker." He pushed.

Surprise widened Sir Feradach's eyes as he stumbled back. The warrior steadied himself, then attacked.

The cacophony of angry steel screamed over and again, the roar of the sea and howl of wind an ominous setting.

His enemy swung.

The razor-sharp blade slid across Rónán's arm, caving a fresh gash atop one received two days before. At the next blow, he ducked. Though he may never have Lathir, if naught else, the bastard wouldn't win.

With his body trembling from exhaustion, aware he had but one chance, and hoping to draw Feradach closer, Rónán sagged, as if barely able to stand, a stance too close to the truth.

Twisted glee on his face, his nemesis raised his sword to deliver the fatal blow.

"Charge!" a deep, vaguely familiar voice boomed.

"We are under attack!" one of the guards shouted from the ledge above. Feradach's eyes flared with outrage. "'Twas a trap!" He lunged, swung.

Rónán ducked and rolled, shoving to his feet directly behind his foe.

As Feradach's blade cut air, he lurched back, lost his balance, and tumbled toward the edge. The knight's fingers caught a jagged stone as he slid over the side. Feet dangling above the slam of waves far below, his breaths blasting out in frantic gasps, through the snow-smeared gusts, he met Rónán's gaze. "Help me."

"Aye, I will give you what you will deserve." Sword in hand, Rónán started up the cliff to where the clash of blades screamed from above.

"You canna leave me to die!" he strangled out.

'Twould be fitting penance. On a muttered curse, Rónán spun on his heel. Aye, 'twould be proper as well to let him rot in the dungeon for the harm he'd served so many. He strode over. As he reached down, the warrior's fingers slipped.

Eyes wild with fear, Feradach's scream entwined with the lash of wind as he plummeted past sheer rock. As if a hand from Hades, a large swell rose up, engulfed him as he reached the sea. Water exploded on the side of the cliff; then the enormous wave receded in a violent snarl of white.

Within the angry churn, naught remained but the blueish-green surge of the next incoming swell.

'Twould seem God had made his own decision on the cur's fate. Rónán looked toward where the men were fighting, unsure who had arrived to help him, but thankful braced his leg against the pain, and started to climb.

As he crested the rocky incline, Rónán stilled. His Templar brothers and Bran, along with warriors he didn't recognize, drove the enemy back. After a quick prayer thanking God for the miracle, he jumped into the fray.

A short while later, with Lord Ardgar's men defeated, Rónán stared at his friend, Stephan MacQuistan, Earl of Dunsmore. Throat raw with emotion, he shook his head. "I canna believe you are here." He scanned his fellow Templar knights—Sir Thomas MacKelloch, Earl of Kincaid, Sir Aiden MacConnell, Earl of Lennox, Sir Cailin MacHugh, Earl of Dalkirk, and other brave, loyal men he'd fought with over the years. "How?"

"A while back, a pirate—Bran, as he asked to be called—sailed to King Robert with news of the attack upon the *Aodh* and Lord Sionn's capture." Stephan paused. "The Bruce ordered that I take two crews and free the nobleman."

"Since then, I, as others, helped Lord Sionn escape," Rónán said, his mind whirling as he tried to take everything in.

"Aye." Stephan wiped his sword clean, "Which we discovered was your intent as we came across the same pirate en route to inform King Robert."

Men parted as Bran swaggered forward, a salty grin on his face. "After a brief misunderstanding—"

"We thought we were under attack," Stephan said dryly.

The pirate chuckled. "Once I ordered the flag lowered, I explained that Lord Sionn had been freed."

"I thought it prudent," Stephan said, "more so with the Lord Ardgar's interference in the Bruce's seizing of Scotland, to seize Murchadh Castle. Bran insisted on joining us."

Mirth twinkled in the pirate's eyes. "Canna miss a good fight."

Rónán stared in disbelief. "You captured the earl's stronghold?"

"Aye," Thomas said, stepping forward. "Believing there to be no threat about after his knights rode off to attack you, the lackwit left the portcullis open." He glanced around, frowned. "I had assumed you were traveling with a large force."

"I was." Rónán nodded, his head still reeling as he fought to take it all in. "'Tis a long story."

"One," Cailin said as he moved next to Thomas, "you can tell us after we get you to the castle and tend to your wounds."

"Aye," Stephan said. "Now we must finish taking care of matters here." He scanned others within his force who were rounding up Lord Ardgar's men. "Those who refuse to swear fealty to King Robert will be imprisoned."

Rónán grunted. "A kind fate when all they offered those seized was death."

Stephan nodded. "Indeed."

\* \* \* \*

The scent of roast venison, onions, herbs, and bread filled the great hall as Rónán lifted his goblet and drank deep. With his wounds tended to, though exhausted, he felt better. However anxious to depart to see Lathir, to let her know he was alive, 'twas imperative to ensure Murchadh Castle was secure, with a trusted guard in place before the Templars sailed away. As they would soon set sail, neither did it make sense to send a runner. Nor with Lathir's focus turning to Kieran, was it wise to allow his mind to linger on her.

Rónán took in his Templar friends, stunned by the turn of events. The strategic stronghold that days before had belonged to his enemy was now King Robert's. No doubt a fortress his sovereign would leave to his brother, Edward, who held aspirations of becoming king of Ireland.

After another sip, Rónán set aside his goblet, recalling his friends' shock as he'd explained how they'd snuck through the secret tunnel and rescued Lord Sionn.

After a comment to one of their fellow Templars, Stephan took a long drink of his wine, glanced over. "I pray the Earl of Torridan's son survived."

"As I. His marriage to Lord Sionn's daughter will end the strife between the two realms, both of whom support our king." A fact, regardless of the pain of letting her go, Rónán must remember. Their realms' stability in this time of strife, more so united to stand behind King Robert, was vital.

The entry to the keep scraped open. Snow swept inside the great hall as a reed-thin woman with scraggly brown hair pushed the door shut.

A guard strode over.

She shook her head at the guard, then pointed toward the dais. "I must see the Earl of Dunsmore!"

Stephan frowned at Rónán. "Do you know the lass?"

"Nay." Rónán wiped his hands with a cloth. "With your having passed word that all within are to come forward with claims against the Earl of Ardgar, I can only wonder what we will learn now."

Frown darkening, Stephan nodded. "Since we took control of the castle, the atrocities I have learned of pile atop the other. Once charges are brought before Lords Sionn and Torridan, Lord Ardgar will see naught but a noose." He motioned to the guard. "Bring the lass forward."

Those seated on the trencher tables shot her a curious glance as she made her way forward.

Her face pale, hollowed with lack of food, the bedraggled woman halted before the dais, bowed. "Lord Dunsmore."

The noble nodded. "What brings you here, lass?"

Nervous eyes lifted to his. "I–I was abducted by Lord Ardgar's men years ago, my lord. I wish to be freed so that I can return to my family."

"A request I will honor," Stephan said.

"I thank you, my lord."

"Your name?" Stephan asked.

"Máire Ó Conaill."

Rónán's hand setting aside the cloth stilled. It couldn't be. His fingers tightened on the woven fabric. "Your husband's name?"

"Tighearnán."

God's truth! "Your daughter's name is Órlaith," Rónán said, "is it not?"

Disbelief flickered on her face, then hope. "You know them?"

Emotion tightened in Rónán's throat. "Aye, lass. Your husband saved my life."

A smile trembled on her lips. "Tighearnán was always a good man and helped those in need."

Mind reeling, Rónán glanced to the hearth, where Bran was talking with one of his men. "Bran."

The pirate glanced over.

He waved him over. As he neared, Rónán stood. "I—"

Bran's eyes flickered on the lass, widened. "Máire?" Disbelief, then joy swept his face as he strode forward and swept her into an embrace. "G–God in heaven, lass, we thought you were dead." Eyes misty, he held her at arm's length. "I canna wait until Tighearnán and Órlaith see you!" Tears running down her cheeks, she sniffed. "As I. I miss them desperately."

Tenderness swelled within Rónán. "We depart at dawn for Wynshire Castle, lass, where your husband and daughter now reside. You will sail with us."

With a shaky nod, she wiped the tears streaming down her face. "I thank you, but..." The joy on her face collapsed in mortification.

"Lass, there is much to discuss, things we will address en route," Rónán said, softening his voice. No doubt she'd suffered abuse beneath Feradach and his men's hands and worried her husband would look at her with shame.

Having spent time with her husband, knowing the depth of his love for his wife, and being a man of honor, Rónán understood that Tighearnán would never regard his wife with anything but affection. "Go now; we depart at first light."

She hesitated, then a weak smile touched her mouth. "I thank you." After hugging Bran one last time, the woman hurried away, disappearing in a swirl of snow as she stepped into the bailey.

The hewn door thudded shut. Rónán shook his head. "Incredible."

"'Tis bloody amazing. I canna wait until Tighearnán and Órlaith see Máire." Bran stepped back. "I need to finish ensuring the ship's supplies have been refilled before we sail in the morning." With a light step, he departed.

Stephan shook his head. "Never have I seen the like. And I am thankful we arrived in time to save you."

Somber, Rónán met his gaze. "Which I will never forget."

"I believe there was a time or two in our past"—Stephan refilled his goblet, then glanced over—"when you saved my life. 'Tis the way of the Templar to be there for our Brothers."

"'Tis." The depth of friendship within the Brotherhood, something for which Rónán was forever thankful. He motioned for the lad to remove his trencher. "Once we reach Wynshire Castle, we are to bring the arms Lord Sionn was to retrieve to King Robert."

Stephan waited until the servant had removed his food and stepped away. "Which our sovereign explained. I will see you at first light, when we depart." He stood, headed toward the turret.

Rónán pushed to his feet, ready to see Lathir, damning that in the end he'd leave her wed to another.

**\* \* \* \***

The lazy crackle of the hearth entwined with the healer's humming as Lathir settled beside Aíbinn in her hut. Over the years, she'd enjoyed her visits, appreciated the time the elder had taken to explain herbs and the use of them. She smiled as she recognized the dried sage, rosemary, and other plants hanging in neat rows from pegs in the ceiling.

"That should take care of the herbs I will be needing for the next week." Aíbinn held out a sack of ground powder. "Place a couple of pinches in Lord Craigshyre's drink."

"Aye." Lathir hesitated. "Should he not have opened his eyes by now?"

Eyes dark with regret held hers. "There is nay telling how long 'twill be before he completely awakens. Be thankful he is alert enough that we have been able to coax him to drink wine and broth. They are signs that his body is healing."

Sage words Lord Torridan, along with the healer, Imag, had said. Lathir took a slow, steadying breath. But how could she be calm when each day that had passed since their return, Kieran lay there unmoving?

Despite her worry over him, she was thankful naught but a touch of swelling and bruises from her father's imprisonment remained, that her father was recovering quickly, and he now walked without a stick.

"I thank you for changing your betrothed's bandages," the healer tsked. "I would be doing it myself, but for the smithy's wife having gone into labor and with this her first child, I need to be there if naught else, to calm her." Aíbinn winked. "One day I hope to be tending to you."

Her and Kieran's child. She wanted to be pleased, knew when the babe came, she would love their son or daughter, but a part of her was saddened it wouldn't be Rónán's.

Heart heavy, Lathir stood. "Where is Lord Torridan's healer? I would think Imag would want to tend to her lord's son."

"She is out gathering more herbs and told me that she would be gone for a good part of the day." A spark popped in the hearth, faded into the whirl of smoke up the chimney as Aíbinn handed her another sack. "'Tis for your father. He willna admit to still being in pain, but I can see it in his eyes."

"And you think I can convince him to take anything more? That I talked him into taking anything at all was a miracle."

The elder chuckled. "You have a better chance than I."

"Mayhap." En route to the stronghold, sadness swept Lathir as she glanced over the land, searching for any sign of Rónán. Waves rippled on the water. Naught but several ducks flew into view.

"Lathir."

At Lord Torridan's voice as she entered the bailey, she looked toward the stable.

The noble said something to the knight at his side, then headed toward her. Fatigue and sadness filled his grayish-green eyes, his worry at his son's condition taking its toll.

He arched a brow at the herbs in her hand. "For your father?"

She held up the secured pouch. "Only one. The others are for Kieran."

A frown lined his brow. "Where is Imag? When I saw her at dawn, she said she would change my son's dressings this afternoon."

"Your healer realized she needed more herbs and is out picking them."

"Aíbinn?"

"My healer is tending the smithy's wife, who is in labor." Lathir smiled, wanting to ease his worry. "As Kieran's betrothed, I will see to the task."

"I will accompany you."

"I thank you." Lathir remained silent as they headed toward the keep.

Golden candlelight entwined with the flicker of flames from the hearth cast Kieran's chamber in a warm glow as they stepped inside.

Grief squeezed her chest as she walked to her betrothed, tucked beneath the quilt. Though she had helped to aid many a knight, she hesitated as she reached for the cover. Irritated at her foolishness, she placed a bowl of water on a nearby table. 'Twas naught intimate about tending to a wound.

After she'd drawn the covering back to expose his outer thigh, she carefully began to unwrap the bandage.

Dark bruises of purple and black came into view.

His father grunted. "The wound is healing well."

"Aye. Thank God there are nay signs of infection." Lathir started to set the old bandage aside, stilled.

On the outside of his upper outer thigh lay an uneven brown path of skin, like a smeared line a thumb's width, the end fading into a curl.

Her fingers fisted on the cloth as she stared at the discolored skin.

"What is wrong?"

Heart pounding, she glanced over. "T–the mark on his upper thigh."

The frown on his brow smoothed. "'Tis naught but a birthmark, one all within my family carry," he said with pride.

She stilled. "All?"

"Aye."

"Have you ever heard of anyone outside your family carrying the same birthmark?"

"Never." His hesitated. "Why are you asking?"

The immensity of this moment shaking her, Lathir fought for calm, failed. "Lord Torridan, Sir Rónán has the same birthmark on his outer thigh."

"Impossible," the earl blustered.

"'Tis there. I saw it." She paused. "How old is Kieran?"

At the earl's reply, air rushed from her as the full impact of the revelation sank in. Legs unsteady, she collapsed into the chair as her chest tightened. "My lord," she forced out, "Rónán is almost two years older. And when I first met Kieran, as he stood alongside Rónán, I couldna help but see similarities between them."

The noble's knuckles whitened as he clutched the bed. "God in heaven, are you saying that you think Rónán is my son?"

"I believe 'tis a possibility. In addition to having similarities with Kieran, Rónán has your grayish-green eyes and brown hair."

His face raw with emotion, the noble shook his head in disbelief. "It canna be. Imag informed my wife and I that my son had died shortly after his birth."

She damned the old pain she'd brought up, more so as Kieran lay injured before them, but after the horrific youth Rónán had endured, to learn that he had a family, one who had loved him, 'twas worth the risk.

Lathir gave a slow exhale. "But you never saw the babe?"

"Nay."

"I swear to you," she rasped, "Rónán bears the same birthmark."

"I am not doubting you, lass," he said, his face growing red with fury. "By God, I will summon my healer and get to the bottom of whatever trickery is about!" Body tense, he strode to the door, jerked it open, faced the guard stationed outside. "Bring Imag here immediately!"

# Chapter Seventeen

Fury pouring through her, Lathir glanced out the window of Kieran's chamber to where snow meandered earthward in the dismal gloom. If Imag had indeed stolen Rónán as a babe, Lathir had little pity for the consequences Lord Torridan's healer would face. The audacity of abducting a woman's babe, of casting a child who was wanted and loved into a brutal life was unthinkable.

Lord Torridan paced to the hearth, then glared at the door. "By God, where is my healer!"

The quick tap of steps from outside the chamber grew.

He stiffened, appeared every inch the ruler of the realm of Tír Connail.

A sharp knock sounded at the entry.

The earl drew himself to his full height, folding his arms across his chest. "Enter."

The door opened and the guard escorted a slim, older woman inside. Worry lining her face, she rushed to Kieran.

The noble lay unmoving.

Brows drawn in confusion, she faced the earl. "My lord, the guard said 'twas urgent, though, sadly, I see naught has changed with your son's condition."

"Kieran's health isna the reason you are here," he snapped. "'Tis about my first son, Dáire McKelan."

"I dinna understand, my lord. Dáire died at birth."

"Then why—" Lowering his arms, eyes narrowed, Lord Torridan stalked toward her, halted several paces away. "Why does the knight, Sir Rónán, carry the Torridan birthmark?"

Imag shook her head, but Lathir caught a flicker of fear, one she would have missed had she not been watching the woman closely. Her heart ached for the misery Lord Torridan's family had suffered at the healer's treachery.

"I dinna know." The healer hesitated. "Are you sure the birthmark is the same shape?"

"I saw both," Lathir stated, outraged that the healer would dare continue to lie, wanting to shake her until she admitted the truth.

"Nor," the earl said between clenched teeth, his face red with fury, "has it escaped my notice that Sir Rónán is almost two years older than Kieran."

Breath coming fast, Imag's face paled. She darted a glance toward the entry.

"You will be caught before you are halfway across the chamber," Lord Torridan warned.

Tears plopped down the healer's cheeks, wobbled on her chin before spilling onto her simple brown garb. Body trembling, she dropped to her knees. "Have mercy on me, my lord."

"Tell me!" he shouted.

"I–I never..." She gulped several broken breaths. "I–I never meant any harm."

If possible, the earl's face grew redder. "You abducted my son!"

"'Twas wrong of me, my lord," she sobbed. "and I deeply regret my actions."

"I dinna give a damn about your regrets." He stepped closer, towered over her pathetic form. "Tell me why!"

"I–I was young and foolish, my lord." She wiped red-rimmed eyes. "My head was turned by a man loyal to the Earl of Ardgar."

Torridan's nostrils flared. "My enemy?"

"T–the man told me that he loved me, wanted to marry me, wanted to take me away to where we could both live happy lives. But"—she sniffed—"that he had little coin."

On a curse, the earl seized her garb. Knuckles white, he hauled her to but a breath before his face. "What does his lack of coin have to do with Dáire's disappearance!"

Imag's throat worked in frantic swallows. "He said Lord Ardgar would pay gold for your child once it was born."

Veins popped on the noble's brow, angry, dark purple lines tinged with red as his eyes narrowed to merciless slits. "You sold my son to our enemy?"

Face stained with tears, her breath stumbling out, she shook her head. "The man I loved swore the babe wouldna be harmed. He explained that once Lord Ardgar attacked and seized your castle, 'twould be simpler if you had nay heirs."

"Did you ever care about the horrific life you sentenced Dáire to?" Lathir demanded. "Care that because of your selfishness and greed, for years he was mistreated and suffered daily at the hands of a monster?"

"He suffered?" Fresh tears flooded her cheeks. "I swear I never knew, my lady. As I said, the man I loved assured me the babe would be well cared for."

Lathir's hand tightened around the hilt of her *sgian dubh*, aching to draw it, to serve justice. "And where," she hissed with disgust, "is this man you loved? Why are you not with him now?"

"Once I had given him the babe, he took it away and never returned. Terrified Lord Torridan would discover what I had done, I made up the story that Dáire had died at birth and I had buried him. Please, my lord," she whimpered. "I beg of you, have mercy on me."

"Mercy?" the noble roared. "Guard, take Imag to the dungeon where she is to remain for the rest of her miserable life!"

Fear flared in her eyes. "Nay, my lord. Please do not let me die there!"

"Punishment you deserve after sentencing my son to a life in Hades!" he roared.

The guard reached for her.

Face ashen, with a cry, she bolted through the open door.

The guard ran into the corridor. "She has run up to the turret." His mouth flattened. "She willna escape, my lord, that I swear."

Against the fading slap of boots down the hallway, Lathir secured her dagger, rushed to the entry.

A distant door thudded closed.

Moments later, a scream sounded from the courtyard.

Lathir ran to the window.

Imag's body lay sprawled on the ground.

Jaw tight, Lathir angled her jaw. "What anger and heartbreak you have caused with your duplicity. Mayhap God can forgive you, but I never will."

Fists clenched, Lord Torridan stepped up to her side. "Amen."

\* \* \* \*

Hours later, seated in the chair beside Kieran's bed, his chamber illuminated by candles and the flames in the hearth, Lathir drew the blanket tighter around her. The tension thrumming through her far from eased by the scent of new rushes or the soft crackle of the fire.

Rónán—nay, Dáire McKelan—as the eldest son of Lord Torridan, was first in line to become the next Earl of Torridan. Had it not been for the healer's treachery, they would have wed.

Heart aching, she stared at Kieran. And Dáire's younger brother could have married the woman he loved.

The door scraped open. Expression weary, Lord Torridan entered, paused. "'Tis late. You should be abed."

"After today's events, I doubt if I could sleep."

"Indeed." On a tired sigh, he walked over. "Has my son tried to open his eyes?"

"Nay."

He settled in a nearby chair. "I didna see you at the evening meal."

She shrugged. "I couldna eat."

"I can have a guard bring you—"

"I thank you, but I am not hungry." Lathir scanned Kieran's face, hoping to catch a flicker of his lids. After losing Rónán—no, Dáire—she prayed Kieran's condition didn't deteriorate and Lord Torridan lose his remaining child.

Face pale, he closed his eyes. His lips moved as he whispered a prayer, and Lathir bowed her head, pressed her hands together, and silently followed along.

On a broken sob, the noble's body began to shake. "Bedamned!" He wiped his eyes. "I stand here praying my son will live, and somehow try to accept that his brother, who I believed had died at birth, lived. More, was abused, horribly."

Tears clogging her throat, aching at his heartbreak, she crossed to him. "But you didna know, couldn't."

Stricken eyes met hers.

"Dáire grew into a fine man," she said, her voice breaking. "One whom you would have been proud to know."

He gave a shaky nod. "From the brief time that we spent together, I discerned he was a man to respect. I curse that he was taken from me before I learned the truth."

Throat burning with tears, she lay her hand upon his Lord Torridan's arm, needing to give him something to cling to. "Your son was of the Brotherhood."

Surprise flickered in red-rimmed eyes. "A Knight Templar?"

"Aye, a man who'd earned notice and respect from King Robert. The reason Dáire was chosen to sail with my father and me to Ireland, to bring the arms my father has hidden to our king. Sit, let me tell you all I know."

"I--I..." He gave a rough breath. "I would like that."

A while later, flames crackled in the hearth as Lathir finished telling him what she knew about his eldest son, the pride on Lord Torridan's face a humbling gift.

"I–I thank you." He cleared his throat. "I know you will wed for duty, buy I regret it willna be to Dáire, who will always hold your heart."

Throat thick with emotion, she struggled to accept she'd never see Dáire again. "Though I dinna love Kieran, he is a fine man. I swear to you, I will be a good wife."

"Aye, I will be proud to have you join our family." Weary eyes shifted to his son, widened, then filled with tears. "Kieran?"

Lathir glanced over. Confusion shimmered in her betrothed's eyes as he held his father's gaze. "W–where am I?" he rasped.

"Thank God you are awake!" His father leaned over and gave his son a fierce hug, then sat back. "You are in Wynshire Castle. While freeing Lord Sionn from Murchadh Castle, you were seriously hurt. As the healer treated your injury, you fell unconscious. You havena woken since."

Kieran tried to move, grimaced.

Lathir helped him sit up. "You will be weak. Thank God you are awake."

"Your father?"

"Because of your help," she said, forcing a smile, "he is alive. And if his grumbles are any indication, healing well." She filled a goblet with wine. "Here, your throat must be dry."

Once Kieran finished a long drink, she set the goblet aside. "How many days have I been asleep?"

"Almost a sennight," his father replied.

"No doubt you are hungry." Lathir stood. "I will bring you a warm meal." And leave them time to talk.

"I thank you. I could eat."

A smile lit his father's face. "Half a boar, no doubt."

Elation that Kieran was awake warred with grief that she'd never again see Rónán, no, Dáire. Her heart in her throat, she crossed the chamber, opened the door.

"Lathir."

At the compassion in Lord Torridan's voice, she turned. "Aye."

"While you are away, I will tell Kieran about Dáire."

Tears burned her eyes and she nodded. Before she began to weep, she hurried into the corridor.

* * * *

A while later, satisfaction filled Lathir as Kieran finished the last of the stew, then a slice of thick-cut bread slathered with butter. Since he'd awoken, his color had returned. With the healing of his wounds, he should be well soon.

The church bell began to ring, and Lathir froze. Pulse racing, she turned to Lord Torridan. "I am expecting nay one."

Jaw set, the noble stood. "Nor I."

Please God let it not be an attack. She ran to the window. Framed within the fading wash of orange-red filling the sky as the sun sank on the horizon, three cogs sailed shoreward.

She gasped. "The first ship is Bran's."

"Aye," the earl said as he stepped beside her, "but I dinna recognize the other two."

Hands upon the cool stone, she took in the vessels sailing in the pirate ship's wake, then relaxed. "Nor I. As they travel with Bran, though, they are men who will bring us nay harm."

"I agree. After all he has done to aid us, I trust him, regardless if he is a pirate."

"One," Kieran said, "who is loyal to King Robert."

His father nodded to his son. "He is that. I will meet them."

"As my father is asleep, I shall go with you." Lathir glanced toward Kieran. "I will ask the healer to stay with you while I am gone."

"'Tis unnecessary. I shall be fine." Kieran yawned. "Nay doubt I will be asleep before you reach the gatehouse."

A short while later, within the wavering of torchlight, Lathir kept pace at the earl's side.

He rode through the gatehouse, as when they first met, accompanied by his knights. Though Lord Torridan suspected no trouble, he'd insisted on taking precautions.

However wonderful to see Bran, 'twould evoke painful memories of Dáire. Tugging her cape tight against the bite of cold, she guided her mount toward shore.

In the distance, outlined within the last wisps of the fading sunset, men climbed down a rope ladder dangling from cog to a small boat.

She squinted. "In the fading light, I canna make out which of the men is Bran."

"Nor I."

The ship dropping an anchor next to Bran's lowered a small boat. A ladder thudded as it unfurled down the side, and several men scrambled to the small craft.

Mouth grim, Lord Torridan halted at the shore's edge. "Whoever 'tis, we will soon learn."

\* \* \* \*

Heart ready to burst, Rónán made out Lathir's figure in the last shimmers of sunset entwined with the torchlight as she stood on shore. How he'd envisioned this moment, wanting to embrace her, tell her that he loved her and would never leave her. An ache built in his chest. Words, with her betrothed to Lord Craigshyre, he could never say.

Had he not promised King Robert to retrieve the much-needed arms from Lord Sionn, he would have remained at Murchadh Castle and allowed Stephan to inform Lathir that he lived. In the end, seeing her, aware that she loved and wanted him, would do naught but cause them both further heartache.

Rónán had dismissed Stephan's understanding offer to remain onboard. Regardless of the hurt, he was here. He wouldna hide like a coward. However difficult to sail away, he would be thankful for his time with Lathir while at her stronghold.

The soft curl of waves spilled along the shoreline as the hull scraped the crush of small rocks. Water splashed as he, along with his Templar brothers, jumped out. The brisk air, rich with the tang of cold and turf spilled past as they pulled the dinghy farther up the beach.

On a hard swallow, he fell in with his friends as they started toward Lathir and Lord Torridan astride their mounts. Stepping over stones, he searched for Kieran and Lord Sionn. Nor was he surprised by their absence. Given their injuries, both would still be recovering in their chambers.

Shadows from several large oaks swallowed Rónán, along with Stephan MacQuistan and the other Templars as they made their way up the rocky sweep of land.

With each step, Rónán's nerves wound tighter.

Several paces before the powerful noble, Lord Dunsmore halted. "Lord Torridan."

A favorite adviser to King Robert, Rónán wasn't surprised Stephan knew the ruler of the realm of Tír Connail.

"Lord Dunsmore—" Lord Torridan nodded to Lathir. "May I introduce to you my son's betrothed, Lady Lathir."

"Lord Dunsmore, I regret the circumstance, but 'tis good to see you again." She glanced toward Lord Torridan. "We met briefly at St Andrews." Lathir faced Stephan. "I regret that my father isna here. He was injured and is recovering. Nay doubt once he awakens in the morning, he will be wanting to speak with you."

He nodded. "'Tis excellent to hear the earl is regaining his health." Stephan's gaze shifted to Lord Torridan. "And your son, my lord?"

"Thanks to God, this night he has awoken."

Rónán released a sigh, thankful he lived.

Lord Torridan's brows twisted together in confusion. "How did you know? Though Bran captains the ship you sailed with, he didna know Kieran was injured."

Caught off-balance by the question, Rónán looked around, realized Lathir and Lord Torridan hadn't seen him as he stood in the shadows. Drawing a deep breath, he stepped into the wavering torchlight. "Because I informed Lord Dunsmore, my lord."

Disbelief glittered in Lathir's eyes. Her body swayed, and the noble's face paled. On shaky legs, she rushed toward him; Rónán met her halfway, caught her shoulders, wanting her with his every breath.

Tears streaming down her face, she curled her fingers on his chest. "You are alive!"

Rónán gave her hand a gentle squeeze, wanting to tell her how much he loved her. "W–why…" He cleared his throat. "Why would you think otherwise?"

"One of the guards who fought with you as we were escaping rode back," she choked out, "and explained you were surrounded by the Earl of Ardgar's knights."

All this time she'd been terrified that he was dead. God's truth. Never had he meant to cause her such pain. "Knights I managed to evade for two days until I was trapped on the cliffs." He shoved back the surge of emotion. "'Twas where Lord Dunsmore and his men, along with Bran's, found me after they seized Murchadh Castle."

Lord Torridan shook his head. "'Tis hard to believe!"

"Aye." Tears pooled in Lathir's eyes. "Are you hurt?"

Tenderness filled Rónán. "Naught of importance."

With a bluster, Bran swaggered forward. "He almost died, but the lad is too ornery."

Lord Torridan cleared his throat, and Rónán was shocked to see emotion welling on the powerful lord's face. Why? He'd overheard that Kieran was alive and well. "What is wrong?"

"Naught. Everything is right," the noble's voice broke at the last as he dismounted, then stepped toward him. "You see, this night I learned that you arena Rónán O'Connor, but Dáire McKelan, my firstborn. A son I was told had died at birth."

His son? Rónán stared at the lord, whose height and build matched his own, struggled to accept his words. He glanced around, found his Templar brothers' expressions ranging from shock to amazement much like, no doubt, what was reflected on his face.

Though he wished 'twas true as it would grant him the dream of a family, of being wanted, he refused to lie. "I dinna know why you believe such," Rónán forced out, "but 'tis untrue. I am an orphan."

"Nay," Torridan stated, his voice rough with emotion. "You were stolen moments after your birth by my healer. Your lineage is proven by your birthmark."

Rónán frowned. "My birthmark?"

A fragile smile danced on Lathir's lips as her tear-filled eyes brightened. "On the outside of your upper thigh. Show him."

Stephan, as the other Templars, crowded in.

'Twas absurd. Heat swept Rónán's face as within the waver of golden torchlight, he lowered his trews slightly, exposing the uneven brown patch of skin like a smeared line a thumb's width, the end fading into a curl.

Pride on his face, Lord Torridan pushed down the garb covering his own thigh, exposing the familiar symbol. "'Tis a birthmark all within the McKelan family share."

Gasps and excited murmurs erupted around them.

Mind reeling, with the evidence undeniable, Rónán secured his garb and stared at the man who had sired him. "Father?" he whispered, the word he'd never believed he'd ever say, rough on his tongue.

"Aye." After repairing his garb, with shaky steps, Lord Torridan embraced his son.

Joy surged through Rónán as he returned the hug. Dáire, his name was Dáire. All the horrific memories of the vile man who'd abused him faded beneath his father's love, and the fact that he had a family.

"I love you, my son. Welcome home." Clearing his throat, Lord Torridan's arm around his son's shoulders, he faced the others. "I am honored this day to present my oldest son, Dáire McKelan!"

Cheers filled the air.

"Never—" Rónán swallowed the surge of emotion. "Never did I believe this day would come."

In the torchlight, tears ran down his father's cheeks. "Nor I, my son. Nor I." Chest tight with emotion, Dáire turned to Lathir, with but one wish left.

As if reading his mind, his father smiled. "As firstborn, 'tis your duty to end the tension between the realms of Tír Sèitheach and Tír Connail, which means—"

"I must wed Lord Sionn's daughter." Heart pounding, Dáire strode over, knelt before her, and took her hand. "I love you, Lathir. You have stolen my heart, and I canna live without you. Marry me. I would be proud to be your husband."

"And I," she said, her eyes shimmering with love, "your wife."

A fresh round of cheers erupted as he stood and swept her into his arms with a heated kiss.

As the shouts died down once he stepped back, his father nodded. "Come, let us return to the castle. You and the others will be hungry and weary. And," he said with a warm smile to Dáire, "on the morrow, we have a wedding to plan."

Dáire laced his fingers with Lathir's. Aye, let them return. He was more than anxious to wed the woman he loved.

# Chapter Eighteen

A fortnight later, with Lathir at his side and surrounded by his friends, Dáire took in the crowd gathered in the great room of Wynshire Castle for their wedding.

Lathir smiled up at him. Her golden hair was plaited with a weave of silver, the adornment complementing the silver torque clasping an emerald at the base of her throat.

Memories warmed him as he glided the tip of his finger along the honed silver. "You were wearing this when we met."

Her eyes misted. "You remembered."

"There is naught about you that I could ever forget." He claimed her mouth in a tender kiss, then skimmed his thumb against the curve of her jaw as he drew back. "More so as our first meeting was with your *sgian dubh* at my neck."

"A memory I shall forever carry." Mirth twinkled in her eyes. "Mayhap the reason you look a bit dazed?"

He laced his fingers with hers. "How can I not be? In but a few weeks my life has changed, and this day, you and I will wed. And as if that was not enough, I have a family."

"One that loves you very much."

"'Tis as if," he breathed as his heart squeezed tight, "a wish granted."

Laughter sounded from the front of the large chamber.

Dáire glanced up. Paces away, Máire stood beside Tighearnán as Órlaith, seated on her father's hip, was chuckling at something Bran had said.

"Nor was my wish the only one that came true," he said as he smiled at the small crown askew on Órlaith's head, remembering how Tighearnán had teased Lathir that his daughter would be asking for a princess crown. "'Twould seem you granted the lass hers as well."

Tenderness filled Lathir's eyes. "A small token. The gift naught compared to finding Máire alive."

He nodded, skimmed his thumb against her palm. "Tighearnán told me that except for sleep, Órlaith hasna left her mother's side since her return."

"Nor can I blame the lass." She arched her brow. "Why are you smiling?"

Dáire shook his head. "Shortly after we first arrived at Wynshire Castle, I remember seeing one of your maids with Tighearnán. From the way they spoke privately, I believed Tighearnán had found more than a woman in his life, but a mother for Órlaith."

"When," she said with a laugh, "all the while 'twas my maid who was taken with Bran and sought out Tighearnán to learn more about his friend."

"Indeed. 'Twould seem Bran is equally taken. After meeting you, I know how he feels. Nor did his good fortune end there. 'Twas wonderful to see the surprise on his face at the arrival of the Bruce's missive, commanding that Bran be knighted for his service to his king."

"A well-deserved honor," Lathir said, "One my father was proud to fulfill."

Laughter echoed from the back of the celebratory crowd.

Aching to touch her, wanting her alone, wanting her in his bed, Dáire claimed her mouth in a deep kiss. Blood pounding hot, he drew back. That time would arrive soon after their vows.

"Nor have the blessings ended there," he said. "I still shake my head that your father as well as mine gifted us with Murchadh Castle, and I with the title of Earl of Ardgar stripped from the previous lord."

Pride shimmered on her face. "A decision our king sanctioned. And with Lord Dunsmore and his Templars bringing the arms to King Robert, I am confident the weapons will make their journey safely."

"And be used to finally bring all of Scotland beneath King Robert's rule." Dáire frowned. "A fight that I fear will take many more years, one that could come to a head at Bannockburn, or another strong Scottish foothold."

Lines of worry creased her brow. "I pray it doesna last that long."

"As I," Dáire agreed.

"Let us talk no further of war this day."

"Aye." Throat tight, bursting with pride, Dáire looked at his fellow Templar knights, Stephan MacQuistan, Earl of Dunsmore; Sir Thomas MacKelloch, Earl of Kincaid; Sir Aiden MacConnell, Earl of Lennox; and Sir Cailin MacHugh, Earl of Dalkirk; loyal men he'd fought with over the years. Brave men with whom he'd sailed from France after King Philip's betrayal.

When they'd reached Scotland less than two years before, never could any of them have imagined they'd be standing together not only bound by the Brotherhood, but as nobles, men who were blessed with incredible women they loved.

"But celebrate—" Lathir said, drawing him from his musings as she pressed a soft kiss on his mouth, lingered with slow, devastating intent. Eyes dark with desire, she drew back. "That you willna have to leave."

"God's truth," he whispered in a rough hiss, "I should haul you upstairs to our chamber right now and—"

The priest cleared his throat as he stepped before them.

Lathir's eyes danced with mischief before she faced the priest.

Bloody hell, the lass knew she was driving him mad. Nor did he mind. This night he would find sweet satisfaction in giving back, teasing her, until they both found their release, only to begin again.

"We are here before God's eyes to unite Dáire McKelan, Earl of Ardgar, and Lady Lathir McConaghy." Wrapping a woven green silk ribbon around Dáire's wrist, then Lathir's, the cleric regaled a passage of faith, loyalty, and love. As he finished, he made a knot. Face beaming with joy, the priest raised their bound hands. "I now pronounce you man and wife!"

Cheers roared within the great hall, the force making the golden chalices and flagons of bronze and silver upon the dais tremble.

The love in Dáire's eyes filled Lathir. "I love you, my husband."

"And I love you." He claimed her mouth. Cheers again swept the room, but the voices faded as she sank into the kiss, let his touch, his taste fill her. With him 'twould always be so.

After accepting congratulations from all within the chamber, Dáire found himself anxious to be with his wife. He leaned close, whispered in her ear, "I am not a patient man."

Her eyes darkened with desire. "What I am counting on." She shot a glance toward the turret. "Do you think they would notice if we slipped away?"

Dáire gave her a dry look, then swept her up in his arms. "My lady wife, with the Brotherhood in attendance, any who tried to stop us would be a fool."

"Then, my husband," she said with a saucy wink, "'tis time we take our leave."

He took her hand, and they sprinted toward the stairs. Once he reached the second-floor corridor, the shouts below demanding their return growing louder, he set her down. "Run!"

Moments later, he slammed and barred the door as Lathir held her sides, laughing. Her laughter faded as he drew her close, backed her against the door, then trapped her body with his. As he locked her wrists over her head, the need in his gaze ignited a matching ache inside her.

"I believe before our vows you meant to tempt me to distraction," he breathed as he pressed slow kisses along her jaw, down her neck. "A dangerous move."

Her entire body burned, but she enjoyed his teasing, savored the way he made her feel. Still, never had a man touched her, and whispers of the joining were far from the reality of this moment.

"I have never been with a man," she admitted, holding his gaze.

"I know and swear that I will be slow, take you with naught but love in my heart." Dáire took his time, and true to his word, used his hands and mouth in a slow, tantalizing journey, leaving them both wild with need. At what moment he'd released her, carried her to their bed, stripped her as himself, she wasna sure, a sense of fulfillment coursing through her as she welcomed him into her body.

Lathir moved with him, his every stroke, whispers of love, taking her higher, making her mind spin until she exploded, his cry of release following hers.

As he collapsed atop her, breath coming fast, she pushed on his chest. With a chuckle, he rolled with her onto his back.

Instead of curling in his arms, she shoved to her knees and straddled him, his full length still deep within her heat.

Grayish-green eyes darkened with confusion. "What are you doing?"

A slow smile curved her mouth. "This." She lifted her body, took all of him.

\* \* \* \*

Hours later, as the first rays of sunlight painted the skies in soft wisps of gold, Lathir lay her head against Dáire's shoulder, never feeling so complete. Aye, he may have discovered his family, but she'd found a man she could respect, build a home and have children with, and most of all, love. Aye, as he'd said before their wedding, 'twas indeed as if a wish were granted, one she'd cherish forever.

# Author's note

Regardless whether hundreds of years have passed, questions remain of where the Knights Templar fled, what treasure they took, and how so many valiant knights were able to disappear without a trace. As a major plotter in The Forbidden Series, I enjoyed weaving my characters' journeys, where they face challenges and in the end fall in love, around these mysteries. I also include my speculation as to where the Templar fleet and many of the Brotherhood could have escaped to prior to the arrests beginning in France on the 13th of October 1307.

Sincerely,
Diana Cosby
AGC(AW) USN, Ret.
www.dianacosby.com

# ABOUT THE AUTHOR

A retired Navy Chief, AGC (AW), Diana Cosby is an international bestselling author of Scottish medieval romantic suspense. Diana has spoken at the Library of Congress, appeared at Lady Jane's Salon NYC, in *Woman's Day,* on *Texoma Living! Magazine*, *USA Today*'s romance blog, "Happily Ever After," and MSN.com.

After retiring from the navy, Diana dove into her passion—writing romance novels. With thirty-four moves behind her, she was anxious to create characters who reflected the amazing cultures and people she's met throughout the world. Diana looks forward to the years ahead of writing and meeting the amazing people who will share this journey.

Diana Cosby, International Bestselling Author
www.dianacosby.com

# FORBIDDEN KNIGHT

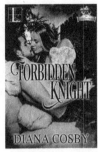

*Deep within Scotland, a healer and a warrior join forces to protect Scotland's future . . .*

There is an intruder in the woods near King Robert Bruce's camp, but when Sir Thomas MacKelloch comes face-to-face with the interloper, he is shocked to discover his assailant is a *woman*. The fair lady is skilled with a bow and arrow and defiant in her responses. The wary Knight Templar dare not allow her beauty to lower his guard. Irritated by his attraction, he hauls her before his sovereign to expose her nefarious intent.

Outraged Sir Thomas dismissed her claim, Mistress Alesone MacNiven awaits the shock on the arrogant knight's face when he learns that she has told the truth. But it is she who is shocked, and then horrified, as it is revealed that her father, the king's mortal enemy, has betrothed her to a powerful noble, a deal that could jeopardize the king's efforts to unite Scotland. Robert Bruce orders Sir Thomas to escort Alesone to safety. As they embark on a harrowing journey through the Highlands, Alesone tries to ignore her attraction to the intimidating warrior, but as she burns beneath Thomas's kiss she realizes this fearless knight could steal her heart.

# FORBIDDEN LEGACY

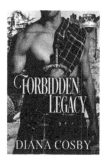

*A betrothal neither wants . . . a passion neither can resist.*

When the English murder Lady Katherine Calbraith's family, she refuses their demands to wed an English noble to retain her home. Avalon Castle is her birthright, one she's determined to keep. After Katherine's daring escape, she's stunned when Scotland's king agrees to allow her to return to Avalon, but under the protection of Sir Stephan MacQuistan . . . as the knight's wife. To reclaim her heritage, Katherine agrees. She accepts her married fate, certain that regardless of the caliber of the man, Stephan may earn her trust, but he'll never win her love.

One of the Knights Templar, Stephan desires no bride, only vengeance for a family lost and a legacy stolen. A profound twist of fate tears apart the Brotherhood he loves, but offers him an opportunity to reclaim his legacy—Avalon Castle. Except to procure his childhood home along with a place to store Templar treasures, he must wed the unsuspecting daughter of the man who killed his family. To settle old scores, Stephan agrees, aware Katherine is merely a means to an end.

The passion that arises between them is as dangerous as it is unexpected. When mortal enemies find themselves locked in love's embrace, Stephan and Katherine must reconsider their mission and everything they once thought to be true . . .

# FORBIDDEN VOW

*In battle-torn Scotland, a castle's mistress awaits her groom, a
warrior she has never met . . .*

Lady Gwendolyn Murphy's fiancé has finally arrived at Latharn Castle,
but she expects no joy in their introduction. Gwendolyn is well aware of
Bróccín MacRaith's cold reputation. Yet from first glance, she is drawn
to the intimidating stranger. Impossible! How could she be dazzled by
such a callous man?

Little does she know, Bróccín is dead. The man Gwendolyn believes to be
her intended is actually Sir Aiden MacConnell, a member of the Knights
Templar and her enemy, masquerading as the earl to gain access to the
castle. His soul is dedicated to God and war; he has no time for luxuries
of the flesh. But Gwendolyn's intoxicating beauty, intellect, and fortitude
lures him to want the forbidden.

With the wedding date quickly approaching and the future of Scotland
at stake, Aiden gathers critical intelligence and steels himself for his
departure, vowing to avoid an illicit liaison. But a twist of fate forces him
to choose—move forward with a life built on a lie, or risk everything for
the heart of one woman?

Printed in the United States
by Baker & Taylor Publisher Services